ALSO BY KATIE RUGGLE

Fish Out of Water

ROCKY MOUNTAIN SEARCH & RESCUE
On His Watch (free novella)
Hold Your Breath
Fan the Flames
Gone Too Deep
In Safe Hands
After the End (free novella)

ROCKY MOUNTAIN K9 UNIT
Run to Ground
On the Chase
Survive the Night
Through the Fire

ROCKY MOUNTAIN COWBOYS
Rocky Mountain Cowboy Christmas

ROCKY MOUNTAIN BOUNTY HUNTERS
Turn the Tide (free novella)
In Her Sights
Risk It All

The Scenic Route

KATIE RUGGLE

sourcebooks
casablanca

Copyright © 2024 by Katie Ruggle
Cover and internal design © 2024 by Sourcebooks
Cover illustration © Carina Guevara
Internal design by Tara Jaggers/Sourcebooks

Sourcebooks and the colophon are registered trademarks of Sourcebooks.

All rights reserved. No part of this book may be reproduced in any form or by
any electronic or mechanical means including information storage and retrieval
systems—except in the case of brief quotations embodied in critical articles or
reviews—without permission in writing from its publisher, Sourcebooks.

The characters and events portrayed in this book are fictitious or
are used fictitiously. Any similarity to real persons, living or dead,
is purely coincidental and not intended by the author.

All brand names and product names used in this book are trademarks,
registered trademarks, or trade names of their respective holders. Sourcebooks
is not associated with any product or vendor in this book.

Published by Sourcebooks Casablanca, an imprint of Sourcebooks
P.O. Box 4410, Naperville, Illinois 60567-4410
(630) 961-3900
sourcebooks.com

Cataloging-in-Publication Data is on file with the Library of Congress.

Printed and bound in the United States of America.
VP 10 9 8 7 6 5 4 3 2 1

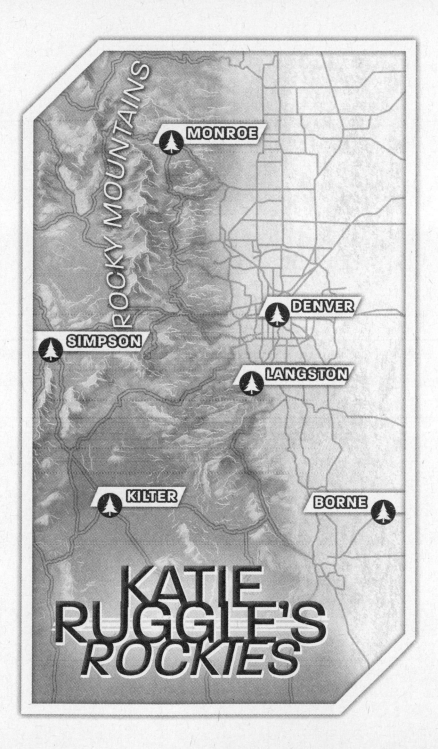

ROCKY MOUNTAINS

MONROE

DENVER

SIMPSON

LANGSTON

KILTER

BORNE

KATIE RUGGIE'S ROCKIES

MEET THE CHARACTERS

The Scenic Route is the first book in Katie Ruggle's latest series, Beneath the Wild Sky...but along the way we get the chance to see some familiar faces. If this is your first time dipping into Ruggle's extended quirky-yet-uniquely-action-packed universe, here's a handy run-through of everyone you'll meet:

LOU & CALLUM FROM *HOLD YOUR BREATH*

Lou, a chatty East Coast transplant determined to make her own way in the Rockies at any cost.

Callum, a taciturn (and charmingly uptight) dive rescue instructor who doesn't know whether he wants to strangle her or kiss her. (Spoiler: He wants to kiss her.)

These opposites attract when Lou stumbles across a headless dead body and begins a mystery that will lead to hijinks, danger, drama, and the formation of a certain Murder Club.

RORY & IAN FROM *FAN THE FLAMES*

Rory, a highly competent, no-nonsense gun shop owner. Raised by mountain doomsday preppers, Rory knows how to do just about anything but deal with people.

Ian, an almost impossibly hot firefighter struggling to reconcile his criminal background with where he wants to be in life. He's been head over heels in love with Rory since they were children.

These childhood sweethearts have their hands full when the local MC comes calling and strange arsons begin spreading out of control.

ELLIE & GEORGE FROM *GONE TOO DEEP*

Ellie, a sweet city girl with zero survival skills but enough grit to have her going toe-to-toe with the most grizzled survivalist.

George, a towering mountain of a man with a reputation for being something of a gruff hermit…until he falls in love at first sight.

This virgin lumberjack of a hero will do anything to help his heroine survive a trek through the Rockies in search for her father: even if he has to wrestle a bear to protect her.

DAISY & CHRIS FROM *IN SAFE HANDS*

Daisy, a kindhearted woman struggling with agoraphobia who witnesses a crime nobody will believe.

Chris, the devoted best friend who will stand by her side no matter who turns against them as a result.

When Daisy witnesses a leader of the community committing a shocking crime, only her best friend is willing to believe her. But the secret that has kept their mutual spark from truly igniting for years may be enough to end their story before it can ever begin.

MOLLY & JOHN FROM *IN HER SIGHTS*

Molly, the oldest of five sisters, is a bounty hunter by both necessity and choice, keeping her family afloat despite the way people whisper about them.

John, a rival bounty hunter and the biggest pain in her rear. He's always underfoot and getting beneath her skin with that obnoxiously handsome grin and cheeky wink.

When her criminal mother puts up the family home as collateral for her latest legal trouble—and then immediately skips town *with* the stolen jewels in tow—Molly and her sisters vow to track her down and save the lives they worked so hard for. Too bad Molly's archnemesis is determined to stick by her side every step of the way.

CARA & HENRY FROM *RISK IT ALL*

Cara, one of five bounty hunter sisters, always dreamed of becoming a kindergarten teacher. But if she can bring in a target with a high payout, maybe she can retire from the family business guilt-free.

Henry, the man Cara is determined to bring to justice, is innocent. If only he could convince the beautiful bounty hunter on his trail of that…

When Cara goes after a high-level criminal, she never anticipated him to be so gentle…or so protective of her when the true villains came back for revenge.

NORAH FROM *CROSSING PATHS* (COMING SOON)

Nervous and shy bounty-hunting sister **Norah** will meet her match in the intimidating visage of the man determined to teach her how to defend herself at all costs.

CHARLIE FROM *TAKE A HIKE* (COMING SOON)

Wild child sister **Charlie** loves nothing more than working for her family's bounty-hunting business…until she's pulled into a mystery that'll have her losing her heart and her head.

PROLOGUE

BENNETT GREEN PEERED BETWEEN THE scraggly branches of the pine tree he was using for cover. In the past few days, it had become his usual spot, and he was getting quite attached to the lopsided evergreen. The tree provided a good view of the side and even an oblique front angle of the Pax house while being bushy enough to hide his substantial frame. It was even close enough for him to see into the kitchen and living room windows using his binoculars, but he didn't do that. It'd be crossing the line from professional stalking to *creepy* stalking.

And Bennett had been struggling to stay on the right side of that line since he'd gotten his first glimpse of Felicity Pax.

As if that thought had summoned her, Felicity emerged from the trees about thirty feet from Bennett. Just the sight of her made his heart rate speed up. She was in her usual running gear—leggings and a thin, long-sleeve shirt—and her straight black hair swung in its high ponytail as she walked across the side yard toward the front of the house.

During his years as a PI, Bennett Green had surveilled a lot of people. He'd never had trouble staying in the background, doing his work, and then leaving the case behind…until now. The Pax sisters—well, this *specific* Pax sister—had somehow managed to break through his thick shell of objectivity, all without even speaking with him.

Or even knowing he existed.

She got nearer to his hiding spot, passing just fifteen feet from him, and he tensed even as he took the chance to admire her up close. Although her mom, Jane, was a tall, pale-skinned redhead, Felicity must've gotten her diminutive height and warm brown skin from her Native Hawai'ian dad, Lono Hale. According to his file, Jane had married and divorced the guy twice, with two other husbands—and three kids—in between, so Felicity, Jane's youngest, and Molly, the oldest, were full sisters. That left remaining sisters Charlotte, Cara, and Norah to round out the family.

Bennett watched as Felicity walked away from him toward the front of the house. He reveled in the surge of adrenaline sharpening his vision and making all the early fall morning colors more vibrant. He could hardly believe it had only been a week ago that his whole life had felt muted and dull, his daily routine just a pointless, repetitive slog.

Then Maxwell Insurance offered him a case. On paper, it would've been fascinating—a small-time criminal, Jane Pax, allegedly stole a necklace from famous sculptor Simone Pichet's hotel room—but Bennett's deadened emotions hadn't let him feel anything more than mild interest. Since the diamond-and-sapphire piece of jewelry was worth twelve million dollars, the insurance company responsible for the payout was very invested in finding this Jane Pax—and therefore the necklace.

When Bennett had started looking into Jane, he'd discovered that her five adult daughters ran a bond recovery company—bounty hunters, in other words. Until the theft, Jane's main residence had been the same Langston, Colorado, house where her daughters lived. Bennett wasn't sure how that worked—the lawbreaking mom with the bounty-hunting daughters—but he hadn't really cared much then.

It wasn't until he'd gotten his first glimpse of Felicity Pax that the fascination had hit.

Fascination? his brain scoffed. *More like obsession.*

Felicity wasn't the Pax sister most people immediately noticed, but Bennett had. And as he'd continued watching her, he'd seen how matter-of-factly she supported her family. She was the one who trained them, pushing them through endless running and self-defense drills. Felicity also kept her more impulsive sister, Charlotte, in check, ensuring both stayed safe even as they operated as an impressively efficient bounty-hunting team. Felicity Pax wasn't just smart and loving and beautiful, she was loyal to her very core.

His phone vibrated against his leg, and he reluctantly melted deeper into the national forest that ran along the Paxes' yard before fishing his phone out of one of his many pockets. When he saw the screen, he slipped farther through the trees until he was far enough away from the Pax house to not be overheard.

"Hi, Zena," he answered quietly.

"Oh, you're using your quiet voice," his foster mom whispered in solidarity, which almost made Bennett smile. "Is this a bad time? Are you on a stakeout?"

Although Zena wasn't wrong, he'd rather get the call over with rather than have the obligation of a future return call hanging over his head. He loved the foster parents who'd cared for him since Bennett was sixteen, but he hated all phone calls. "It's fine," he said, still keeping his voice low. "What's up?"

"I just want to make sure you're coming to Dean's retirement party."

He frowned, confused. "Yeah, but that's over a month away."

"I know." Her voice had returned to its usual volume. "I just want to make sure it's etched in stone in your schedule. Dean would be so disappointed if you can't make it."

"I'll be there," he promised, itchy to get back to watching the house…and Felicity. "It's in stone. Better go. I'll text you later."

"Good. Keep it in stone," Zena said. "Now go catch that cheating husband."

His huff of amusement was almost soundless. "That's not *all* I do."

"I know. But you won't tell us stories about your cases, so I have to go off movies and private dick clichés."

He held back a groan. "Please don't say that."

"What?" Her innocent tone was ruined by giggles. "Private dick?"

"Please stop."

Still laughing, she said, "Okay, fine. Go catch that cheating *wife* then. Bye. Love you."

"Love you too." Even after twelve years of practice, it was still hard to say, coming out more as a grunt. After he ended the call, he returned to his favorite hiding spot. He got back in place just in time to see Felicity and two of her sisters—Molly and one of the twins, probably Charlotte—leave the house.

Molly and her new boyfriend—John Carmondy, another Langston bounty hunter—got into his car and drove off, while Felicity and her half sister hurried toward the trees. Bennett frowned, wondering why they'd be heading out for another trail run right after finishing their usual morning workout. He decided to follow them, silently making his way through the trees until he reached a path that he knew would eventually bisect the trail the sisters had taken.

His pulse jumped in excitement, and he allowed himself a smile. For some reason he couldn't define, Felicity Pax had woken him up, and he couldn't get enough of her. Setting his jaw, he felt determination fill him. Today he'd talk to Felicity. It was time to move the investigation forward…and past time to meet her face-to-face. Buzzing with anticipation, he started to jog.

ONE

Earlier that morning...

FELICITY PAX INCREASED HER PACE, pulling ahead of the rest of the group. Her sisters were reluctant runners, and she knew they'd be happy to slow to a shuffling jog that was barely faster than a walk once Felicity wasn't there to prod them on. Weaving through the trees, she let her mind go blank, focusing only on the way her thighs burned and her heart raced and the crisp air filled her lungs.

Despite her trembling legs, straining lungs, and a rather ridiculous amount of sweat, Felicity smiled as she finally slowed to a walk. As masochistic as it might be, there was nothing like a trail run to settle her brain. The trees thinned as she reached her backyard, and Felicity was grateful for the gazillionth time that their family's house sat right up against national forest land. Circling around to the front porch, she jogged up the steps and yanked open the squeaky screen door as she pulled out her key.

When she turned it in the lock, however, the dead bolt was already disengaged.

Felicity went still for just a moment before sliding the key out and turning the knob. It was too late to be sneaky, since the screen door hinges had already announced her presence, but she still tried to be quiet as she pushed open the door and stepped cautiously inside.

Pulling out her phone, she quickly silenced it before tapping out a three-word text—front door unlocked—and sending it to her sisters.

The alarm didn't give its usual warning beep to let her know she had to enter the code before it started blaring. Instead, the control panel sat blank and eerily silent. The living room appeared empty, the early-morning sunlight just starting to filter through the blinds on the east-facing window. She crept into the kitchen, relieved to see the family dog, Warrant, crouched— scared but safe—under the table. Soundlessly, she yanked open the door to the pantry, only to find it empty.

Upstairs then.

Felicity climbed the steps, knowing exactly where to place her feet to avoid the creaks from a lifetime of going up and down these stairs. As she reached the top, she heard the lightest of thuds to her left.

Mom's bedroom.

It wasn't really a surprise. That was the room the cops had focused on the hardest when they came with a search warrant looking for the priceless necklace Felicity's mother had suppos- edly stolen before she skipped town and left her daughters to pick up the pieces. It made sense that any opportunistic thieves wanting to snatch the necklace would focus there as well.

Just another mess Jane Pax had left her five daughters to clean up.

Felicity moved down the hallway, trying to keep her steps as light as possible on the hardwood floor. She was grateful for her running shoes as she soundlessly approached the closed door of her mother's bedroom. Carefully, keeping her body flat against the wall in case someone were to shoot at her through the doorway, she turned the knob and cracked open the door.

No one was visible through the tiny opening, so she took a deep breath and shoved open the door, rushing inside to keep the element of surprise.

Instead of jumping on the intruder, however, she stopped abruptly and stared at the person digging through the small closet. All those searches, all that research, all those nights away from home searching for her mother so she could drag her back home before they lost everything, and nothing...until now.

"*Mom?*"

Jane jumped and spun around, her elbow making the plastic hangers rattle together. "Oh! Felicity, you startled me." Pressing a hand to her chest, she sent her daughter a chiding look. "Shouldn't you be out training your sisters instead of here trying to give me a heart attack?"

Even after twenty-two years of experience dealing with her mother's gaslighting, Felicity was still a little thrown by Jane's casual attitude. After a silent moment, however, a thousand questions pressed forward, making it almost impossible to speak. Felicity finally managed to ask, "Mom, where've you been?"

Jane waved a hand, brushing away the question. "Oh, here and there. Figured it was time to see some old friends." Tugging a phone from her back jeans pocket, she glanced at the screen and frowned at Felicity. "You usually train the other girls until seven. Have you been slacking off?"

Again, Felicity was struck speechless for a long moment at the sheer audacity of the woman in front of her. All the frustrating days on the road, all the sleepless nights in thin-walled motel rooms, all the dangerous and life-changing moments her sisters had experienced that she'd missed…all because of the selfishness and greed of the person who'd given birth to them.

Something snapped inside her, and the last strands of guilt for hunting her own mother like she was just another skip slipped away. She reached for Jane's wrist, calm settling over her as she prepared to take the bail jumper in front of her down. Her mom was taller than she was, but Felicity was stronger, and she knew she could keep Jane contained until her sisters arrived to help.

Jane's well-developed sense of self-preservation must've kicked in, since she took a step back and yanked her arm out of reach. "Don't you dare put your hands on me, Felicity Florence Pax. I am your mother."

"You're a thief and a skip," Felicity stated grimly, moving to grab Jane again. "It's my job to bring you in. Plus, it's the only way to save our home." Bitterness surged through her at the reminder of yet another terrible thing her mother had

THE SCENIC ROUTE 11

done—putting the house her children lived in, the house *they* had paid for with their own blood, sweat, and tears, up as collateral for her bail bond only to skip town immediately. If Felicity didn't get her mother to her next court appearance, she and her sisters would soon have nowhere to live.

Her mom's gaze flicked over Felicity's shoulder. Stomach tightening with instinctual dread, she started to turn around when pain radiated from her temple and everything went black.

———

"Fifi! Open your eyes."

The command sounded like it came from far away.

"We're going to sit here eating Cheetos and Ben and Jerry's ice cream until you wake up." That was her sister Charlie's voice.

Annoyance gave Felicity that extra push she needed to raise her weighted eyelids. The bright light felt like a laser cutting directly into her brain, and she squeezed her eyes closed again with a groan.

"I knew that would work." Charlie's voice was filled with satisfaction. "She'd come back from the dead to keep us from eating junk food."

"Thank you, baby Jesus," Molly said on a long exhale from directly above Felicity. "I'm really glad you didn't die on us."

Although Felicity agreed in theory that she was happy to be alive, her pounding head made her wish she'd at least stayed unconscious. She tried opening her eyes again, more slowly this time. The bright morning light still sent spikes through her brain, but the pain dulled as she adjusted. Once her head settled on a steady throb, she remembered the cause of her unconsciousness.

"Mom," she gasped, sitting up abruptly.

"Wait… What?"

"Mom was here? Our mom?"

"Of course our mom. What other mom would she be talking about? What happened, Fifi?"

Before she could answer, John and Henry—Molly's and Cara's partners, respectively—crowded into the room. "Rest of the house is clear," John said.

That meant her mom had slipped by them. "How long was I out?"

"Out?" Henry's eyebrows drew together in a frown. "You need medical?" He pulled his cell phone out as if he was preparing to call an ambulance.

"No!" By the way her timid sister Norah jumped, Felicity realized she'd gotten a little loud. "No ambulance. Thanks though." When Henry, looking unconvinced, didn't put away his phone, Felicity shoved to her feet, determined to show just how fine she was. Her head hurt, but it definitely wasn't enough to warrant a 911 call, since that would just bring the wolf in detective clothes to their door.

As she stood, swaying slightly, Molly grabbed her arm to help her balance. "I'm not sure how long you were unconscious, although we just found you, and your text came through when we were about a mile away."

"You would've been proud of our sprint time," Charlie added.

Felicity offered her the best attempt at a smile she could dredge up at the moment. "You didn't see Mom or anyone else leaving the house then?" Since four women and two oversize men blocked her exit, she waved everyone toward the door. "Let's go. We need to search for her and at least one of her friends, since someone knocked me over the head before I could tackle Mom. There wasn't a car out front—besides ours—which means they're on foot for at least a couple blocks."

As everyone moved out of the bedroom and toward the stairs, John asked, "What's the plan, Pax?"

Molly didn't even pause before she started rattling off orders.

Despite her tension and aching head, Felicity had to smile. Her oldest sister loved having a plan.

"Okay, Norah and Cara, you're holding down the fort here. Henry, you stick with them. I'm not thrilled that everyone and their mother…" Molly gave a humorless snort before rephrasing. "*Too many people* have bypassed that security system for comfort."

"Also," Felicity chimed in as she crossed the living room, heading toward the front door, "Mom was searching for something in her closet when I walked in on her. If it's important enough for her to risk coming here, she may wait for us to leave and then double back for it."

"We'll keep our guard up as we do a deep dive into Mom's closet," Cara said, stopping next to the couch.

Henry was silent, but he took a protective half step closer to her.

Norah, looking pale and tight around her eyes, gave a wordless nod.

Molly yanked open the door, looking at John over her shoulder. "Carmondy, you're with me in my car, checking the roads. Charlie and Felicity, you take the forest." She paused to give Felicity an assessing look over her shoulder. "You feeling up for this?"

"Yes." She put all her resolve into her answer. There was no way she was missing out on this search. Her throbbing head just gave her extra motivation.

Molly frowned but gave a small dip of her chin. "Stick close to each other." She and John headed toward the colorful Prius parked in the driveway.

"Let's take my car," John suggested, side-eyeing the painted pot leaves with *Weed on Wheels* in large pink bubble letters that decorated the passenger door. After Jane had taken the necklace, she'd had one of her shady friends steal the Prius and sell it for cash. Molly had gotten it back, but not before a marijuana delivery service had given it a new, distinctive paint job. "It's less…conspicuous."

Molly barely hesitated before switching directions. "Fine. I really need to get that repainted. Be careful, you two."

Already focused on the hunt, Felicity gave her sister a distracted wave as she picked up a jog toward the trees.

"Ready, Fifi?" Charlie gave her a grin filled with anticipation.

"Beyond ready." Felicity didn't even complain about the hated nickname. All she cared about at the moment was finding Jane and finally finishing this endless search.

Before they reached the tree line, the hum of a garage door opener caught her attention. She stopped and turned to see her neighbor across the street, Mr. Villaneau, slowly back his white Cadillac SUV down their driveway and into the road. He paused just to shoot a glare out his window at them before rolling forward. For some reason, this struck Felicity as amusing, and she gave a huff of laughter as she entered the forest.

"Why do all our neighbors hate us?" Charlie asked whimsically. "We're all extremely likeable—well, except for Jane, I guess."

The reminder killed Felicity's amusement, and her smile fell away. "At least we're not invited to any of the neighborhood barbecues, so we don't have to come up with excuses to explain why we never go."

"True."

They'd both dropped their voices as they started moving through the trees, and Felicity barely heard Charlie's response. The only sound was the occasional soft scuff of their trail-running shoes against the rocky path. Even the birds and small animals were quiet, as if everything in the forest was holding its breath.

It was too early in the fall for the trees to have dropped their leaves, and the underbrush was still heavy, which made it hard to see very far in any direction. Felicity kept her head swiveling, her gaze scanning the forest for any colors or movement that didn't belong. Her phone vibrated almost silently against her thigh, startling her. Still keeping her gaze up, she slid her phone from the pocket of her running pants and saw a text from Charlie.

Taking the trail fork toward Bear Creek.

Felicity turned toward her sister and frowned, but Charlie was already mostly hidden by greenery. Felicity hated that they weren't in view of each other, but the fork was a narrow one, and the paths ran almost parallel for over a mile. The trees would block the visual, but they'd at least be able to hear each other if they yelled loud enough. Plus, they *did* have their phones. Instead of protesting, she just responded OK and returned her cell to her pocket.

The woods felt different without her sister right next to her. Every rustle and snapping twig was ominous now. Her feet wanted to slow, but she made herself up her pace, forcing down her apprehension. This was probably pointless anyway, she figured, since her mom could be anywhere by now, and an entire national forest made a pretty big haystack to find that needle in.

A flash of orange up ahead and to the left caught her eye. She left the path and headed in that direction. Off the trail, she was forced to slow down so she didn't crash through the underbrush and tree branches like an elephant. Slipping around a scrawny aspen, she saw the orange again, bobbing along fifty feet in front of her.

Her adrenaline surged, making it hard to keep each step quiet and deliberate. She fished her phone out again and paused for a few seconds to tap out a message to Charlie.

Spotted someone, no ID yet, following

The orange patch was farther ahead now, and she upped her speed, giving up some of her stealth in order to narrow the gap between them. Closer now, she could see that the orange was actually a tuft of hair escaping a beanie. Although Jane was a redhead, it was too light to belong to her. Also, the person she was following was taller and thicker than Jane, and the way they walked was different, more lumbering than Jane's usual graceful stroll.

Mentally running through Jane's cohorts for a ginger, she winced as the obvious culprit came to mind. She quickly texted the name to Charlie.

Zach Fridley

Although he normally kept his carrot-red hair shaved close to his scalp, the shade of it matched, as did his body type. Of course it was Zach. He'd been up to his eyeballs in Jane's mess since the night she stole the necklace. It wasn't a surprise that he'd been involved in her latest break-in. In fact, he'd probably been the one to knock Felicity over the head. Leave it to Zach freaking Fridley to attack her from behind like the cowardly man-slug he was.

Ignoring the multiple vibrations coming from her phone, which she assumed was Charlie demanding more details, Felicity put her cell away. With her gaze locked on Fridley's back, she unzipped the pocket on the inner part of her waistband and fished out her folded knife. Keeping it tucked in the top of her leggings for easy access, she upped her speed.

Once she was fifty feet behind him, she dropped any attempt at keeping her footfalls quiet and started to sprint. Zach twisted around to look at her, his cold blue eyes annoyed, before bolting away. She gave chase, the thrill of the potential capture buzzing in her veins. Maybe she would've preferred finding her mom, but Zach Fridley had been a huge, felonious pain in their collective asses for as long as Felicity could remember. Bringing him in would be sweet, even more so because he was guaranteed to have several arrest warrants out on him. There might even be a bounty, a financial bonus to the bone-deep satisfaction she'd feel.

Despite his long legs, Felicity was gaining on him. She ran in this forest every day while Zach was drinking at Dutch's, the local bar, or committing crimes. There was no way he could escape her now. His back was thirty feet away, then twenty-five, twenty… She dug for more speed, needing to close the gap between them before she'd be able to leap on him and tackle him to the ground.

As she rounded an evergreen in a full-out sprint, her toe caught on the edge of a rock, sending her flying. She immediately tucked her chin and transformed her fall into a graceful dive roll. Using the momentum of her fall, she rocketed to her feet, feeling just a tiny bit smug that her fall wouldn't cost her any time. Zach Fridley was still within her grasp.

Then a huge shape loomed right in front of her.

Going too fast to change course, she hit hard, bringing whatever it was down with her as she fell. Somewhere in the shocking blur of motion, she realized that the large thing she'd run into was a person. Muscle memory from thousands of training sessions kicked in, and she rolled clear of his grip once they hit the ground. Her freedom didn't last long though. Before she could push up to her feet—or even sit up—he was straddling her hips, holding her down.

Ready to send him flying, she forced herself to pause

and take stock. Ever since this person stepped into her path, she'd been reacting blindly, and she hated doing that. She gave Molly a hard time about loving her plans, but Felicity was almost as bad. She didn't like winging it. That was when people got hurt.

She looked—really looked—at the person straddling her hips for the first time, even as she palmed the knife she'd tucked into her waistband earlier. The guy was huge and objectively hot. His rough-hewn features, shaggy black mop of hair, and liquid dark eyes somehow merged together into a whole look that was obnoxiously perfect in a messed-up way. She also knew that he was a total stranger. If she'd ever gotten a glimpse of him before, she would've remembered. There was no forgetting that face. Her fairly reliable instincts told her he wasn't a threat—at least not to her life. Her dignity was another matter.

He was staring back at her, his expression baffled, as if he hadn't been the one to bring her down and then sit on her. The reminder shifted her from information-gathering mode back to full annoyance.

"What the heck?" It wasn't the most productive question she could've started with, but she still felt the shock of the sudden end to her foot chase. Her gaze snapped up, but of course there was no sign of Zach Fridley. The guy was nothing if not an opportunist, and he'd happily taken the opportunity to get far away from her. The knowledge that he'd slipped through her fingers again made her glare even harder at the guy who was *still* sitting on her. "What are you doing? Get off me!"

The stranger glanced down as if surprised to see that he was, in fact, sitting on her. He stood and reached down to help her to her feet. Ignoring his outstretched hand, Felicity stood under her own power, brushing dirt and bits of twigs and other forest debris from her backside and legs.

She quickly gave up trying to get clean and turned to the still-silent giant in front of her. "What was…*that*?" She gestured toward the general direction that Zach was running in, indignation building as the shock abated a bit.

Instead of answering, the guy blinked at her, making her notice that his eyelashes were ridiculously long. Irritated with herself for focusing on such a random and definitely not-important detail, she made an impatient gesture with the hand not holding her knife. Taking a breath, she concentrated on asking a simple, clear question.

"Why did you stop me?" Suspicion crowded in, making her narrow her eyes at him. "Are you working with Zach?" She almost added *and my mom*, but she swallowed the words before they made it out. No sense in giving the guy information that he might not know yet.

"Who's Zach?" The words rumbled out of his deep chest, the smooth bass of his voice twanging a muscle in her chest, kind of like when she walked into a club with the music turned up so loud she could feel it internally. Shaking off her strange reaction, she focused on his actual question.

She had to give it to him. The man had a good poker face. "Zach Fridley? The guy who got away, thanks to you?"

He was back to just frowning at her silently.

"If you don't know who Zach is, then why did you stop me

from chasing him?" She held on to her patience with extreme effort as she looked him up and down. "And then sit on me?"

That got a reaction—just a slight twitch of discomfort, but at least he wasn't just watching her, stone-faced and silent. "You fell."

"Yes, and I got back up again." She narrowed her eyes at him. "How was knocking me down again supposed to help me?"

"I didn't mean to…" Trailing off, he switched gears abruptly. "I need to talk to you."

It was her turn to stare, thrown by how easily he'd dodged her accusation. "You need to talk to me."

His chin dipped slightly in the smallest of nods.

"You need to talk to me." Her voice went up to a higher pitch, but she couldn't stop it from happening. She'd almost had Zach Fridley literally in her grip, but this random guy decided to plant his mountain of a body in front of her because he wanted to talk to her. "If you need to talk to me, you come to my house or call my cell or even follow me into the grocery store, but you don't tackle me in the middle of a chase!" Her voice grew louder toward the end, and she sucked in a breath, trying to regain her calm—or at least the outward appearance of calm.

Before he could respond, Charlie popped into view as she ducked under a hanging branch. "Where's Zach? Did you get him?"

"No." A fresh wave of aggravation rolled over Felicity at the reminder. "I was really close, but then this rando sat on me."

Charlie looked at the stranger and then back at Felicity. "What?"

"Yeah, he couldn't just stalk me like a normal person." With a final, longing glance in the direction Zach Fridley had run,

Felicity huffed a frustrated sigh and forced herself to let go of her disappointment. "We might as well head back. Hopefully Molly and John had better luck finding…um, better luck." She almost mentioned their mom but remembered at the last minute that letting this stranger know their mom was in the area—and that they were trying to hunt her down—was a bad idea. The fewer people who knew she had basically jumped bail, the better.

Chasing Zach had taken her off the trail, but Felicity had a general idea of where she was. Turning around, she started tromping back toward the house, taking a sour satisfaction in making all sorts of noise as she walked now that she didn't have to be stealthy.

"Wait," the stranger protested. "I still need to talk to you."

"Nope." Felicity didn't pause or even glance behind her, even though she felt Charlie's curious gaze on the back of her neck. "I don't talk to treasure hunters who ruin my takedowns and sit on me."

"I'm not a treasure hunter." From the closeness of his voice, the guy was following her.

"I don't talk to cops who skip-block me either."

"Not a cop." A hint of frustration leaked into his even tone, which lifted Felicity's spirits somewhat. At least she wasn't the only one annoyed. "I'm a private investigator."

Although she really wanted to continue ignoring him, that piqued her interest. She glanced at Charlie, who was being unusually quiet. Her sister was looking positively gleeful as her gaze bounced between the stranger and Felicity. Charlie always did love drama.

When the stranger didn't elaborate, Felicity couldn't stop herself from asking, "A PI? Who hired you?"

"Maxwell Insurance. They insured Simone Pichet's necklace."

Felicity's head dropped back as she groaned at the sky. "Great. Yet another person lurking and getting in our way."

Charlie finally broke her silence. "You're so feisty right now, Fifi. I love it."

"I won't get in the way," the stranger said, sticking close to their heels. "Don't you want help proving your mom's innocence?"

Felicity met Charlie's incredulous gaze and almost laughed. "Why would we do that? She's guilty as sin."

"Fifi," Charlie muttered warningly, and Felicity rolled her lips between her teeth, regretting her words. In her defense, it had been a really rough day for her so far.

The PI seemed to roll with it though. "Don't you want help finding the necklace then?"

What she could really use help with was finding her mom, but she couldn't say that. After all, they were pretending that Jane hadn't skipped bail so they could hold on to their house for as long as possible. All they needed to do was make sure Jane made her first hearing in a few weeks. Unfortunately, that was proving to be harder than they'd first thought.

Realizing she hadn't answered him, she twisted her shoulders in an uncomfortable shrug. Finding the necklace would just bring the hordes of treasure hunters and cops down on their heads. They'd already had a slew of break-ins, despite their new security system. If there was even a hint that the necklace was in their possession, things would get a thousand times worse.

With a slight shudder, Felicity narrowed her eyes at the PI. "How about you do your investigation, and we'll stick to ours. If we find anything of interest to you, we'll text."

She broke through the tree line and strode across the yard, but the PI dogged her steps all the way to the porch. "Here." He thrust a card at her. "Let me know what you find out."

Knowing he'd probably camp out on the porch swing if she didn't at least play along, she accepted the card and then went inside, Charlie close behind. As the screen door slammed after them, Felicity glanced back through the wire mesh to see the PI still standing at the base of the steps, eyeing her thoughtfully.

Flustered for some reason, she tore her gaze away and closed the inner door a little too firmly.

TWO

"Your private dick is back," Charlie said, smirking behind her coffee cup.

Felicity shifted in her chair so she could see across the street where the large PI was indeed lurking, leaning against the brick front of the pharmacy, pretending to read something on his phone. He snuck a peek at Felicity through those mile-long lashes before hurrying to drop his gaze. She barely resisted the urge to bang her head against the small café table in front of her. "If he's going to stalk us, he should at least have the decency to be a little sneakier about it."

"You," Charlie corrected. "His stalking is most definitely focused on you."

Even though Felicity glared at her sister, she really couldn't argue. She'd had an unwanted shadow for the past two days, ever since the guy had sat on her in the woods. Mr. B. Green, according to his business card, had been following her everywhere, even when she just wanted to sit on the coffee shop patio and enjoy some caffeine and early autumn sunshine in peace.

"I did tell him to stalk me like a normal person."

Charlie pursed her lips. "That probably wasn't wise."

With a quiet groan, Felicity turned so she couldn't see Mr. Green anymore. "I was having a bad day and was slightly concussed. I shouldn't be responsible for what I said."

Felicity's phone buzzed, and she glanced at the name on the screen before answering. "What's up, Molly?"

"So remember how there was no sign of Mom after she left the house?"

"Yes, I remember that thing that happened two days ago." Felicity felt a little bad at her snarky tone, but she blamed her sour mood on Mr. Green. Pretty much everything that'd gone wrong since she'd literally run into him had been his fault.

To her credit, Molly ignored her sarcasm. "But who was leaving his house right as we started searching?"

Felicity thought back to that unpleasant day. "Who was leaving—oh! Mr. Villaneau." Even as she said the name, realization dawned, and she wanted to smack herself for being so oblivious. She'd watched the guy leave and all she did was make a joke about his glare. "Mr. Villaneau, the man Mom had an affair with five years ago and then lightly blackmailed."

By the way Charlie was staring at her, she'd figured out what the conversation was about, just from Felicity's half. "She was hiding in that SUV that drove right past us, wasn't she?"

"Need us to have a chat with Mr. V?" Felicity asked, giving Charlie a grim nod.

"Already did. Carmondy and I played good cop/bad cop, and I finally got to be the bad cop." Molly sounded positively chipper. "He eventually admitted he'd brought her to that truck stop out by the interstate. Guess who she met up with there?"

Felicity rubbed her forehead, feeling an echo of her headache returning. "Zach Fridley."

"Yep. But the good news is that we got a vehicle description from him, and our darling Norah is already working on getting the security video footage. Hang on—she's handing me a sticky note wiiiiith...the license number and direction of travel."

"Nice." When Charlie gave her an inquiring look, Felicity said, "Norah has the plate number for Zach and Mom."

"Way to go, Nor!"

There was mumbling on the other end of the call before Molly's voice returned. "Our genius sister has managed through only slightly less than legal methods to access the State Patrol cameras on the interstate. Mom and Zach took the first Colorado Springs exit."

Relieved to have a new lead after letting both Jane and Zach slip through her fingers, Felicity pushed back her chair and stood. "Thanks, Moo. We'll stop home before heading out."

"Um, Fifi?" Charlie followed her off the coffee shop patio toward where they'd parked on the road a half block away. "What are we going to do about Mr. Lurky McStalkerson?"

Letting her head drop back, Felicity groaned. "I forgot about him." She couldn't resist glancing over at Mr. Green. Although he was still pretending to look at his phone screen, his big form was almost vibrating with interest now that she and Charlie were on the move. His body language reminded her of Warrant when he spotted a squirrel.

"I don't think it would be a good idea to lead him to Mom," Charlie said, serious for once.

"Agreed." Felicity resisted the urge to stomp her feet as she headed toward the driver's door of her car. "Just what we need— another complication."

"I know, right?"

An idea took root in her mind. She didn't like it at all—hated it, in fact—but there was just one solution she could think of. "Guess I'm going to be goose bait."

Eyeing her over the top of the car, Charlie asked, "What?"

"Goose bait." Felicity waited until they were both in the car and the doors were closed to explain. "We're going to lead Mr. B. Green on such a wild goose chase, he's going to regret stalking the Pax sisters."

With a grin, Charlie held up her fist. Felicity bumped it with hers, unable to hold back her own smile. Private Investigator B. Green didn't know who he was messing with.

———

Norah and Cara both lit up like sparklers when Felicity mentioned her plan—at least the rough outline she'd come up with.

"Ohhhhh," Cara said, shuffling through the files they had on various bail jumpers they were currently investigating. "We need to pick a believable destination so your stalker won't figure out what you're doing and drop you to chase after Charlie instead."

"I don't know," Charlie said around a bite of apple. "He's pretty fixated on Fifi."

Giving Charlie a glare—both for the comment and the hated nickname—Felicity turned back to her other sisters. "Any skips with out-of-town connections worth checking out? Preferably in the opposite direction of the Springs? Might as well be productive so it's not a waste of time and gas."

Norah's fingers tapped on her laptop and then paused. "How about Douglas Fletcher? Before he moved here, he spent a few years with some militia group in the mountains."

"Douglas Fletcher?" Charlie leaned over Norah's shoulder to look at her laptop screen. "Oh, Dino! The meth dealer. Pretty good payoff if you bring him in too."

"Perfect." Felicity was starting to get excited about the detour. As much as she wanted to help track down her mom, a mini vacation in the mountains sounded really nice. She'd been working on the same case for weeks, and a temporary change in target would be a relief. Also, the aspens would be changing color, and she'd get a couple of days to herself—well, by herself except for her PI stalker. It would be satisfying to lead the annoying Mr. B. Green astray, so his presence was almost a bonus. "I'll go do some nosing around...where exactly?"

"Just about three hours west of here." Norah peered at the map on her screen. "Right outside a town called Simpson."

"Simpson, huh?" Felicity peered over Norah's shoulder at the small dot right in the middle of the Rockies and then made a smug face at Charlie. "While you're chasing Mom and Zach,

I'll be relaxing in a sleepy little mountain town. Guess there's an upside to being stalked."

"Ugh." Charlie frowned at her half-eaten apple, not looking quite so cocky now. "Suddenly, this plan doesn't seem so great for me."

With a light step and growing excitement, Felicity headed upstairs to pack for her mini vacation. Maybe being goose bait wouldn't be so bad after all.

THREE

By the time Felicity passed the *Welcome to Simpson* sign, the sun was just starting to peek over the mountains to the east. She rolled slowly into town, eyeing the quirky homes and businesses that made the place look like an Old West film set on acid. The low-slung buildings—many made of logs and the others painted in unexpected bright pastels—balanced on the line between adorable and unsettling. It was equally possible to imagine a cheery lumberjack or a suspicious doomsday prepper emerging from one of the doorways. Since she was in such a good mood, Felicity decided to go with cheery lumberjack. Sharp, rocky peaks loomed over the hamlet on all sides, somehow managing to create a feeling that was both cozy and claustrophobic.

The extra-early start to her drive hadn't fazed Felicity, especially since she was in her nice, normal dark blue compact car, and Charlie had to borrow Molly's Prius so she could remain incognito on her way out of town. After all their planning, they didn't want Charlie to catch the PI's attention, so Felicity got her usual ride, while Charlie was in the "Weed on Wheels" car.

The town was quiet, with no one around to disturb the early-morning peace, and Felicity slowed even more as she thought about what her plan of attack should be. She hadn't worked out any details yet—just lure Mr. B. Green out of Langston and away from Charlie's brightly painted weedmobile. It was much too early to check in at the motel, too early for anything really, except for…

Felicity smiled when she spotted the coffee shop with its prominent *Open* sign in the window. She turned into the small lot adjoining The Coffee Spot and parked next to the other two vehicles—both dusty, older pickups. As she got out, she immediately shivered and reached back in the car for her fleece jacket. The air felt thin and a lot colder than Langston, which had an elevation about three thousand feet lower than Simpson.

She grabbed her laptop bag too, since she couldn't imagine a coffee shop existing that didn't have Wi-Fi available. This was perfect—she'd have breakfast and plan out her research into Dino's old militia at the same time.

Closing her car door, she turned to look around, only to have her view blocked by a black SUV that pulled into the spot right next to hers. Her stomach sank even before she got a good look at the driver.

Mr. PI himself. Great. He's not even trying to be sneaky anymore.

With a sigh, Felicity gave him a flat stare before heading toward the coffee shop entrance. There was no reason to bemoan B. Green's presence. After all, he was the main reason she was in Simpson at all. She was the bait, and he was the goose. Or was she the goose and he the goose chaser? She frowned, trying to figure out her metaphor as she walked inside.

The smell was universal of all coffee shops—roasted beans and sweet pastries and steamed milk. Her good mood returned. Charlie was probably grabbing a gas station fake cappuccino from a machine right now. Felicity really had gotten the best part of this assignment. A couple of people were seated at the small tables scattered around the shop. They glanced up when she came in and then returned to their phones and drinks.

"Welcome!"

Felicity turned her attention to the pretty blond barista and headed to the counter. "Hello…" Her gaze flicked to the woman's shirt, checking vainly for a name tag.

"It's Lou." Her smile was quick and easy. "If you were looking for my name, that is. If you were just checking me out, then thank you, I'm flattered. What can I get you?"

"Hi Lou. I'm Felicity." She had to smile at the barista's chatter as she slid onto one of the stools at the counter. Lou reminded her a little bit of Charlie—the two tended toward the same unfiltered brain-to-mouth monologue. "A probiotic smoothie would be great." Her gaze snagged on the pastry case, and she had a seldom-felt urge to indulge. "And one of those white-chocolate raspberry scones."

"Excellent choice," Lou said approvingly, plating the scone before ringing up the order. "Baked them myself, so you know they're good."

As Felicity paid in cash and stuffed a few bills into the tip jar, she glanced toward the door as casually as possible. It seemed as though Mr. B. Green was just going to wait for her in the parking lot. She mentally shrugged. No amazing-smelling scone for him then. His loss.

"You're just gorgeous, by the way."

The out-of-the-blue compliment made Felicity pause before saying, "Thank you."

"I'm not hitting on you or anything," the barista chattered on as she made the smoothie. "I'm just saying it as a completely platonic and objective fact. I get the same people in here every day, so it's nice to see someone new for a change."

Felicity accepted her drink and thanked Lou again. She took a bite of her scone, and her eyes half closed in sugary bliss. "You make a mean pastry, Lou."

"Why, thank you." Lou sketched a curtsy. "So what brings you to our weird little town?"

"I needed a few days of peace," Felicity said, fairly honestly. "Plus I'm doing a little research."

"Research?" That one word seemed to grab all Lou's attention. "What type of research?"

Felicity paused, considering her options. Just from the short conversation she'd had with the barista, Felicity had a feeling that Lou could be a good resource. "I'm investigating someone who used to be in the militia group outside town, the Free—"

"Freedom Survivors," Lou said with her. "Isn't that the stupidest name?"

"It really is." Felicity'd had the same thought. "It sounds like they're survivors of freedom."

"Exactly!" Lou smacked the counter with her open hand.

"It doesn't make any sense. They should've called themselves Freedom Upholders or something."

"That sounds a little stiff. Freedom Promoters?"

"Eh," Lou scrunched her nose. "That sounds like a country music agent."

"You're right." Felicity accepted the constructive criticism good-naturedly. "Freedom Builders?"

"Super PAC."

Felicity winced. "Uncomfortably accurate. Freedom Growers?"

"Pot producer."

"Freedom Winners."

Lou clapped her hands. "That's the one."

Felicity put her hands up in victory, reveling in the moment of being in complete sync with a stranger who didn't feel like a stranger.

"We're going to be best friends, aren't we?" Lou echoed her thoughts.

"Yep."

"Better buckle up." Lou's smile was positively devilish. "Being my friend is a wild ride."

———

It wasn't until Lou had a run of customers and Felicity was knee-deep in research on her laptop that Mr. B. Green made his way into the shop.

"Hey," Felicity greeted him without looking away from her laptop screen. "Finally got sick of sitting in your car?"

He didn't respond as he took the seat on the stool next to hers. He was close enough for Felicity to feel the heat radiating from his flannel-clad shoulder. She was tempted to lean away, since his proximity made her stomach feel fizzy in a way she didn't want to analyze too closely, but that felt like letting him win. Instead, she held her ground and kept her gaze fixed firmly on her laptop, even though the words that had made perfect sense before he'd taken up all the space in the room were now a meaningless jumble.

"Who's this?" Lou asked, eyeing the newcomer.

"My stalker," Felicity answered matter-of-factly.

"Oh." Lou looked back and forth between the two of them. "Is that a pet name or a cry for help? Because I can call the sheriff as easily as I can make this guy a coffee. You just say the word."

Felicity finally looked at the mountain of a man on the neighboring stool. "You going to cause me any trouble, Mr. B. Green?"

"Nope."

She'd forgotten what a nice bass voice he had. The memory of it just didn't hold the full impact of hearing it in the moment.

"No trouble. I can even help," he promised.

After another long pause, Felicity turned to Lou with a small shrug. "Let's go the coffee route for now, but keep the sheriff option in our back pocket, just in case we need it later."

"Got it." Turning to the PI, Lou put on a big customer-service smile, as if she hadn't just been discussing the possibility of calling the cops on him. "So what can I get you?"

"Large coffee, cream and sugar, please."

Lou poured the coffee and set it in front of B. Green along with containers of cream and sugar. "I'll let you doctor it up to your liking."

Felicity could feel both Lou and the PI staring at her, but she refused to look up. She hadn't decided how much to share with either of them, but she had a strong feeling that neither was going to quit looming until she told them something.

Lou was the first to break. "C'mon, Felicity, my new friend, my buddy, my sister from another mister. You need to satisfy my curiosity before the parents get done dropping their kids off at school."

That caught Felicity's attention. "Why is that the deadline?"

"This is their next stop after Simpson Elementary. I'll be slammed for a good hour, and my curiosity will kill me within ten minutes. Spill, for the love of Pete!"

Felicity's gaze slid to the big silent man next to her. He sipped his coffee while watching her closely, and she rolled her eyes back to Lou.

"You don't understand," Lou continued. "It's been months—*months*, I tell you—since something exciting has happened here. Not even a hint of a mystery, no dead guys, headless or otherwise, just…nothing except making coffee for the boringly normal locals. My murder-solving whiteboard is covered in a layer of dust." She grimaced a little. "Okay, fine. It'd be covered in dust if I wasn't married to Mr. Clean-Freak Callum."

This time, when Felicity glanced at B. Green, their gazes met in a look of confusion and an odd sense of solidarity. She looked away quickly, uncomfortable with any sort of bonding with this stranger, and met Lou's begging eyes.

"My research here is boring." Felicity didn't want to raise Lou's hopes just for her to be disappointed. "Just a run-of-the-mill meth dealer who skipped out on his bond. Everyone has their heads attached, and everyone will *keep* their heads—and all other critically important body parts—attached during the course of my investigation." It felt a little like a vow.

Despite Felicity's attempt to keep Lou's expectations low, the barista's eyes lit up. "Ohh, you're a bounty hunter?" At Felicity's nod, Lou looked at B. Green. "How about you? Are you a bounty hunter too? Maybe a rival one who's stalking Felicity so you can steal her rightful bounty out from underneath her?"

As amused as Felicity was by the accusatory frown Lou was directing at Mr. Green, her sense of fairness couldn't let that go uncorrected. "He's a PI, not a bounty hunter." Felicity had to snicker a little at Lou's disappointed expression. "What you just described did happen to my sister though. Except he wasn't trying to steal her skips. He just had a crush on her."

At this, Lou was positively dancing in place. "Really? Are they together now? Please don't tell me she didn't feel the same way and had to let him down easy, and now he's nursing a broken heart."

Felicity was glad she could give Lou good news. "They're together."

Lou cheered before focusing on B. Green and returning to her initial line of questioning. "So, Mr. PI, are you after the same meth dealer as my new bestie then?"

With a short shake of his head, he took a sip of coffee, obviously using it as an excuse not to talk.

THE SCENIC ROUTE   39

"He's following me because he's looking for a stolen necklace, and he thinks I can lead him to it."

Cocking her head to the side, Lou looked back and forth
between them. "And can you?"

"No."

B. Green gave a quiet, disbelieving grunt that made Felicity
want to smack him.

"Then why is he following you if you don't know where the
necklace is?"

"My mom stole it." Felicity wasn't sure why she was sharing
that information with an almost stranger. In her defense, she
was used to everyone and their grandma not only knowing what
Jane did but also a good percentage of them breaking into their
house in order to search for the necklace themselves.

"Wooow." Lou pulled out her phone. "You two don't mind
if Callum joins us, do you? He pretends he's not a nosy gossip
queen, but he really hates missing out on any drama."

"Uhh…" Felicity found herself glancing at Mr. Green and
giving him a wide-eyed look before she caught herself. *He's not
my partner.* She mentally repeated the reminder, but there was
just something so solid and reassuring about the man that was
completely opposed to the reality of their relationship. He'd
skip-blocked her, sat on her, then stalked her. Why couldn't she
seem to remember that?

Shaking off her distraction, she noted that Lou was putting
her phone back in her pocket. Apparently, Lou had taken her
silence as permission, and the drama-loving Callum had already
been summoned. With a sigh, Felicity resigned herself to having

an audience, her brain already working on information she could get out of these Simpsonites. If she was going to be the entertainment for half this small town, she'd at least use them as a resource. She smothered a grin, imagining herself with an army of odd mountain people under her command.

"Who's this meth dealer?" Mr. Green asked.

Pausing, she considered the PI. Might as well make him into a lieutenant in her bounty-hunting army, she figured. If he was going to be underfoot, he may as well be useful. "Douglas Fletcher. He goes by Dino. He was caught with a whole lot of meth, arrested, paid his bond, and disappeared."

The door swung open, letting in a chatty crowd of customers that filled the shop. As they formed a somewhat orderly line at the register, Lou made a face that only Felicity and Mr. Green could see. "*This* is what happens when you don't get right to the good stuff immediately. Now the hordes of parents are here." She backed toward the register, pointing at Felicity and then Mr. Green. "No talking about interesting things while I'm busy."

Despite her early mental lecture, Felicity's gaze found Mr. Green's again, and this time he quirked an eyebrow, making her want to laugh.

No! No laughing. No camaraderie. He's my stalker. S-T-A-L-K-E-R. Stalker.

Forcing her gaze back to her sleeping laptop screen, she woke her computer and returned to reading the file. It was a bit slim. Researching Dino Fletcher obviously hadn't been a priority for Cara or Norah. In their defense, all five of them had been running around like headless chickens ever since Jane had stolen that necklace.

At the reminder of the object of interest to the big guy sitting silently next to her, Felicity looked up, studying the side of his face until he turned to meet her gaze.

"Why are you still here?" she asked and got the questioning eyebrow quirk again. "I'm obviously not anywhere near my mom or the necklace—at least I'm pretty sure neither is close by—so why are you still lurking? You have no interest in Dino Fletcher, so why aren't you zooming back down the mountain to Langston?"

One of his burly shoulders lifted in a slight shrug. "You're my best lead."

"I'm a *terrible* lead. You need to find a better one."

The corner of his mouth twitched. "We'll see."

"Humph." She turned back to the bare-bones bio on her screen. "We *will* see. We'll see that I'm right, Mr. B. Green."

"Bennett."

"What?"

"My name. The B," he clarified. "It's Bennett."

She frowned. Knowing his name wouldn't help keep him at a distance. It would've been better to keep calling him Mr. B. Green in her head. Formal and impersonal. Just how things should stay between them. "Oh. Okay."

Her attention was drawn away from what a really bad idea getting friendly with a lurking PI was when another man settled on the stool at the end of the counter. Even though there was an empty stool between them, Felicity still felt a little overwhelmed with a big man on either side of her. She eyed the newcomer, turning her laptop slightly to hide the screen from the stranger.

"Don't worry," Lou called from her spot at the cappuccino machine. "That's just Callum. You can tell him everything."

Somehow, that wasn't as reassuring as Lou probably thought it would be. Felicity eyed the newcomer as she felt Bennett shift slightly closer to her. Callum didn't seem to fit Lou's description at all. He had a poker face that even beat out Bennett's for implacability, and his eyes, shadowed by a worn baseball hat, were serious and piercing.

"Hmm," Felicity hummed as she studied him. "You don't look at all like a gossip-loving drama queen."

She felt a sense of satisfaction when his eyes widened for a fraction of a second. She might not be able to discomfit PI Bennett Green, but she'd at least managed to throw this new stone-faced man off-center.

Callum quickly regained his composure and turned toward his milk-steaming wife. "A gossip-loving drama queen." His flat delivery made Felicity snort.

"You deny it," Lou said, pouring the hot milk into a coffee cup. From the heavenly smell, there was vanilla involved. "But I know how happy you are to have the scuttlebutt before the firefighters find out. You love that they think you're some kind of all-knowing oracle rather than just a gossip fiend."

Instead of taking offense, his expression softened as he gave her a glare that even Felicity, who'd barely met the guy, knew was an attempt to hide a smile. "Scuttlebutt? Are you channeling the spirit of my great-grandma?"

Lou just made a face at him as she capped the cup and handed it to a bearded man who wasn't even pretending not to eavesdrop.

Callum refocused on Felicity and Bennett, the soft expression disappearing in an instant, replaced by the sharp lines of suspicion. "What's going on?"

Rather than answer immediately, Felicity studied him. Despite Lou's description of her husband, he really didn't seem like someone who'd spread gossip all over town, but Charlie was always telling her that she gave people the benefit of the doubt, even when there was very little doubt that they were shady—including their mom, who'd proven herself morally bankrupt over and over again. If word got around and Dino heard she was looking for him, he'd disappear, and she might never find him.

"I don't spread gossip," Callum said, as if he could read her mind.

"He doesn't," Lou chimed in, leaning on the counter in front of them while her current customer studied the whiteboard menu, ignoring the impatient grumbly noises the people in line behind her were making. "He loves hearing things before everyone else, but he doesn't spread it around, just packs it away so he can make smug, knowing faces when the firefighters find out and try to shock him."

"Thank you for that compliment." The man really was the king of deadpan.

Felicity glanced over at the silent man on her other side and mentally awarded him the commendation. Bennett was the king of deadpan, and Callum was runner-up. Prince? Vice king? She shook off the distracting thought as Callum focused on her.

Felicity paused for only another few seconds before giving in. After all, she didn't even know where the militia's compound was located. It's not like they sent out an email newsletter with their address printed on the bottom. "I'm a bounty hunter, researching one of my bail jumpers."

"I know what I want to order," the woman at the counter announced, and Lou silently sighed. She moved to the register with a smile that was only slightly strained.

Callum's expression didn't change. "Go on."

"Douglas 'Dino' Fletcher. He is—or was—a member of the Freedom Survivors."

The corner of his mouth twisted down in the slightest frown of distaste.

"I know," Felicity said. "It's a terrible name."

"Most of the members aren't great either."

"Figured." With a small shrug, she said, "It's a militia. They're not known for being...great."

"What was he arrested for?" Callum asked.

"Dealing meth."

That slight frown came again. "You want Sparks's help?"

"Sparks?"

"Lou."

"Oh." Pushing aside the urge to ask if that was a nickname or a last name, she focused on the initial question. "Sort of. I mean, I won't drag her out to the compound, shouting Fletcher's name. Just basic information, if you two have it. An address would be handy."

His expression had turned glacial about the time she

mentioned dragging Lou into a militia compound. It didn't really warm up any as she continued.

"They can use my whiteboard," Lou offered eagerly, using the excuse of pulling out a new package of cups to lean into their low-voiced discussion. "And I can call up the other murder club ladies."

Once again, Felicity found herself meeting Bennett's gaze for a *what?* moment before she forced herself to look away. "Um…murder ladies?"

"Murder *club* ladies. Three friends of mine. We're strictly amateurs in the investigation business, of course, but we've solved every murder we've looked into." Lou turned back toward her line of customers, leaving Felicity no choice but to give Callum a questioning look.

He glanced briefly at the ceiling in what was almost an eye roll. "Give me your number."

Felicity's eyebrows drew together at the unexpected request.

"This isn't the place." Callum glanced meaningfully around the shop, crowded by customers who looked much too interested in what they were talking about. "We'll meet up after Lou's shift is over."

With a shrug, Felicity rattled off her cell number. Out of the corner of her eye, she saw Bennett tapping at the screen of his phone. It probably wasn't the best idea to give her phone number to her stalker, but he was turning into more of a… helper, maybe? At least a neutral party. So it would probably turn out okay in the end.

She hoped.

FOUR

FELICITY SPENT THE REST OF the morning and the early part of the afternoon at The Coffee Spot. Immediately after getting her cell number, Callum had leaned over the counter to kiss Lou on the cheek and left, so Felicity only had one stone-faced giant to deal with. To her surprise, Bennett was an unexpectedly relaxing companion. Once he had Dino Fletcher's details, he focused on researching on his own laptop while she studied maps of the town and surrounding areas.

When Felicity gave a little shiver, Bennett turned his head to look at her questioningly.

"It's this." She turned her laptop so he could see the topographic map she'd pulled up.

He frowned at the screen for a solid minute before giving her another look that clearly said he didn't get it.

"All this." She circled her hand over the map. "It's so... mountainy."

He still looked confused. "We're...*in* the mountains?"

"I know." She turned her computer so it faced her again. "But I'm a Front Range girl. I'm used to mountains being more of a pretty backdrop than a…"

When she paused, Lou stepped closer and filled in the blank. "A predator-filled, ice-coated, shifting rock pile of death?"

Felicity pointed at her. "Exactly."

His snort sounded amused, making Felicity raise her eyebrows at him. "You disagree?"

"Nope." He leaned back on his stool, his dark eyes gleaming at her in a way that made her want to smile back at him. "That's actually a really good description."

"I'm from the East Coast, so this"—Lou drew a circle over the map with her palm, imitating the motion Felicity had just made—"took a while to get used to. I love it out here, but it'll never not be terrifying."

For the first time since they'd hatched this plan, Felicity envied Charlie. Knowing Jane, she'd never venture out of civilization. At least Charlie wouldn't have to chase *her* skip through snow-dusted cliffs littered with mountain lions.

Swallowing a sigh, Felicity made herself look on the bright side. At this altitude, she could test her lung capacity, plus she did love a good adrenaline rush. The extra helping of mountain danger would just add to her buzz.

"Find out anything useful?" she asked Bennett, deciding a subject change was in order.

He twitched his shoulders in an awkward shrug as he bent over his laptop again.

Something about him seemed so familiar, but Felicity

couldn't put her finger on what. She would've definitely remembered meeting—or even getting a glimpse of—Bennett, so he had to be reminding her of someone else. Pushing the thought to the side for the moment, she focused on what he was saying.

"I found a few names connected to the Freedom Survivors," he said. "Clint Yarran seems to be the current guy in charge…at least for the past six months."

"Yarran," Lou repeated thoughtfully. Now that the lunch rush was over and everyone else except the three of them had left, she'd been chatting with Felicity while clearing tables. "That sounds familiar. Who was the boss before him?"

"I just have a nickname." Bennett scrolled down as he peered at the screen. "Cobra Jones."

"Hmm…" Felicity said. "Those are always the guys who started life with names like Eugene Balzac."

Lou winced. "Oh, poor Eugene."

Leaning over to get a better look at Bennett's laptop, Felicity blinked and then turned to give him a condemning look even as she tried to hide her grin. "Field County Sheriff's Department? Why, Mr. Bennett Green! Did you hack into the local sheriff's records?"

Placing her hands over her ears, Lou called out, "La-la-la! My law enforcement–adjacent self can't hear you talking about doing illegal stuff!"

"Maybe?" Bennett guiltily peeked at Felicity out of the corner of his eye, and she decided there should be a law against looking so adorable while also being such a big mountain of muscles and hard jawline. "Their security is terrible. It's almost like they *wanted* me to access the records."

"Norah!" Felicity said suddenly as the thing she'd been struggling to think of all day finally popped into her head. Bennett reminded her of Norah, which changed her entire perception of him. Maybe he wasn't an ass—or at least as much of one as she first thought. Maybe, like Norah, he was just really socially awkward.

"What?" Lou asked.

"Your sister?" Bennett said at the same time.

"Yes, sorry." Flushing a bit, Felicity waved her hand in an attempt to dismiss it. "I was just reminded of my sister. Going back to the militia, what happened six months ago?"

"Six months ago?" Bennett repeated, still looking slightly abashed from being caught hacking.

"When management changed." Filing her speculation about Bennett into a file marked *Things to Think About Later*, Felicity refocused on her current case. "Why did Yarran get promoted? Did the militia guys just take a vote?"

Looking thoughtful, Lou paused in stacking some used plates. "I've never thought about how a militia's structured. Is it led by democratically elected officials? A board of directors? Do they fight for the alpha position like a pack of werewolves?"

The last suggestion made Felicity stare at her before looking back at Bennett, who was scrolling through the records on his screen, apparently unfazed. "I'm not seeing anything."

"Hang on." Felicity did an internet search on Cobra Jones from Simpson, Colorado, but nothing relevant came up. He hadn't died, been arrested, or anything else newsworthy—at least according to the internet. Disappointed, she sat back, thinking for a moment before asking Lou, "You mentioned being law enforcement–adjacent? What's up with that?"

"I'm on the county's rescue dive team," Lou explained. "Callum too—he's our brave leader, in fact. On calls, we work with lots of different departments: fire, search and rescue, sheriff's office, even the Colorado BCA—Bureau of Criminal Apprehension—occasionally."

"Anyone discreet and willing to share info at the sheriff's office?" Felicity asked, wishing she was back in Langston with all her and her sisters' contacts.

"Hmm…maybe?" Lou already had her phone out and was texting someone. After a few minutes, she spoke again. "Okay, so Daisy has to work until four tonight, but she said we can use her office for a murder club meeting anytime after that."

That made even stone-faced Bennett blink.

"She does know this is just a boring meth dealer, right?" Felicity was questioning the wisdom of building her bounty-hunting army. "I can't promise any murders."

Waving a dismissive hand, Lou went back to clearing tables. "Don't worry about disappointing the crew. They're so hungry for some excitement, any crime will do."

"That's…reassuring?" Felicity found herself seeking eye contact with Bennett yet again. She really couldn't help herself. It appeared they were the only two semi-normal people in a town of rather odd ducks, and Felicity wasn't used to that. She and her sisters—with their bond-recovery business and felonious mom—had always been the strange ones. It was disconcerting, to say the least.

Glancing at her phone, she cleared her laptop screen and powered down.

"Heading out?" Lou asked, looking a bit anxious, as if she was worried that Felicity would take her investigation—as tame as it was—and leave town altogether.

"It's a little early to check in at the motel, but I'm going to try." Felicity swallowed a yawn as she gathered her things, tucking everything neatly into her laptop bag. "My extremely early morning is catching up with me."

"Callum has your number, right?" After Felicity nodded, Lou continued, "I'll have him text you the address for Daisy's gym. Not that you really need the address—it's the only gym in town, and the town's pretty small. Want to meet there around five? That way, we'll be done before dinner. I highly recommend going to Levi's after the murder club meeting."

"Levi's?" she asked.

"Barbecue place." Lou clarified. "You'll love it. Bring your stalker if you like."

Felicity raised her eyebrows at him. "If I don't, you'll just show up anyway, won't you?"

His shrug was definitely a yes.

———

The Black Bear Inn wasn't much, but Felicity had seen a lot worse over the past couple weeks hunting for her mom. At least it was cheap and looked clean, plus not having to share with

Charlie was a nice bonus. The security on the place was a joke though. The room key was an actual *key*, with the room number attached. In all her bounty-hunting travels, she'd never seen that before—except in horror movies.

She'd barely put her bag down when a heavy knock at the door made her jump. Blaming her atypical nerves on her earlier scary-movie thoughts, Felicity exhaled in a laugh and headed for the door. After checking the peephole, she rolled her eyes and unlatched the dead bolt.

"Really, Mr. Green?" She swung open the door, revealing the man in all his mountain-size glory. "It's been five minutes. Even real stalkers aren't this dedicated."

His frown appeared even more pronounced than usual as he peered over her shoulder into her room.

"What's wrong?" she asked, following his gaze and not seeing anything except outdated furniture and her couple of bags.

"This place."

She waited, but he didn't seem inclined to elaborate.

"I mean, I've stayed in worse." She gave a shrug as she leaned against the frame, holding the door open with her shoulder. When his frown deepened even more, she took a guess at what was bothering him. "Is it the furnishings from the seventies or the ancient plumbing that's making you extra grumpy?"

"I'm not grumpy." He had the gall to look surprised by that.

"Well, you give a really good impression of a Grumpy Gus then." Her brain and body were protesting her early-morning wake-up, and she could feel her nap-time minutes slipping away. "What specifically is bothering you about this place?"

"The security." He held up his key, dangling it between two fingers as if it were something nasty he didn't want to touch. "This is a *key*."

Amusement edged into Felicity's tired impatience. "Very good," she said in a slow, encouraging tone, one she would use when praising Warrant for retrieving his ball after she'd thrown it.

By the way Bennett's eyes narrowed, he'd obviously caught her sarcasm. "This is my room number." He gave the key still dangling from his fingers a shake, and the attached wooden piece—which indeed had *#4* carved into it—rattled against the metal key and chain. "*With* the key."

She sighed, resigning herself to the fact that she probably wasn't getting any sleep until after the murder club meeting and dinner. "I need you to get to the point, B. Do you want to borrow my pepper spray?"

"What? No." His hand holding his key dropped back to his side. "*I'll* be okay."

Felicity caught the slight emphasis he'd given the word *I'll* and folded her arms across her chest. "Mm-hmm. So if *you'll* be okay, what's the problem?" She bared her teeth in something she knew looked nothing like an actual smile.

"You're—" As oblivious to social cues as he seemed to be, he did catch himself after only one word. He studied her uncertainly before carefully rewording whatever he'd been about to say. "I wanted to make sure that you felt safe here."

She couldn't hold back an actual smile at that. As much as she wanted to keep him at arm's length, the man could be

obnoxiously sweet at times. "Thank you. I'll be fine. I appreciate your concern, but I really need a nap."

As she stepped back and moved to close the door, Bennett
caught the edge to stop it. "Do you need any...protection?"

Her mind immediately went to condoms, and her face got
fiery hot. "Umm...what?"

"Weapons?" he clarified, appearing to be thankfully unaware
of her misunderstanding. "Trip wires? Small explosives?"

It was her turn to study him. She was too tired to determine
whether he was joking or not, so she forced a polite smile and
shook her head. "No, thank you. I'm all set with explosives *and*
trip wires. Come back around quarter to five, and we'll drive to
the murder club meeting together."

His eyebrows shot up underneath his shaggy black bangs.
"Together? Really?"

"No sense in taking separate cars." She tugged on the door
handle, and he released his grip, allowing her to close the door
almost all the way between them. At the last second, she leaned
back out. "Besides, you'd just follow me anyway." At his affirmative
shrug, she snorted and closed the door with a firm click. "Stalker."

She wasn't sure what that said about her that she said it
almost...fondly.

———

The gym was surprisingly new and expansive. Even though
Simpson was a tiny place, the machines and weight room were
much better than anything her hometown of Langston had
to offer. Felicity was quickly learning that there were lots of

hidden details in this quirky little mountain town, both nice and not so nice.

Just like a certain PI, she thought with a quick glance at Bennett. He'd offered to be the one to drive, and Felicity had agreed. Not only did she—probably unwisely—trust the guy for some reason, but she also knew that the motel was within a fairly reasonable walking distance if things went south and she had to find her own way back. Also, she may not carry small explosives, but she wasn't completely defenseless.

"Felicity!" Lou called out from the other side of the space. When Felicity looked over, the blond woman waved them toward an open door in the corner behind a line of heavy bags. Just a couple people were using the equipment—a woman doing dead lifts in the weight room and a man running on a treadmill.

Felicity led the way toward Lou, sensing that Bennett was following behind her. It was strange how much it felt like he was watching her back.

Felicity paused in the doorway, taking in the three women already sitting around the office. She wasn't shy in any way, but walking into something casually called a *murder club* was a bit disconcerting. Two of the women were smiling, however, and the other had a serious expression that seemed neutral rather than hostile. "Hello," Felicity said.

"Daisy, Ellie, Rory," Lou introduced quickly. "Where's the peanut, Ellie?"

"Home with George." Ellie had a sweet expression, big dark eyes, and long dark hair. "I figured she's a little young to be an active murder club member."

Although Lou looked disappointed, she said, "You're probably right. Everyone, this is Felicity and Bennett."

"No Callum?" Felicity asked, giving a general wave of greeting to the room before finding an empty seat between Ellie and Rory. Daisy sat behind the desk, leaning back in her chair and idly turning the seat back and forth. The movement made Felicity think that, had Daisy been alone, she would've been spinning the chair around.

"The fire chief grabbed him for an impromptu budget meeting," Lou said, hopping up to sit on the corner of the desk. "I promised to tell him everything I learn tonight and also that I wouldn't let anyone drag me to the militia compound—*or* drag anyone else there."

"Knowing you," Daisy said, "that promise isn't nearly comprehensive enough."

"I know, right?" Lou shook her head. "It's like he doesn't know me at all."

Felicity glanced toward the doorway, where Bennett was leaning against the wall. "Daisy, is there another chair we can pull in here?"

"Right, sorry!" The woman was halfway to standing when Bennett shook his head.

"I'm fine here," he said, back in poker-face mode.

Felicity studied him, wondering if he ever really left poker-face mode or if she was just getting better at reading his slight changes of expression.

Daisy remained hovering above her chair, half sitting and half standing. "You sure? It's no problem to grab a chair from the front."

Bennett gave a slight but firm affirmative dip of his head, and Daisy settled into her seat again.

"Pretty nice promotion," Lou said to Bennett with just the slightest suspicious edge to her vivacious tone. "From stalker to partner."

Felicity found herself inexplicably bristling. Pressing down the urge to defend the big guy, she managed to say mildly, "Not quite a partner. More of a lieutenant in my brand-new bounty-hunting army."

"You're a bounty hunter?" Ellie asked.

"Yes!" Lou answered excitedly before Felicity could say a word. "She's after a meth dealer and needs our help finding him."

"Just research help." Felicity had a feeling she needed to slow the runaway train that was Lou before everyone in the room ended up breaking into the militia compound at two in the morning, rappelling down the walls in black catsuits like the mountain version of Charlie's Angels. "And you'll be researching somewhere safe and far away from the actual militia."

Lou laughed, not appearing to take offense. "Callum will be relieved to hear that. Why don't you tell us who and what you're looking for, and we'll share what we know?"

"Okay." Felicity resisted the urge to clear her throat. With all the stares fixed on her, she felt like she was back in high school, about to give an oral report. "Before I do, I'd ask that you keep what I tell you to yourselves—"

"Callum and Chris, Daisy's husband, already know," Lou broke in. "And Ellie and Rory tell their husbands everything."

"That's fine." It wasn't really fine, but Felicity knew it was inevitable that they share the news with their respective partners. "If you can just limit it to the eight of you, I'd appreciate it." She waited for nods all around before continuing. "My skip is a member of the Freedom Survivors…"

A groan from multiple people interrupted her.

"Do you think we could start a petition to change that name?" Daisy asked. "It's so dumb that it's embarrassing for everyone involved."

Hopping off her perch on the desk, Lou grabbed a marker from the ledge of the whiteboard propped on an easel in the corner of the office. She wrote *Create petition to change name from Freedom Survivors to something better* on the bottom of the board. "Not a priority right now, but I agree it's something we need to do as soon as Felicity gets her guy. A name that bad reflects poorly on the whole town."

Bennett gave a soft cough, drawing Felicity's attention. Although his expression hadn't changed, she had a feeling he was amused.

She swallowed her own smile and asked, "Okay for me to continue?"

Lou waved a hand in an expansive gesture before lifting the marker to the top of the board and pausing there as if waiting to record whatever Felicity was about to say. All the focused attention was throwing her off a little, but she gamely plunged back in.

"Dino Fletcher is a meth dealer who was arrested in Langston." She paused as Lou wrote *Dino Fletcher—meth dealer,*

Langston, CO. "He was released on bail but never showed up to his first court date. Before he came to Langston two years ago, he was a member of the...Freedom Survivors." After the previous discussions, she couldn't help pausing before she said it.

Lou used her marker to tap the note about the petition.

"Do you have a picture?" asked the serious one of the four— *Rory*, Felicity remembered.

Felicity pulled up Dino's mug shot on her phone and handed it to Rory. She studied the photo before passing it across Felicity to Ellie as Daisy and Lou moved to where they could see the screen over Ellie's shoulder.

"Tall guy," Ellie commented, and Felicity nodded. At six four, the guy should be easy to spot in a group. He could change his hair color or length, grow a beard, or even disguise his face, but he was stuck being tall.

"Have any of you seen him around Simpson before?" Felicity asked.

"Don't think so," Lou said, and the other three shook their heads.

Ellie handed Felicity's phone back to her. "Sorry."

Waving off the woman's apology, Felicity gave her a small smile as she returned her phone to her pocket. "It was a long shot anyway. Since the guy just skipped bail, he's going to be doing his best to stay out of sight."

"What information do you need from us?" Rory asked.

"To start, where the militia compound is located."

"I've got this." Daisy sent a text, and her phone rang seconds later. "Hey, what's up?" She paused and then answered whoever was on the other side of the call. "Because I figured you'd know where our Freedom Survivor friends hang out. Do you?" Smirking a little, she spoke again. "*I* don't need to go there. My new friend, Felicity, needs to go there."

Felicity was a little surprised she'd been elevated from *brand-new acquaintance* to *friend* so quickly.

"Because her bail jumper is there—well, it's likely he's there." This time, the pause was shorter. "She's a bounty hunter. How awesome is that?" Daisy smiled at Felicity, looking positively delighted. "Lou met her first, and then she got the murder club back together."

Whatever the person on the other end of the call said made Daisy's smile disappear.

"Oh, don't worry," she assured the person. "Dino isn't a murderer. He's just a meth dealer." She sighed at the response. "That's okay if you don't want to tell us. Rory's pretty sure she knows the general location. We'll just go there and wander around a bit until we find it."

Everyone looked at Rory, who looked mildly surprised at this news.

"Uh-huh." Daisy's grin was back, triumphant this time. She jumped up from her chair and hurried to the whiteboard, accepting the marker Lou offered her and scribbling directions on the empty top left corner of the board. "Uh-huh. Got it. Love you. I will. See you at home tonight. Bye." As she ended the call, she looked proud. "Chris gave me the location." After a glance at Felicity, she clarified, "My husband is a deputy for the Field County Sheriff's Department."

Felicity thanked her as she copied the notes from the whiteboard into her phone. Apparently, she'd picked the right murder club to ask for help.

"Does anyone know the new leader of the militia?" she asked. "Clint Yarran?"

Rory frowned. "What happened to Cobra?"

"Cobra?" Ellie repeated. "Someone's trying a little too hard to compensate for something."

Felicity snorted at the comment but focused on Rory. "Clint took over the position six months ago. You knew Cobra?"

"I don't know him well." Rory was beginning to look uncomfortable with everyone focused on her. Felicity could relate. "He just bought a couple of shotguns from me." Her gaze moved to meet Felicity's. "I own a gun store."

"Gun store?" Felicity smiled in surprised delight. She knew she didn't fit the bounty-hunting mold, and people were always shocked when she told them what she did for a living. She imagined this quiet, slight woman got a similar reaction.

Rory didn't elaborate. She just watched Felicity with wary light eyes.

Letting her curiosity slide since she figured Lou would give her all the details later, Felicity asked instead, "Have you seen Cobra since Clint took over?"

Rory's gaze turned thoughtful before she shook her head. "Not for almost a year."

"Know what his legal name was?" Felicity asked.

"Cobra Jones." As hard as it was to believe that any parent would name their child Cobra, Rory's voice was confident.

"That's what he used for the background check, so if it's a nick-name, he had it legally changed to Cobra at some point."

While they'd been talking, Lou had listed Cobra and Clint on the whiteboard, and she'd sketched out a timeline with Rory's last sighting of Cobra on it.

"Are we going to be researching the Freedom Survivors' leadership?" Ellie asked, sounding hopeful.

"Possibly." Lou added Clint's takeover of the militia to the timeline. "I'm curious now. Did Cobra willingly give up control, or did something more nefarious happen? Did Clint literally kill for his new position?"

"It's more likely Cobra bought an RV and retired in Texas." Bennett's bass voice came unexpectedly from his spot by the door and made them all jump.

"Do you know something we don't?" Felicity asked.

His eyebrows drew together. "No?"

"Your hypothetical was just very specific." Turning back to the women, she said, "He's right though." She hated to ruin their fun, but she also felt responsible for her little bounty-hunting army, and she didn't want them poking around in the local militia and making potentially dangerous enemies. "It's most likely he's safe somewhere else."

The other four women exchanged a look with one another, but the only response was a half-hearted "maybe" from Lou.

"So what's our next step?" Daisy asked, changing the subject with more enthusiasm than smoothness.

Felicity let it slide, reminding herself that she was not these women's mother. If they were going to investigate the Freedom

Survivors' regime change, there was really nothing Felicity could do except warn them of the dangers. "I'm going to the address your husband gave us and poke around a little. If I'm lucky, Dino will be there, and I'll nab him."

"Is it usually that easy to find a bail jumper?" Ellie asked.

Turning her hand from side to side in a *sort-of* motion, Felicity said, "Sometimes. Most skips aren't geniuses, so they're pretty easy to track down. Others..." She trailed off as she thought about some of their harder, more dangerous cases. "Others are more work." She didn't elaborate more than that, not wanting to quash their enthusiasm with the less-fun reality.

"What can we do in the meantime?" Lou asked, capping her marker.

"Anything you can find out about Dino or the Freedom Survivors would be helpful." Felicity hesitated, conscious of the possibility she might be leading these very nice ladies into trouble. "Try to be discreet, however. If Dino finds out we're searching for him, he'll be gone. You don't want to rile up Clint and his buddies either. I have a feeling they'd make uncomfortable enemies." All four women nodded their agreement, and Felicity stood. "You were all really helpful. Thank you."

"You're welcome," Lou, who was apparently the group's spokesperson, said. "Good luck out there."

Felicity moved toward the door, but the other women stayed in place. "Well...bye," she said a bit awkwardly before unlocking and opening the door. Bennett followed her out into the main gym, and Felicity realized that she was looking forward to discussing what they'd just learned with him.

She swallowed a groan. As much as she fought it, the guy continued inching his way closer to being her partner. Charlie was never going to let her forget this.

FIVE

ONCE THEY WERE OUTSIDE THE gym, Bennett moved to her side as they headed toward his SUV. "They're going to be trouble."

"Soooo much trouble." Even as she said it, though, she had to laugh. "They're so eager to fight crime. I'm surprised they don't make themselves superhero capes and patrol the town at night."

"Don't suggest that," he warned, making her chuckle again.

Felicity reached into her bag and pulled out a case with two earpieces inside. After the slightest hesitation, she handed one to Bennett and stuck the other in her right ear.

Glancing down at the small piece of electronics in his hand, his eyes widened for a moment before he huffed out what sounded suspiciously like a laugh.

"What?" she asked, watching him insert it into his ear.

"If this doesn't work, we can use mine."

She stared at him for a moment before snorting her own laugh. "You bugged the office too?"

His amused look was her only answer.

Still smiling, Felicity climbed into the passenger side of Bennett's SUV and concentrated on listening to Lou's voice. Although audible, the sound quality wasn't the best, and she wondered if Bennett's was better.

"…check out Felicity's story?" Lou was asking, making Felicity frown. She should've expected some suspicion—deservedly so, since she'd just bugged the office—but it still stung.

"Chris said there's a Felicity Pax with Pax Bond Recovery out of Langston, Colorado, who's licensed as a bond recovery agent." That sounded like Daisy, the one married to the deputy.

"Good." Even with the poor sound quality, Felicity heard Lou heave a sigh. "I would've been really sad if she turned out to be a criminal or scammer or something. We bonded at the coffee shop today."

"There's no guarantee she was telling the truth about her skip though," Rory's serious voice warned.

"The Dino details check out." That was Daisy again. "A Douglas 'Dino' Fletcher did skip out on his bail after being charged for meth possession with intent to distribute."

"Ask Chris if Dino used to be in the Freedom Survivors," Ellie suggested.

"Ugh, that name," Lou groaned. "I hope we solve this quickly so we can move on to that petition."

"He says we'd need the Langston Police file on him for info on his known associates." Daisy sounded disappointed by that. "You'd think a cop would know how to hack the records of another cop."

The women laughed, and Felicity couldn't help but join them. She covered her mouth with her hand, even though they couldn't hear her.

"What about the guy with her, Bennett... Do you know his last name?" Ellie asked.

"Mr. Creepy and Silent?" Lou asked, making Felicity bristle with protective fury. She glanced over at the man under discussion, but he didn't look fazed by the insult. "He's a PI, Bennett Green. Does Chris have anything on him?"

"I didn't think he was creepy," Ellie said, and Felicity decided that Ellie was her favorite of her bounty-hunting soldiers. "I thought he was nice."

"That's because you have a thing for the big, quiet guys," Lou said affectionately. "Compared to George, this Mr. Green was positively chatty."

Ellie protested, "George talks."

"We only have your word on that," Daisy said in a teasing tone before returning to the topic under discussion. "Chris said there's a Denver address, but nothing much else. Not even a speeding ticket. Either this guy's a total Boy Scout, or... Actually, I don't know what the alternative is. A fake identity?"

"It's my real name. I just don't speed," Bennett said, sounding sulky in a way that was strangely adorable.

Felicity turned her head to hide her smile from him, mentally scolding herself for finding her stalker—ex-stalker—much too appealing.

"I don't have any speeding tickets," Rory said in protest, "and I don't have a fake identity."

"Exactly," Bennett muttered.

"That's because you never left your bunker until you started dating Ian," Lou said matter-of-factly. "Is this Mr. Green—totally made-up name, by the way—a licensed PI?"

"No license required in Colorado," Daisy reported.

"I wouldn't have picked Green," Bennett huffed, making Felicity look at him in question. "If I picked my name, I would've chosen something better than *Green*. It sounds like a Clue character."

Felicity couldn't hold back her laugh at that, and she missed a chunk of the women's conversation. When she tuned back in, Ellie was talking about needing to get home. Felicity lifted her eyebrows at Bennett, who plucked out his earpiece, handing it back to her and then starting the SUV.

Although she kept hers in for the trip back to the Black Bear Inn, Felicity didn't learn anything new or interesting. Various male voices arrived, and everyone chitchatted so casually she had the paranoid suspicion that they'd found one of the listening devices. When Bennett parked in the spot in front of her room, she pulled out her earpiece and put it in its case with the other.

"Do you agree?" Bennett asked.

"With what?" she asked, wondering if she'd missed whatever it was she was supposed to be agreeing with. He spoke so rarely, and his voice was so mesmerizing, that she couldn't imagine not listening to everything he said.

"What Lou said?" When she gave him a look, he elaborated. "About me being creepy?"

Surprised, Felicity didn't answer immediately.

Bennett tensed, his mouth drawing into a tight line. "Fair. I did stalk you, after all."

"No."

"What?" he asked, his body still tense.

"You're not creepy." It was the truth, but Felicity still found herself blushing when she said it. "You remind me of Norah."

"Norah?" he repeated. "I remind you of your *sister*?"

"You're both really smart and good at your jobs, but neither of you is exactly…socially proficient." Felicity winced, hoping that hadn't sounded as insulting to him as it did to her.

It must not have, since Bennett relaxed slightly, leaning ever so slightly closer to her. "So not creepy."

"Not creepy."

"Even though I stalked you."

"It was more of an annoying stalking, not a creepy stalking." *This is one of the weirdest conversations I've ever had.*

For a long, quiet moment, he searched her eyes as if determining her sincerity, and then he sat back and smiled faintly. "Good."

Realizing that she'd been staring right back at him, Felicity fumbled for the door handle. She popped it open as her stomach gave a pang of complaint. "So…dinner?"

With a nod, he glanced at the dashboard clock. "Out here in fifteen?"

"It's a date." It took enormous effort to hold back her flinch at those words. "Or a plan. It's a plan then. Let's call it a plan."

He actually chuckled. "Who's not socially proficient now?"

"Fifteen minutes." She gave him her best glare, which usually managed to shut down even irrepressible Charlie. Bennett didn't look too bothered by it, to her great annoyance.

Getting out of the SUV, she slammed the door to release some of her awkward frustration, but the only sound was a soft *thunk*. "Where's a beater car when you need one?" she grumbled, heading for her door.

———

Levi's looked just like what Felicity would've guessed a barbecue joint in a small, weird, mountain town would look like. The place was packed, so she figured they either had good food or this was the only restaurant in town.

As the harried server led them toward a table toward the back, Felicity checked out the customers, the image of Dino at the forefront of her mind. It would be a very convenient and unlikely thing if she managed to run into her skip her first night in town, but it was possible.

The only familiar face was the serious frowning one attached to Lou's husband, Callum, who was sitting with three other men. Lou didn't appear to be with him.

As soon as the server waved them toward their table, Felicity and Bennett scuffled over the seat with the best view of the room. She won, despite Bennett's surprising speed, but she had a suspicion that he let her have it. After all, as strong and big as he was, he could've just lifted her right off the prime-viewing spot and deposited her wherever he wanted to put her. Instead, after their minor tussle, he moved to the other side of the table, grabbed the free chair, and wedged it right next to her.

"This is going to be awkward," she warned him as he settled in, close enough that his shoulder pressed against hers.

His only response was a tip of his head toward the opposite side of the table.

"And put my back to the room of strangers?" she responded with an exaggerated shudder. "I'd rather sit on your lap."

Even in the atmospheric restaurant lighting, Felicity could see that his cheeks had reddened, which made her flush in turn. When she ran what she'd just said back in her mind, she realized it sounded less like the platonic teasing she was going for and more like...flirting.

She was almost relieved when Callum approached their table with his companions in tow. He hadn't seemed like the most convivial person when she'd first met him at the coffee shop, but anyone who'd break the thick, tension-filled atmosphere she'd unintentionally created was welcome.

"Hey, Callum," she greeted with a relief she hoped wasn't too obvious. "Sorry you couldn't join us for the murder club meeting."

It wasn't until he gave a slight wince that she realized how that'd sound to anyone *not* familiar with murder club. The older two of his companions looked interested in a startled way, and the youngest one looked irritated, but he'd looked that way since they'd walked over, so she thought that might just be his face's natural state.

"Murder club?" The one who looked a bit like Santa was the first to speak.

Callum gave her a *you did this, so you fix it* look.

Felicity forced a laugh that she hoped sounded convincing. "Just an inside joke for a group of friends getting together. No one was murdered, I promise."

"Ah," skinny Santa said with a nod, apparently accepting that rather weak explanation. "You never know around here. We seem to get more than our share of crime."

"Felicity Pax and Bennett Green." The stern way Callum said their names nearly made her jump. She was half expecting to be arrested. "This is Fire Chief Winston Early and firefighters Finn and Kieran Byrne."

He pointed at the skinny Santa first, then at the smiling older man, and ended on the young, cranky-looking one. His frown hadn't lightened during their conversation, so she decided that at some point during his short life, his face had indeed stuck like that. Although the chief and Finn looked to be in their early sixties, all three of them had the well-muscled look she associated with firefighters. Kieran could've posed for a calendar if he was capable of losing his scowl. Or maybe there was a calendar featuring cranky yet fit firefighters?

"What brings you to Simpson?" Finn asked. From the age difference and his resemblance to Kieran, Felicity was guessing they were father and son. Both had black hair—although Finn's was graying—blue eyes, and the strong jawline of a Disney villain.

"Just seizing an opportunity to get some work done while enjoying the mountains." She purposefully didn't mention her hunt for a certain meth-dealing bail jumper. It was bad enough that the entire murder club and their spouses knew. If the whole town learned she was a bounty hunter, Dino was sure to hear about it, and then he'd be gone. "The aspens are beautiful this time of year."

Finn seemed to accept this, but Kieran continued his silent glaring, and the chief's eyes narrowed slightly.

"What do you do for work?" the chief asked. His tone was casual, but she still sensed an interrogation was beginning and felt the accompanying nervous tension start to coil in her stomach.

She waved a dismissive hand. "Nothing interesting—a mix of public relations and bonds." It wasn't quite a lie, but it skirted the edge. It was only because Bennett was still crammed up against her side that she heard his almost inaudible snort. She made sure her glance at Callum was quick and casual, but his expression hadn't changed, except for the slightest amused quirk of his mouth. It looked like Lou had been telling the truth about her husband's ability to keep things private...so far at least. "Nothing nearly as interesting as firefighting. That must have its exciting moments."

"Not today." The chief grimaced. "It was hours of budget meetings." She made a sympathetic face as his attention turned to Bennett. "Do you two work together then, or are you here for the 'enjoying the mountains' part?" the chief asked.

Felicity drew in a breath to answer, but Bennett spoke before she could. "We're working together on a project."

"Ah." The chief looked like he was ready to ask a whole new slew of questions, but Callum pointedly looked at his watch.

"Didn't you tell Dory you'd be home early tonight?" Callum asked.

The fire chief checked his watch and winced. "I'd better go. Nice meeting both of you. Enjoy your stay, wear sunscreen, and remember to drink lots of water. We don't want to be seeing you on an altitude sickness call."

"We'll remember that," Felicity said, giving him a wave as he turned to make his way toward the exit.

Callum focused on the two remaining firefighters. "Finn, Kieran." His tone and short nod were so beautifully dismissive, Felicity vowed to remember how he did it and practice in front of a mirror. The thought of having the power to make people leave with a word and simple glare made her practically giddy.

Although Finn hesitated at first, his curiosity obvious, he eventually caved to Callum's dismissal. Raising a hand, he smiled at Felicity and Bennett. "Good to meet you." Kieran dipped his chin, and both men turned to leave. Before they'd gotten past two tables, Finn was hailed by a middle-aged couple, and the two stopped to talk—well, Finn stopped to talk. Kieran's shoulders dropped in what looked to be a long sigh, and he gazed—scowling, of course—over the heads of the couple.

As Callum pulled an unused chair from a nearby table, Felicity gave him a nod. "Impressive."

He settled across the table from them, angling his chair so his back wasn't fully to the room, and lifted an eyebrow in a way that asked her to elaborate as clearly as if he'd said the words out loud.

Felicity had a feeling she was going to steal all sorts of gestures from him over the next few days. His body language was just so *effective*. "You got rid of them so quickly with minimal talking. Nice."

Bennett shifted beside her, drawing her gaze to him. "I talk minimally." Although his expression was still impassive, she detected a hint of wounded pride in his tone.

She patted his shoulder. "You're both very efficient with your word use. Good job." When he frowned at her, she choked a little on the laugh that wanted to escape before turning back to Callum. "I suppose you want the murder club meeting minutes?"

"Lou already texted me the highlights."

Felicity wasn't surprised or bothered by that information. Apparently this was the week of trusting complete strangers.

"What's your plan?" Callum asked straight-out.

"Depends." When his mouth flattened in what she assumed was dissatisfaction in her answer, she elaborated. "The next step is to check out the militia's compound. After that, it depends on what we learn."

He eyed her for a moment and then dipped his chin in a nod. "Keep us updated."

Felicity snorted. "Do you think for a second that your wife would allow anything except hour-by-hour progress reports?"

His smile transformed his face, making him look sweet and tender for just a second before his impassive expression returned. "Good point." He stood to leave. "Stay safe."

"You too."

As Callum walked away from their table, Bennett eyed her with amusement. "It's not like he's going on the stakeout with us," he said. "He'll be lounging around at home. I think he'll be safe."

She shrugged, settling back in her chair. Her shoulder pressed just a little bit more firmly against his upper arm, and she couldn't bring herself to mind. "He's a rescue diver. I'm sure he needs to take extra care to stay safe. Or even driving home on these twisty mountain roads. Besides, it's a good habit to get into, staying safe."

Bennett snorted, his arm draping behind her chair. It wasn't touching her, but it still gave her the feeling of being surrounded and protected, as if all *she* had to do to stay safe was continue to sit next to Bennett Green with his arm wrapped around her. "Says the adrenaline-junkie bounty hunter."

She grinned, not at all offended. "There's safe, and then there's *boring*."

"Boring is something you'll never be."

————

I might not be boring, Felicity thought, tapping her fingers against the armrest on the SUV's door, *but stakeouts always are*.

Part of the problem was that the single-level, concrete-walled building that made up the militia's home base was sitting on a high plain that stretched, mostly treeless and flat, to the base of the encircling mountains. Even though it was dark, it was impossible to get close to the compound without being spotted. The barbed-wire fence didn't provide any concealment either, and without much of a moon, there was no way Bennett could see well enough to drive without his headlights on. Therefore, they were parked on the side of a dirt road, too far away to see anything except the very occasional flash of headlights from someone passing through the automatic gate providing access to the compound.

Frustrated, Felicity brought her night-vision binoculars up to her eyes, then almost immediately returned them to her lap.

"This is a waste of time," she said.

Even though she'd just broken a five-minute silence in the SUV, Bennett didn't jump at her sudden outburst. Instead, he calmly turned his head to look at her, staying silent.

She took that as a request to elaborate. "Even if Dino strolled out of the compound right in front of us, we're too far away to recognize him. We need to get closer."

He reached for his door handle. "Then let's get closer."

Felicity blinked at the seat where Bennett had just been sitting. "That was easy." For some reason, she'd been expecting him to protest, but he was a PI, after all. It wasn't like he worked at a desk job when he wasn't tailing her around the mountains. He was likely used to action and occasional danger.

She got out of the car as well, easing her door closed soundlessly after her. Bennett was already moving away from the car, and she hurried to follow before the dark could swallow him. The ground looked flat, but the rocks and scrubby plants threatened to trip her. She wished a flashlight wouldn't have revealed their position like a beacon as she squinted at the dark ground. A shallow gully stretched across their path, and they scrambled down to the dry bottom before climbing back out.

A high-pitched yipping howl broke the night's silence, and it was quickly joined by other, similar voices.

"Coyotes," Bennett said, low-voiced.

"I know." She was almost disappointed that the darkness hid her eye roll. PI Green needed to know how ridiculous he was being.

She could feel more than see his gaze on her.

"I'm not *that* much of a city girl." That felt like a lie, so she amended it. "Fine, so I'm like ninety-five percent city girl, but even cities have coyotes."

"Sorry."

"It's fine." His apology knocked all the defensive indignation out of her. "Just don't assume I'm dumb."

"You're not dumb." The absolute certainty in his tone made her stomach warm for some strange reason.

They crested a small rise, and the lights from the militia compound came back into view—although a lot closer than they'd looked from the car. They both fell silent, and Felicity tried to move as soundlessly as she could as the tall fence surrounding the compound loomed closer.

A flash of light in her periphery caught her attention, and she jerked her head around, but there was just darkness there. Splitting her attention between where she was putting her feet and the spot where she'd seen the brief illumination, she caught the moment of light again.

She exhaled in an almost silent huff.

"What?" Bennett asked in a whisper.

"Firefly."

There was a short pause. "Is that a code word?"

"It is," she whispered mock-solemnly. "Your code name, in fact."

The silence extended so long that time that she didn't think he was going to respond. In the meantime, every time one of the lightning bugs flashed, she smiled.

Finally, he said quietly, "I've had worse."

A huff of amusement escaped before she could smother it. She never would've guessed that this big, nearly silent PI would be so funny.

Her phone vibrated in her pocket, the screen lighting up and sending a faint glow through the fabric of her pants. She thought of how she must resemble one of the fireflies darting around them, but then the reality of where she was and what they were doing sank in. As her phone continued glowing and buzzing against her leg, she scrambled to shove her hand in her pocket. Her fingers fumbled blindly, feeling huge against the tiny buttons on the sides of her phone, but she finally managed to make them work. Her phone went dark, and she sucked in a breath, her heart pounding in her chest as her hand remained clutched around the device.

For a second, everything was silent and still.

Then there was a soft thud by her feet, and dirt spattered almost noiselessly against her boots.

SIX

BENNETT GRABBED HER ARM AND yanked her back, hard enough that her feet left the ground. The force of the movement almost dragged a yelp out of her, but she swallowed it down, burning her throat. Although her brain wasn't sure what was happening, she knew that Bennett was sprinting away from the compound, towing her behind him, and that meant there was a good reason for them to be running.

As her feet moved more intentionally rather than just in reflex to avoid being dragged, Bennett's grip on her arm loosened, sliding down to grasp her hand instead. She fell into a fast, familiar rhythm next to him, her boots barely touching down on the rocky ground before they were lifting off again. She moved a half step in front of him, trusting her sense of direction to steer her in the general vicinity of the car.

Then her boot left the ground and came back down, but there wasn't anything underneath it. For a frozen moment, she

felt like a cartoon character after they'd walked off a cliff, suspended in midair, knowing that the long fall was coming.

Sure enough, she started dropping through the air, plum-
meting down until the ground appeared under her again after
what felt like an eternity, her left foot hitting with a jarring
wrench that twisted her ankle sideways. Bennett pulled her up
just a fraction of a second too late as he stumbled on his own
landing next to her.

As pain lanced through her left ankle, she realized she'd just
dropped a short distance into the shallow gully they'd crossed
on their way toward the compound. She didn't let herself stop
to check her ankle, knowing that any attention to it would just
make it hurt worse. She knew if it'd been broken, she wouldn't
have been able to keep running like she was. Even so, the sprain
still shot pain up her leg every time her left foot connected with
the ground, making her gait uneven and agonizingly slow.

After losing her rhythm, every step felt endless. Bennett
stayed next to her despite her hobbling pace, and she turned her
head toward him.

"You okay?" she asked, breathless even more from the pain
than the run.

"Yeah." His voice was low but it was endlessly reassuring to
hear. "You dropping warned me."

"Glad to…" Her breath caught as a particularly sharp
twinge bit into her ankle. "Glad to be of assistance," she managed to get out.

"Need me to carry you?"

"No." The thought of being slung over Bennett's broad

shoulder as he hauled her to safety was both horrifying and weirdly tempting. "No." The second *no* was more for the weak part of her brain rather than for him.

"Let me know if you change your mind." He didn't have any doubt in his tone, which braced her. If he thought she could make it under her own power to the car, then she would make it. His belief in her lent her confidence.

Despite her bolstered faith in herself, her ankle still really hurt. The remaining trek back to the car seemed endless. When she saw the small flashes of light appear in front of her, her clenched jaw eased slightly. The fireflies distracted her a little from her pain and fear.

They were almost on top of the car before it appeared out of the darkness, and Felicity couldn't hold back the tiniest sob of relief. Without asking, she headed for the passenger seat.

Once they were both in the car, Bennett started the engine.

"You don't mind driving, do you?" she asked belatedly. After everything that'd just happened, she could see herself driving the pair of them right into a ditch.

"No." He sent a quick but searching look her way. "How's the ankle?"

"Painful." She didn't see any reason to lie.

In the glow of the dashboard lights, she saw Bennett wince at her answer. His face was definitely relaxing since the first time she'd met him. Maybe he was starting to feel comfortable around her. Maybe he was starting to like her. Maybe—

Reining in her stampeding thoughts, she forced herself to focus on the main issue at hand. "Did someone shoot at us?"

His nod was short and grim.

"From where? The roof?" She ran through the scene in her mind. The compound was a single-story building, and everything around it had been flat. It was dark, but the bullet had hit the ground by her feet. Her skin went clammy as she realized just how close she'd come to getting really hurt—or even killed. "Thanks for getting me out of there."

His nod was a bit stiffer than usual, and she found his awkwardness endearing. Immediately, she pushed the thought from her mind. Now was not the time—if there was a good time—for getting all mushy about her former stalker. Well, now her *lifesaving* stalker, but still.

He turned off the narrow gravel track onto a slightly wider county road.

"The roof wouldn't have been high enough," she said, answering her own question as she thought about the maps and photos of the area she'd gone over earlier. "Oh!" She blamed her still-present shock for her taking so long to make the connection. "They've turned that old fire lookout into a watchtower."

Bennett dipped his chin in a nod.

"I figured that thing would be halfway to falling down." She was a little disgruntled that she hadn't thought of the fire tower immediately. Of course the militia would have someone standing watch. "It hasn't been used in fifty years."

She took his grunt as agreement.

With a sigh, she accepted that she'd been careless and moved on. "My phone lit up right before that first shot. I had it silenced, but they must've spotted the light from the screen. Sorry for almost getting us killed."

"Not your fault." He seemed to be taking their brush with death quite calmly. "Could've just as easily been my phone."

She wondered who'd be calling him. His client wanting an update on his hunt for the necklace? A friend wondering where he'd disappeared to? A girlfriend? A wife? She swallowed through a suddenly tight throat and once again forced her thoughts into a different direction. Pulling out the culprit of her almost death, she saw she'd missed a call from Charlie.

Needing a bit of normalcy—well, as much normalcy as Charlie could offer—she called her sister back.

"How're the mountains?" Charlie answered in her usual way, diving right in as if they were just continuing a conversation from another day.

Felicity tried to think of a concise way to describe the utterly wild day she'd just had. "Interesting."

"Hmm…" Charlie hummed. "Interesting in a near-death kind of way?"

With a blink, Felicity glanced at her phone screen before returning it to her ear. "Are you psychic?"

"No, but I *am* glad you're alive. Any injuries?"

"Twisted ankle, but otherwise I'm fine." Felicity tentatively flexed her foot, grimacing when the movement brought a fresh bolt of pain with it. "Bennett yanked me out of there in time."

The whole close call with death hadn't given Charlie pause, but obviously something Felicity just said had.

"Who's Bennett?" Charlie finally asked.

"Oh, that's right." Their time at the coffee shop felt so long ago, although it hadn't even been a full day. "You missed the big reveal. The B in PI B. Green stands for Bennett."

For some reason, her answer caused an even longer pause. "So…Bennett Green, as in your stalker?"

"Yes, but he's been promoted."

"Promoted? From stalker to…?"

"Lieutenant."

"Lieutenant." Charlie seemed incapable of doing anything other than repeating what she said, and Felicity took a gleeful pleasure in her sister's befuddlement. Normally, Felicity was the practical one, while Charlie was the wild card. It was fun to swap roles—at least temporarily.

"That's right." Felicity let her smile spread across her face, and she knew her amusement was obvious in her voice. "Lieutenant in my bounty-hunting army."

"You had to replace me with an entire army?" Charlie asked. "I'm flattered."

"Pretty much."

Bennett cleared his throat. "I'd like to apply for another promotion."

Felicity raised an eyebrow at him.

"General," he said.

"You can't just go from a lieutenant to a general."

Charlie made a sound of agreement. "That's a big leap."

Although Bennett got that sulky look that Felicity found so stupidly attractive, he blew out a breath and said, "Fine. Colonel."

"Captain, and that's my final offer."

After another deep sigh, he gave a resigned nod.

"I know he saved your life," Charlie said. "But don't forget he's still a PI with his own agenda. If you need help, Moo or Cara could be there in three hours to watch your back."

"Thanks, Charlie, but I'll be fine." Felicity knew she needed to change the subject before it turned into an argument she really didn't want to have in front of Captain Bennett himself. "How are things? You get your hands on them yet?"

"Not yet, but I'm so close, Fifi." A note of excitement lifted Charlie's voice. "Mom and Zach are camped out in a Springs neighborhood, and Norah's watching the State Patrol camera feeds to make sure they don't sneak out. I'm looking forward to taking both of them down."

Felicity felt a wash of the same mix of guilt, anticipation, and bone-deep weariness that dealing with their mom had brought on since she'd stolen the necklace and then disappeared. No, it was earlier than that—maybe since Felicity was a child and first understood that her mom wasn't much of a mother at all.

"Fifi?"

Realizing she'd gone silent for too long, Felicity cleared her throat. "Sorry, Charlie. I was thinking about something."

"Something like, oh, I don't know, the fact that your stalker is suddenly a high-ranking officer in your bounty-hunting army?"

"I don't know that captain is that high-ranking," Felicity grumbled, but Charlie was already off on another tangent.

"Moo's calling me," Charlie said. "Better see what she wants.

Cara and Nor didn't find anything in their first search of the closet, but they were going to dig through it again. There has to be something in there for Mom to risk breaking in. Have fun but don't die in the mountains, 'kay?"

"I won't." Although she said it with conviction, cold washed through Felicity at the thought of the close call they'd just survived. Staying alive in Simpson just got a lot more complicated.

———

By the time Bennett turned the car into the Black Bear Inn's parking lot, the adrenaline had worn off, and Felicity was exhausted.

"All I want is a hot shower and my mediocre motel bed." She stretched her sore muscles as well as she could in the passenger seat of her car.

Bennett gave her a strangely intense look but then hummed what she took as his agreement, so she decided not to ask what that glance meant. Instead, she unbuckled her seat belt in preparation of hobbling to her door as she glanced at the dashboard clock.

"It's not even midnight," she said, swallowing a yawn. "This day feels like it's lasted a thousand years already."

When Bennett stiffened, it was so tiny a movement that Felicity was surprised she'd caught the motion. It was just more evidence that she was focused on him in a way that was probably a bad idea, not to mention how much teasing she was going to get from her sisters when this whole story came out.

Following his gaze through the windshield to the sidewalk in front of her room, she groaned. "What now?"

The elderly woman who'd checked her in was waiting outside her room. As Bennett pulled into the parking space right in front of Felicity's room, she got a better look at the motel owner and groaned again. From the top of her bluish white curls to her white New Balance shoes, the woman was positively vibrating with righteous indignation.

Biting back a few choice words that wanted to escape, Felicity forced herself to get out of the passenger-side door. Plastering on as much of a smile as she could manage, she walked toward the motel owner, trying not to limp too much. The last thing she wanted was questions about how she'd hurt herself. "Hello. Did you need something?"

"I need you to get your things, hand over your keys, and leave," the woman snapped, her arms crossing over her skinny chest.

Felicity felt her eyebrows shoot up to her hairline. "You're kicking us out?"

"I am." The woman's nod held a grim satisfaction. "With pleasure."

Felicity gave herself a few seconds to try to understand the reasoning behind this unexpected ejection, but she honestly couldn't. They'd only been in their rooms for fifteen minutes, and as far as she knew, they hadn't created any loud noises or especially noxious fumes. "Why? We've barely spent any time here."

"I know why you're here." The motel owner's mouth screwed up even tighter than it had been.

Felicity glanced over at Bennett, but he looked as confused as she felt. "To work?"

"Work," scoffed the woman with such disgust that Felicity shifted back a step, a little worried the owner was going to spit on her shoes. "That's what you call hounding an innocent boy until he has to go into hiding?"

"Innocent boy?" Even though she knew it wouldn't help the situation, she couldn't prevent her incredulous tone. "Are you talking about Dino? Because he's about as far from an innocent boy as you can get. He's a meth dealer."

"*Douglas* is my grandnephew, and he doesn't mess with any drugs. He told me himself. He was framed by his no-good ex-girlfriend, poor boy, and you're here to harass him some more."

Figuring it was futile to continue to argue about Dino's innocence, Felicity bit back the words and focused on the important part of what the woman was telling her. "Who told you this?"

"I have my sources," she said smugly before her expression went flat again. "Now get your things and go."

After another speaking glance at Bennett, Felicity let herself into her room. She quickly repacked and scanned it for anything she'd forgotten. Her body—especially her ankle—protested her rapid movements, but she didn't dare slow down. If she did, she didn't think she could get moving again.

Once she'd cleared the room, she left, handing off the old-fashioned key to the owner.

"I want our money back." It wasn't much, but Felicity was feeling helpless and frustrated, tired and sore, and she wanted to win a point in the confrontation, even if it was a small one.

The motel owner looked affronted, as if Felicity had demanded a huge concession, but she pulled out a wad of cash, peeled off some bills, and held it out to Felicity, who accepted it. She made a show of counting it, using the petty activity as a way to hold off her exhaustion.

Once Felicity pocketed the cash, they waited a couple of minutes in stiff silence that made it feel like an hour. Bennett finally emerged from his room with a bag slung over his shoulder and handed over his key.

"I have our money," Felicity said, tiredness dragging at her, making her desperate for the confrontation to be over. "Let's go."

"Good riddance," the motel owner spat, turning toward the office with both keys clutched in her fist. "Pair of jackals, chasing after my sweet Douglas."

"Don't think you're getting a good Tripadvisor review from us." Felicity cringed at her pathetic threat, but then amusement sparked off her irritation as she turned back to Bennett. "Jackal is actually one of the nicer things I've been called."

He made an agreeing sound before turning to escort her to his SUV with a huge hand warming her lower back.

"I really don't want to be driving around the mountains at midnight, trying to find a motel with an available room," she said, fighting the urge to lean into his supportive hand as she limped along. "Want to just sleep in our cars?"

"No."

Glancing back at him, she raised an eyebrow. "No?"

"We're not sleeping in our cars," he said, opening the passenger door of his SUV for her. "We're sleeping in *my* car."

"We're squashing two full-grown adults into one vehicle?" she asked, sinking into the seat with a low groan as her muscles protested, although it was a relief to get off her sore ankle. "Why not use both? We'll have to move my car out of here anyway. I have a feeling Ms. Crabby Pants will be out here with a can of paint, tagging it with creative swears, if we leave it here."

Bennett looked over at her car. From his sigh and the way he held out his hand, he knew Felicity was right. "Keys."

She dug them out and handed them over, too tired to do anything except follow direct commands. Good thing she'd promoted him to captain.

The thought almost made her giggle as he strode over to her car. She watched from her perch on his passenger seat as he moved the car out of the lot and parked it on the street close to the coffee shop. He walked the block back, and her gaze stayed on him. Apparently she was exhausted enough that all her willpower was completely gone. She couldn't resist the urge to watch him—or think about him as someone more than just her stalker.

By the time he climbed into the driver's seat of his SUV, she was half-asleep. He didn't say anything. He just started the engine and eased the SUV out of the lot. Feeling strangely secure and cared for, she allowed herself to doze until the vehicle rocked to a stop and Bennett cut the engine.

"Where are we?" she asked without opening her eyes. In fact, she wasn't sure if it was possible to open them at that moment. Her eyes—and the rest of her—were done for the day.

"Trailhead parking lot."

With a yawn, she opened her eyes a crack with extreme effort. "Aren't those usually closed for the night?"

"Not this one."

She squinted, glancing around, and saw a handful of other vehicles, although the others appeared empty and dark. There was a single sodium light at the back of the lot, but the darkness was thick everywhere the light didn't touch.

"Stay there," he ordered, getting out of the SUV.

Although her eyebrows shot up at his high-handedness, she was honestly too exhausted to move, so she decided to wait until morning to remind him that he wasn't the boss of her. Turning her head to the side, she watched idly, too tired even for curiosity, as he rummaged through a duffel in the back.

Once he'd apparently found what he was looking for, he returned to the driver's seat. "Let me see your ankle."

With a yawn, she rotated until she was sitting sideways, her knees on the center console and her feet in his lap. Gently, he removed her shoe and sock before pushing up her pant leg a little. Almost not wanting to see how bad it was, she forced herself to look at her ankle.

"Oh!" she said, surprised and relieved. "It's not swollen as badly as I thought it'd be."

He made a displeased grumble as he began wrapping her ankle with the ACE bandage. "Bad enough," he muttered.

Warmth flowed from where his careful hands touched her foot and calf all the way up to her face, making her blush. Mentally thanking the universe for the dim lighting, she rested her temple against the seat back and ignored the fact that she was being ridiculous. She just enjoyed the contact and attention as her weighted eyelids fought to close.

Once he finished putting her sock and shoe back on over the bandage, she forced her eyes open and yawned, reluctantly swinging her legs back to her side of the car. Her ankle felt so much better now that it was immobilized, and she gave a sleepy smile as she looked down at the neat wrapping. "Thank you."

"Um."

The single syllable caught her attention with its sheer discomfort, and Felicity turned her tired eyes to Bennett, who was staring hard through the windshield. "What?" she asked, her curiosity pushing back her exhaustion.

"The best way to…" He cleared his throat, darted a quick glance her way, and then continued glaring through the windshield as if he were still driving. "There's only the one…"

Fully intrigued and a little amused now, Felicity sat up from her sleepy slump. "Just say it. I promise not to be offended. After all, I grew up with Norah. You don't have to be tactful with me."

"It's just that we only have one blanket." He stopped again, but at least he managed to get a full sentence out.

At first Felicity wasn't sure why he was so uncomfortable. But then she shivered as the chill from the mountain night air started to invade the interior of the SUV, and she understood. "Oh. One blanket means we have to share."

He made a strangled-sounding grunt that sounded like an affirmative, and Felicity grinned. He was just so adorably awkward that any discomfort she might have felt melted away, replaced by humor. Turning around in her seat, she grabbed the blanket off the back seat of the SUV. When she unfolded it, she saw what was making Bennett so uncomfortable—the blanket was small, much too narrow to stretch between the two front seats.

Looking at the back of the SUV again, she absently bundled the blanket into her lap as she thought. The back bench seat wouldn't fit two sleeping people, especially with as squirrelly as Bennett seemed to be with the idea of sharing a blanket with her. "I know it won't be as comfortable," she finally concluded, "but I think folding the seat down and sleeping on the floor is our best bet."

His only response was another wordless grunt, but when he got out and opened the back passenger door, Felicity concluded he agreed with her plan. Bennett had the seat folded down in seconds, and her tiredness started to overtake her again. Crawling into the back, she settled onto her side, spreading half of the blanket over her and using her arm as a pillow. Bennett locked the doors but then hovered as far as he could get from her.

"C'mon, B," she said on a yawn that stretched his initial into four syllables. "I haven't killed anyone in their sleep in months."

She heard a choked sound that could've been a cut-off laugh, but she was too tired to do more than half smile in return. Her eyes closed, and she instantly fell into a deep sleep.

———

When she woke up, it was too dark to see anything, but she was warm. The bed was hard, though, and her pillow wasn't much better, plus someone who wasn't her was breathing in regular deep almost snores.

After a few blinks, she remembered where she was—the

back of Bennett's SUV—and she realized that her pillow wasn't actually a pillow. Instead, she was pretty sure it was Bennett's muscled biceps supporting her head, and the rest of him was draped over her back and side like an extra-heavy, breathing, weighted blanket.

She went still, not wanting to move and wake him. If he'd been awkward about just the idea of sharing a blanket, the reality of their full-on cuddling was sure to make his head explode.

As if he'd read her mind and wanted to make everything worse, Bennett rolled even closer, plastering his muscled body against her back and side, as close as he could get without stripping out of their clothes. Tossing the arm not under her head over her hip, he pulled her tightly against him, snuggling her as if she were a beloved teddy bear. With a silent sigh, he tucked his face against her neck so his heavy sleeping breaths flowed over her collarbone. She shivered for reasons completely unrelated to the chilly air surrounding them. Despite the stern mental voice telling her that she shouldn't be snuggling with a near-stranger, especially in a public parking lot, Felicity just couldn't bring herself to move. They needed the body heat, she reasoned, and moving away from him would serve no purpose except to make them both cold.

Besides, being snuggled by Bennett Green was really nice.

Feeling warm and completely safe, she started dozing off again when a whisper brought her back to full wakefulness. It came from outside the SUV, and although it could've been from another car camper, there was a menace to the sound that made her tense.

"Which…he…be in?"

Felicity strained to hear the muttered words, but she could only pick up every third or fourth. She tried to push up to sitting, but Bennett's arms tightened around her, pulling her even more firmly against his chest. Trapped, she stayed in place while another person spoke in hushed tones.

"…don't…can't be…just start shooting."

SEVEN

THE "JUST START SHOOTING" MADE Felicity flinch, tensing so suddenly that Bennett woke with a quiet grunt. Felicity knew the very second he remembered where he was and realized how he was holding her, because he went rigid. Any other time, she would've found his overreaction to their closeness hilarious, but right now they needed to deal with the immediate threat.

Before she could do anything, there was a low thud and then another. Felicity recognized the sound as a gun firing with a suppressor attached. Bennett moved as if to rise, but she grabbed the arm holding her, keeping him in place.

"They're shooting," she said, barely audible.

She hadn't thought he could get any stiffer, but he somehow managed it before rolling his body over hers. This time, it wasn't a cuddling, cute movement but a protective action. One arm curled around the top of her head, and she felt like she was completely surrounded in Bennett. Although they were muffled, she still could hear the sporadic thuds and then a loud crack that sounded too close for comfort.

Bennett tucked her underneath him even more, so close that she could feel the rhythmic thump of his heart. It wasn't racing like hers was, and the steady *thud, thud, thud* gave her something to focus on so the shooting didn't make her panic.

After what felt like an eternity but was probably actually less than a minute, the muffled shots ceased, and the low muttering of voices came again. This time, covered in her Bennett blanket as she was, Felicity couldn't make out any of their words. The two voices faded away, and everything was quiet. She strained to hear beyond the rushing of blood through her ears, but there was only silence. Still, Bennett didn't move, which meant Felicity was trapped in place as well—although she didn't mind too much. She didn't have any urge to chase after two armed people who just casually shot up a trailhead parking lot.

Finally, night insects started making sounds again, and Felicity knew the shooters were gone. "You okay?" she asked, keeping her voice to a bare whisper.

"Yeah," he whisper-grunted. "You?"

"A little squashed but otherwise fine."

He immediately lifted his bulk off her, moving to his knees, and she swallowed a half-hysterical laugh as she sat up.

"Kidding," she whispered. "Thank you for the protection, although I get to be on top next time."

Even in the near darkness, she saw his eyes widen as he stared at her. The double meaning of her words belatedly hit her, and she felt blood warm her cheeks and was glad the concealing darkness would hide her blush.

"Next time we get shot at, I mean," she quickly said, even as she knew she should keep her mouth shut and stop digging herself deeper. Deciding to change the subject, she cautiously peeked out the side window. No one was visible in the dim pool of illumination around the single streetlight, but the surrounding darkness was as deep and impenetrable as ever.

She pulled out her phone to check the time, but the screen remained black. Making a face, she realized that she hadn't charged it since before she'd left for the mountains. Charlie had stolen her phone charger yet again, so she needed a wall outlet—like the one she should've had at the motel. Shaking off her renewed irritation at getting kicked out, she focused on their immediate situation.

"We should check to make sure no one's hurt," she said, sliding her useless phone back in her pocket. "What time is it?"

"Four thirty-six." He reached for the side door handle. "I'll check the other cars. Stay here."

As he silently got out of the SUV, she followed, noting that her wrapped ankle gave a minor twinge of pain, but it was a hundred times better than it had been right after she'd twisted it. "You're not the boss of me, and I'm not helpless. We'll both check."

He looked at her for a long moment, but the dark made it impossible to guess what he was thinking. When he finally turned away, he headed toward the closest car without protesting, so Felicity took that as agreement with both of her points.

Pulling a penlight from one of her pants pockets, she moved to the second closest car. She winced when she saw puckered dimples where several bullets had struck the front passenger door, and she hoped that all the vehicles in the lot were as unoccupied as they'd looked when she and Bennett had arrived.

Holding her breath, she peeked through the window, only exhaling when she saw it was indeed empty. Moving to the next car, she did the same thing. Bennett was checking the final three on the other side of the lot, so Felicity pocketed her small flashlight and headed back to his SUV. Despite being glad she hadn't stayed in the car while Bennett went out alone, she felt relieved to be returning to the safety—as dubious as it was—of the familiar SUV.

"Oh nooo," she breathed as she got close. From this angle, she could see that a bullet had hit the bottom right corner of the windshield and entered the dash. Cobwebbing cracks turned the glass opaque, making the whole right side of the windshield unusable. She took a quick walk around the vehicle, checking for any more hits, and found a bullet hole in the driver's door and another in the left fender.

A dark shadow loomed behind her, and she jumped and turned, pressing her back against the SUV as she reached into her pocket for something to use as a weapon. Before she could pull out her knife, she recognized the large shape as Bennett.

"The good news is that all four tires are bullet-hole-free and inflated," she said, figuring it wouldn't hurt to start with the positive. "Plus the important half of the windshield is still intact, so that's good."

From his grunt, he wasn't that thrilled with her optimism.

"Are you comfortable driving like that?" she asked, noticing that the night sky was fading to a dark gray as the very first light of morning approached. After he shrugged affirmatively, she headed for the passenger door. "We should probably go before any of the other car owners return and call the cops. Unless you want to be stuck here until noon, answering questions?"

He climbed into the driver's seat with a grimace that she took as a no. Felicity held her breath as he turned on the SUV, hoping that the engine and all the other important functioning parts still worked. It hadn't looked like anything vital had been hit, but she could've easily missed seeing a hole in the early-morning darkness.

When it roared to life without a protest, Felicity exhaled hard with relief before settling back against the passenger seat. "Those were a couple of our friendly neighborhood militia guys, I'm assuming."

"Yep."

She made a face. "So one of our murder ladies snitched on us?"

Bennett made a thoughtful sound. "Possibly."

Although she knew she was being too trusting because she liked the murder club ladies, she couldn't help herself from grabbing on to the doubt in his tone. "What's the alternative?"

"We haven't been that discreet talking about why we're here."

"True." There could've easily been eavesdroppers in the coffee shop or at the barbecue place. "I wasn't careful enough. But I was more concerned with Dino getting tipped off and running than I was getting shot at."

"The motel owner…"

Felicity made a face. If it weren't for her, they both could be tucked up safely in their respective motel rooms, still snoozing away. "What about her?"

"She heard it from someone."

"Yeah." With a sigh, Felicity let her head flop back against the headrest. "I think we—*I*—underestimated the efficiency of a small-town gossip machine."

Bennett made a sound of agreement. "One good thing."

"What's that?" she asked, eager to latch on to any positive at this point.

"Dino likely isn't skipping town."

Her huff of laughter petered out at the end. "He just sent his buddies after us instead. Way to see the bright side."

They fell silent for a long minute as air whistled through the hole in the windshield.

"Where to from here?"

"Let's check on my car, make sure it survived the night." She braced herself for a mess but hoped it'd been overlooked by any militia guys.

"Then back to Langston?"

"Are you kidding?" she asked, staring at his profile. He turned his head to glance at her with a raised eyebrow. "No meth dealer and his gun-nut friends are going to run me out of town. I'm going to bring Dino in while having a relaxing vacation in the mountains if it kills me."

And it just might, her mind warned.

"You don't have to stay," she said, her conscience warring

with that ridiculous part inside her that would be very sad if he left. "This is my mess. I can deal with it. I'm sure you have PI stuff to do."

"I'm not leaving you." The utter conviction in his tone warmed her from the inside out.

———

Her car hadn't been touched, thankfully, so they moved both vehicles to the coffee shop parking lot. It was still closed, but Felicity figured it'd be the first place in town to open its doors. After parking, she returned to the warm passenger seat of Bennett's SUV.

"What's the plan?" he asked.

She pulled down the sun visor to look in the mirror, made a face at her mussed hair, and then flipped it back up again. "Showers. Then you need a new windshield. I saw a mechanic a few doors down from Levi's, so let's see if they can fit your car in. If possible, I'd like to grab the bugs out of the gym. They're expensive, so Moo yells at me when I lose them."

"Moo?"

"Molly."

"Your sister," he said rather than asked, and she raised her eyebrows at him.

"That's not the first time you knew details about me. What'd my background check show?"

Ignoring the heavy sarcasm in her voice, he rattled off her basic info. "Felicity Florence Pax, twenty-two years old, five feet two inches tall, one hundred twenty-six pounds. Mother is Jane

Pax, father is Lono Hale, sister is Molly, half sisters are Cara, Charlotte, and Norah. Lives in Langston, Colorado, and works for Pax Bond Recovery as a bounty hunter. Never been married, not currently dating anyone, no known close friends—"

"Okay!" She cut him off, the bare bones of her life too depressing to hear out loud, especially after just a few hours of sleep. "And it's five feet two and a *half* inches tall. Just for the record."

He nodded solemnly like he was committing that correction to memory.

Feeling a bit flustered, she decided to change the subject. "You know all my details, but I never did a background check on you." She was kicking herself for that now. "So tell me about yourself."

"Bennett Xavier Green, twenty-eight years old, six feet four inches tall, two hundred fifty-two pounds. Mother was Deborah Dover Green, now deceased. Father is unknown. Foster parents from age sixteen to eighteen were Dean and Zena Roman. No known siblings or half siblings. Originally from Fort Collins, Colorado. Now lives in Denver, Colorado, and works as a private investigator. Never been married, not currently dating anyone, no close friends."

Felicity was torn between fascination and wishing she'd never asked. Somehow, the way he laid out the raw details of his life so starkly made her want to hug him forever. She sat on her hands in order to resist the urge.

When he took a breath as if to continue listing the brutal facts of what sounded like a painfully lonely existence, she was relieved to see the headlights of a pickup cut through the linger-ing dimness of dawn.

"Oh, that must be Lou," she said, again divided between disappointment that their revealing talk was over and relief that her confusing emotions could once again be stuffed in a dark corner to be dealt with later. "Unless she's not working this morning."

Bennett pulled something up on his phone as the pickup turned into the alley behind the coffee shop and parked in a small lot there. "That's her. That truck is registered to Louise Sparks."

Felicity eyed his phone, thinking of all the times she could've used instant vehicle registration information. "You're very handy to have around, do you know that?"

With his gaze still focused on his phone screen, he smiled, looking so sweetly pleased that Felicity felt a squirmy warmth she definitely shouldn't be feeling.

Her emotion-induced panic was interrupted by Lou, who'd opened the shop door and was waving them inside. Grabbing her computer bag, Felicity hopped out of the SUV.

"We're not open for another half hour, but come inside and tell me all about your adventures last night," Lou said.

"Sorry if we stink," Felicity said, stepping into the coffee shop with Bennett close behind. "The motel owner kicked us out."

Lou's mouth fell open. "Whaaat? Marian did that? Why? Were you rowdy? I can't imagine you two acting all eighties rock star, but sometimes people surprise you."

"Is Marian a little old lady who looks super sweet until she chucks you out at midnight because her grandnephew is a piece of trash meth dealer who won't accept the consequences of his actions?" Felicity made a beeline to the bathroom.

"Well, yes to the first part, but I was today years old when I learned about the other bit."

Lou's voice faded as Felicity closed the door. The bathroom was tiny, but it didn't matter—Felicity was just relieved to have indoor plumbing after their night in the car.

Once she was out and Bennett took her place in the bathroom, Felicity collapsed in one of the chairs as Lou bustled around, performing all the opening tasks automatically as she shot questions and demands at Felicity.

"Tell me everything. Did you go to the militia's compound last night? What'd you find out? Why are you limping? What'd Marian say? Where'd you sleep? You're staying at my house tonight. We have a guest room and everything, so we won't have to sleep four to the bed."

Bennett emerged from the bathroom just in time to hear the "four to the bed" part, and he gave Felicity such a wide-eyed look that she had to laugh.

"I said we *won't* have to sleep four to a bed." Lou must've interpreted his panicked look correctly. "You really need to meet Ellie's husband, George. He's your brother from another mother."

Bennett didn't respond. He just blinked a few times while backing toward Felicity. Pulling out another chair, he plopped down next to her, close enough that their shoulders touched. It seemed to be becoming their usual position.

"Back to Marian," Lou said without taking a breath as she poured coffee beans into a grinder. She didn't seemed fazed at Bennett's lack of response. "Tell me everything. No! Go back to your stakeout. Did you find Dino?" She started the loud grinder, making conversation impossible.

"The stakeout was a bust," Felicity admitted once the grinder had fallen silent. She leaned back in her chair, Bennett's shoulder rubbing against hers, giving her that familiar sense of security she was beginning to associate with him. "We couldn't drive close enough to see anything, and when we approached on foot, my phone lit up, so someone in the guard tower shot at us."

Lou stared at her, apparently shocked speechless. It only lasted a few seconds, but Felicity was certain that it was rare for Lou to be silent for any length of time, so she still took it as a victory. "You were *shot* at? Are you okay? Were you hit? Is that why you're limping?"

"We're fine. I just twisted my ankle running away."

Lou finally broke out of her shock-induced paralysis and started filling the first coffee maker. "That's good. I mean, not good about the ankle, but good that you don't have any bloody holes in you."

"Only holes are in the cars," Bennett muttered, but Lou must've had ears like a bat, because she immediately latched on to that.

"What cars? Cars were shot? That's so weird. Who shoots at cars, of all things? Hang on. Callum really needs to hear this directly. This is grade A, prime gossip. The fire station guys are going to be livid they didn't know about this once it all eventually comes out." She tapped out a text as Felicity met Bennett's meaningful gaze. She gave a small nod and turned back to Lou.

"Speaking of gossip," Felicity said, trying to think of a way to ask Lou if she or one of the other murder ladies squealed without sounding accusatory. "Marian heard from someone that we planned to bring Dino in, so she wasn't feeling all that hospitable toward us."

Lou groaned loudly, her head dropping back as she swore creatively at the ceiling. "This town. No one can keep a secret to save their lives. I'm positive it wasn't any of the murder club ladies, but I can ask them if they know anything about who may have overheard and spilled the beans to his auntie."

"Sure, although the damage is done on that end," Felicity said. Maybe it was naive of her, but she believed Lou. Her instincts told her that none of the murder ladies was the loose-lipped culprit, and her gut had proven to be pretty reliable in the past. Besides, she was battling a militia in a strange town with no local sources and only one ally. She needed all the help she could get. "Dino knows we're here for him. Maybe just remind the others of the importance of being discreet when discussing whatever they discover or hear in the future. Less chance of me getting shot at that way." Felicity knew this was good advice for herself too. Who knew who'd been listening in at the coffee shop or Levi's yesterday?

"Definitely." Lou began stocking the pastry case. "Where'd you end up sleeping last night? You should've texted me."

"It was late, and we managed to get a few hours of sleep

in the car," Felicity said, even as her hip gave a throb that echoed the one in her ankle. The floor had been rather hard, especially with Bennett half on top of her. The memory made her cheeks burn again. "A couple of guys shot up the trailhead parking lot where we'd parked this morning, so that wasn't a fun wake-up call."

"Wait, wait, wait!" Lou waved her hands, a paper-wrapped croissant in each. "You were shot at *twice* in twelve hours?"

"More like six hours, but yeah." Felicity knew she was punchy from lack of sleep, because the conversation was making her want to laugh. "Speaking of bullet holes in cars, is the auto shop in town any good? Bennett has a windshield that needs replacing."

"Yeah, Donnie's good." Still clutching the croissants, Lou stared at her. "But how are you so calm? I'd be screaming hysterically if I were you."

"No, you wouldn't," Callum said as he walked in. "Your place was burned to the ground, and you barely missed a beat."

Leaning over to kiss him quickly on the lips, Lou said, "I think your memory is faulty. There was a lot of crying, some screaming, and I threatened to move in with a pack rat." She turned to look at Felicity and Bennett. "Not a euphemistic human pack rat. The literal small, fuzzy, disease-carrying animal."

Felicity blinked, unsure what to do with that piece of information, so she just gave Callum a nod of greeting instead.

"Is that a bullet hole in your windshield?" Callum asked.

"It is," Felicity said.

"Any connection to the damage-to-vehicles call at the Blue Hook trailhead the sheriff's department got this morning?"

She met Bennett's gaze before turning back to Callum and giving him a small shrug. "Maybe?"

"Maybe."

"Probably?" For some reason, she felt like a teenager being interrogated by her father, even though Callum couldn't be much more than ten years older than her. He just had that stern-dad stare down. "We didn't call the sheriff."

"What happened?"

Lou gave him an affectionate bump with her elbow. "I was just asking that. This wasn't the only shooting last night, by the way."

Callum's brows shot up as he turned his attention back on Felicity, and she opened her mouth to speak.

"Hang on!" Lou interrupted, tapping at her phone, and Felicity closed her mouth. "Let's get the murder club ladies over here while I finish setting up for my shift. Only a few people come in before seven, and we can all just stare at them until they get uncomfortable and leave."

"That seems like a terrible business model," Felicity said, resisting the urge to laugh.

Lou shrugged as she headed for the back, emerging soon after with a register tray. "Just for today. Usually I'm a star employee, so I feel like I'm due a few creepy-stare days."

Felicity couldn't really argue with that, so she just exchanged a what-a-weird-place-this-is look with Bennett and settled in to wait for the rest of the murder club ladies. Lou got them all coffee before unlocking the door and lighting up the *Open* sign.

Ellie was the first to arrive, holding the hand of an adorable, serious-faced toddler.

"Mila!" Lou immediately swooped the baby up, peppering kisses all over her face and eventually getting a tiny giggle before setting her back on her feet. The little girl reached up to Callum, and he picked her up, placing her on his lap with a faint hint of smugness ruining his usually excellent poker face.

Lou shook her head in mock disappointment even as she smiled at the pair. "Why does she like you so much more than me? I provide all the best bribes—candy, puppies, toys—and she still picks you. I don't get it."

"Hey, Felicity," Ellie greeted her with concern. "You okay?"

Before Felicity could answer, Lou spoke up. "They're looking rough because they got shot at twice and had to sleep in their car."

Ellie's eyes widened, her gaze bouncing from Felicity to Bennett and back again as her hand rose to rub at her breastbone. "You were shot at? Were you hit?"

"Nope. Just twisted my ankle running away," Felicity assured her. "Bennett's windshield, on the other hand, wasn't so lucky."

"Your skip?" Ellie asked, taking a seat at the counter a few stools down from Callum.

Felicity raised her hands in a shrug. "The militia guys at least. I haven't seen Dino yet though."

Rory and Daisy arrived in quick succession, and the round of hellos and baby kisses interrupted the talk of shooting until everyone was settled with a coffee.

One unfamiliar twentysomething man came in, but Lou

put her creepy stare into action—which Felicity had to admit was truly one of the creepiest she'd ever seen—and the customer decided to take his muffin and cappuccino to go.

"Okay!" Lou announced when the door had closed behind the fleeing customer. "We don't have a whiteboard this morning, but we'll add any pertinent facts to it later. Felicity, why don't you give a rundown of what happened after you left the gym last night?"

Felicity did just that, although she left out the part about bugging the office and listening to the murder club's conversation after she and Bennett left the previous evening. Otherwise, she stuck to the truth, telling her rapt audience about the stakeout, the attempted shooting, Marian's tirade, and the interruption of their short sleep by the shooters at the trailhead. She skimmed over the part about sleeping in the SUV and didn't mention the only-one-blanket issue, even though she was pretty sure the murder ladies would've been enthralled by those juicy details.

"Why didn't you call the sheriff's office?" Callum asked when she'd finished.

All the women stared at him.

"I'm married to a deputy, and I still wouldn't have called them if I'd been in that parking lot," Daisy said. "Well, maybe I would've texted Chris to let him know I was fine when he heard the call come in, but other than that, nope."

"Hard agree," Ellie said.

Rory nodded.

Callum frowned as the toddler played with his shirt buttons. "Going through the proper channels—"

"Usually wastes a lot of time," Lou finished for him, although she gave him an affectionate pat on the arm as she said it. "No one was injured, and the other people parked in the lot called it in soon enough. If Felicity and Bennett get involved in the cops' investigation into the militia, it'll just make things messy."

"Or they'll think Felicity's a suspect," Rory chimed in.

"Exactly," Felicity said, relieved that the murder ladies were on the same page as her as far as involving the police. She already had one detective in Langston dogging her steps. She didn't need a bored sheriff's department in her business as well.

Although Callum let it drop, he still looked unconvinced. Little Mila grabbed a handful of his shirt, and he glanced down at her with a small smile.

Taking advantage of Callum's distraction, Felicity changed the subject. "We need to find a better vantage point to watch the compound—*we* meaning me and Bennett," she clarified firmly, not wanting any of the murder ladies to take that as an invitation. "Dino might not even be there."

"Didn't Marian say that he was?" Rory asked.

Felicity thought back to the confrontation with the motel owner. "Not directly, but she definitely implied it."

"You sure you want to keep pursuing this?" Ellie asked. "The situation seems to have a high risk of flying bullets. Aren't there less risky bail jumpers you could go after?"

"Well, sure," Felicity said. "But now I'm annoyed."

Bennett gave a snort of laughter but sobered quickly when he saw he'd drawn everyone's attention.

"Why don't—" Lou cut herself off as the door opened and

an enormous bear of a bearded man walked into the shop. The guy was even bigger than Bennett, and Bennett was huge.

Felicity looked at Lou, expecting a repeat of her creepy, customer-repelling look, but instead she was smiling. Mila gave a happy shriek—the first loud noise Felicity had heard from her—and wiggled to get down. Once Callum placed her on the floor, she toddled over to the newcomer, her arms outstretched in welcome.

The big man scooped up Mila and crossed the room to give Ellie a kiss. From this, Felicity deducted that this must be George.

"George!" Lou called, confirming Felicity's assumption. "You have to meet Bennett Green. We all think he's your long-lost brother you never knew about."

George blinked impassively at this, one arm holding his baby and his other hand resting on the back of Ellie's neck.

Felicity studied him, her head cocked to the side. Big, burly, silent, most likely socially awkward... "I can see it." She felt Bennett's gaze on the side of her face, so she turned to see him raising his eyebrows at her. Felicity just shrugged. "I'm not saying you're twins separated at birth, but I'm not *not* saying it."

Lou laughed with delight. "I knew the first time I met you, Felicity Pax, that you'd fit right in around here."

I'm not sure if that's a good thing, Felicity thought, looking around at the quirky denizens of this weird, sometimes creepy little town. She had to admit, though, that she indeed felt like she belonged here.

EIGHT

WHEN THEIR IMPROMPTU PROGRESS MEETING broke up soon after George's arrival, Felicity made a beeline to Daisy, walking as fast as her sore ankle allowed.

"Can I ask a favor?" Felicity said once she'd caught up with Daisy by the front door.

Daisy nodded.

"Could we use the showers at your gym?" Felicity gestured at her rumpled self. "It's been a rough night."

"Of course." Pulling out her phone, Daisy shot off a text. "There. I'm stopping by the station to see Chris, but my manager knows you're coming. Just give your names to the guy at the front desk, and he'll show you where everything is."

"Thank you." Felicity's relief wasn't feigned. Although it'd only been a little over a day, she felt like it'd been months since her last shower. Besides, she had tech to retrieve so she didn't hear about it from her sister. Since their mom had committed a felony and taken off, money had been tight.

She waited while Bennett dropped his SUV at Donnie's Auto Shop and talked briefly with the sleepy-eyed mechanic, whom Felicity assumed was Donnie.

As Bennett climbed into the passenger seat of her car, Felicity asked, "Will he be able to get your windshield replaced soon?"

Bennett dipped his chin. "Three days."

Patting the steering wheel, she said, "We'll have to take good care of my baby then. Keep her away from flying bullets and sledgehammers."

"Sledgehammers?" The corner of Bennett's mouth lifted in a half smile that was more intriguing than it should've been.

"Who knows around here?" So far, the town had surprised them several times—in both good and not so good ways.

Bennett made a sound of agreement as Felicity turned the car in the direction of the gym.

The burly guy at the front desk was quiet but helpful, leading them to the doors of the locker rooms and pointing to a shelf piled with clean towels. Felicity watched him walk back toward the front desk, wondering if something in the mountain air made the guys around here so big and silent.

A nudge on her shoulder pulled her out of her thoughts, and she turned to see Bennett's scowling face.

"What?" she asked, looking around to see what had put him in a bad mood.

Instead of answering, he shoved through the door into the men's locker room. With a mental shrug, she grabbed a towel and headed into the women's.

The shower stung scrapes and abrasions she hadn't even

known she'd acquired over the past twenty-four hours, but the hot water still felt amazing. Although the motel owner kicking them out had seemed like terrible luck when it happened, showering in the roomy and sparkling new gym facilities was an improvement over the mildewed ancient bathroom at the Black Bear Inn. Sleeping with Bennett—despite the unpleasant early-morning hail of bullets—had been pleasant too. She paused, her hands stilling in her hair as the water pounded against her head and back. *Pleasant* didn't seem like a strong enough descriptor. *Nice? Cozy? Safe? Addictive?*

She abruptly shut down her musing, scrubbing at her scalp as if she could physically wash away her thoughts. "Head in the game," she warned herself, knowing that what was turning into a pretty sizeable crush on her stalker turned partner would end badly. "You barely know him."

The problem was that what she knew about PI B. Green, she liked. A lot.

She finished showering and dressing quickly in the otherwise empty locker room, trying to keep her mind off a certain private investigator who was currently naked just a wall away. Once she focused on the task of retrieving the listening devices, it was easier to shove Bennett to the back of her mind.

Quietly, she pushed open the locker room door, catching it before it could thud shut. Another much larger hand wrapped over hers on the edge of the door, and she jumped before turning her head to meet Bennett's gaze. After the unruly thoughts about him that'd run wild just minutes before, she couldn't stop her cheeks from heating.

Hoping he thought her face was still flushed from the heat of the shower, she tilted her head wordlessly toward the office, and he gave a short nod. After holding his hand over hers on the door a half second longer than technically necessary, he released her, and she closed the door silently.

Trying to move as quietly as possible while not appearing to be sneaking around was a feat in itself, but Felicity'd had plenty of opportunities to practice. From the way Bennett glided behind her, looking slightly bored to a casual observer, this wasn't his first rodeo either.

It was still early enough that the gym was quiet, but she knew that wouldn't last. Already, there were a couple people walking through the front door and a small line checking in at the desk. Felicity let her gaze slide past the gym patrons indifferently, checking for familiar faces or anyone who seemed interested in her and Bennett, but no one stood out to her. The manager at the desk had his back to them, so Felicity made her way through the weight room with a casual stride that masked her sense of urgency.

"Hey!" a male voice called out, breaking the sleepy quiet of the gym.

She fought down the urge to jump and glanced with studied indifference over her shoulder. The caller was heading toward a woman doing bench presses who finished the set she was on before sitting up and smiling at the man approaching her. They started talking, and Felicity covered the last few feet to the office door.

As she grabbed the knob, she prayed to the breaking and entering gods, sending up a silent *thank you* when the handle turned easily. Reaching back, she grabbed Bennett's hand and hauled him into the office with her.

The setup from the murder club meeting was the same as it'd been the evening before, and Felicity made a beeline to her chair, retrieving the bug from where she'd stuck it on the upper inner back right leg. As she held it up triumphantly, she saw Bennett collect his own electronic device from between the wall and the back of a picture frame.

"Nice spot," she whispered almost soundlessly, and he looked pleased as he pocketed the bug. She moved to follow him out the door when they both froze.

The doorknob was turning.

Bennett turned and grasped her upper arms, twisting Felicity around until her back was against the wall with his considerable bulk pressing against her front. She was confused for the split second it took for the door to open, not sure what Bennett's intent was. Sure, there'd been a lot of bullets flying around them lately, but she doubted that whoever was coming into the office was going to try to harm her physically. He gave her a meaningful look, as if asking permission. Assuming that he was checking if it was okay that he'd pushed her up against the wall, she nodded.

Then his lips crashed down on hers, and her thoughts stopped completely.

She froze, barely aware that the door swung wide and that someone else was in the room with them. All she could focus on was the press of his mouth on hers, the heat and hardness of him trapping her against the wall, as well as the shocking softness of his lips. Her own parted automatically, and he deepened the kiss in response. It turned from a mannequin fake embrace to something real and intense and incredible.

"Oh sorry!" The words yanked Felicity out of her kiss-induced daze, and she jerked back from Bennett. His mouth followed her at first, but then he seemed to recall himself, and he retreated.

Blinking lust-shocked eyes, Felicity looked blankly at Daisy and an unfamiliar man, both of whom looked equal parts amused, surprised, and bewildered.

"Oh!" Felicity didn't have to feign her shock—or her embarrassment—as she scrambled to come up with a reason for them to be in Daisy's office. *So that's what Bennett had been silently asking.* "Sorry! We were just… This is all new, and… Um, we didn't mean to…"

Daisy finally took pity on her. "Don't worry. I get it. Chris has pulled me into a random room or two."

The uniformed guy next to her—who must be Chris, her deputy sheriff husband—looked at Daisy with a mix of humor and heat that made Felicity think the other woman would be pulled into another random room in the near future.

"Sorry," Felicity said again, sheepish now as she extricated herself from Bennett's hold. "The gym just got busy, so we…" She shrugged, still feeling flustered by the whole thing. Although she didn't want to admit it, the kiss was the main reason she was a babbling mess. The threat of getting caught retrieving listening devices wasn't even an issue at the moment.

"I get it." Daisy waved her hand as if dismissing the whole

situation from her mind. "Felicity Pax and Bennett Green, this is Deputy Chris Jennings, my husband and main information source."

Although Chris winced at the "information source" part, his smile came easily enough as he nodded at both of them. "Nice to finally meet you. I've been hearing all about you and your… work here."

Bennett raised his chin in the universal guy greeting.

"Same," Felicity said, ignoring the way Chris had paused on the word *work*, as if he had a whole slew of questions for them. "I appreciate your help with finding the militia's location."

Chris made a noncommittal humming sound. "Things seem to have gotten a little riled up over there. We'll see if I regret passing on that bit of information or if I thank you in the end."

Unable to hold back a grin, Felicity said with assurance, "Oh, you'll definitely thank us. I'm sure of it."

His repressive cop look was ruined by the way his lips wanted to twitch into a smile. "We'll see," he just repeated before giving Daisy a kiss on the cheek and a much more serious look. "Please stay away from the militia's compound and any trigger-happy Simpsonites today, sweetheart."

"Of course," Daisy said, her wide-eyed expression almost too innocent for comfort. "I don't know why you'd even need to say that. Safety is my middle name."

With a snort that managed to be both amused and loving, he gave her another kiss—this one on the lips—and turned to leave.

"Wait," Felicity said, suddenly aware that she and Bennett were *still* in Daisy's office uninvited. "We're heading out if you two were going to…talk." *Aaaand now I've made things awkward again*, she thought, feeling her cheeks heat. She'd blushed more on this short trip to Simpson than she had during the rest of her adult life. Grabbing Bennett's hand, she towed him past Chris out the door, calling over her shoulder, "Sorry again! Bye! Thanks for the showers!"

"Wait!" It was Daisy stopping them this time. "Do you need to use my office for research? I'll be stuck at the front desk all day after my manager leaves at eight, so you're welcome to this." She spread her arms wide, indicating the entire office space.

"Thank you, but I think we're going to camp out at The Coffee Spot," Felicity said, realizing that she was still holding Bennett's hand and that it felt really nice enveloping hers. "We've monopolized your office long enough." The blush was back, so she gave an awkward wave and started pulling Bennett away again. "Thanks again! Bye!"

The weight room had filled up while they'd been busy— her blush flamed hotter—in the office, and everyone turned to watch them leave. Bennett caught up so they were walking side by side, still holding hands. He gave her fingers a gentle squeeze, and suddenly everything seemed less mortifying and more like an adventure.

Felicity turned her head to smile at him, and he gave her one of his half grins back. Tugging her closer with their linked hands, he leaned way down so he could whisper in her ear.

"Operation Bug Removal successful."

———

"This isn't all that much better," Felicity said quietly, lowering her binoculars to her lap.

"It's not worse."

She couldn't disagree with Bennett there. "True. At least from here, we can get a good look at the traffic coming and going." She glanced around at the surrounding area and couldn't hold back an impressed smile. "Plus the views are pretty fantastic."

Bennett gave a grunt of agreement. They'd decided to try their luck on the other side of the compound during the day this time. The late-afternoon sun lit up the edges of the cliffs and highlighted the clumps of hard grass and shrubs dotting the ground. Even the razor wire surrounding the compound glowed gold, burnishing something inherently ugly with an odd touch of beauty.

Since Bennett's SUV was getting a new windshield at Donnie's Auto Shop, they'd parked Felicity's car in a small copse of scraggly evergreens on a rocky hill a quarter mile from the militia headquarters. It was the only decent stakeout spot they could find after poring over maps for most of the day. Their view of the compound was limited, but they faced the gravel drive leading to the entrance and were close enough to see license plates with the help of her binoculars if they peered through gaps in the greenery.

"Honestly, at this point, I just want to know if Dino is even here." Felicity pulled her gaze off the entrancing view of the mountains and focused on what she could see of the compound again. "If we're going to get shot at, we should at least know we might get a bounty at the end of all this."

Bennett just gave her a raised-eyebrow look, and she lifted her free hand in a small shrug.

"I know," she admitted. "I have a slight adrenaline addiction. Even so, I don't want to do dangerous things without a payout."

Wearing one of those partial smiles that she was starting to look forward to seeing, he opened his mouth to respond but then closed it again. His face returned to seriousness as he gestured toward the compound. "A vehicle's coming."

Sure enough, she heard the faint hum of an engine as soon as he said that. Finding a gap in the trees in front of them that was at a good angle to see oncoming cars, Felicity focused her binoculars through the clear space and waited. The engine sound gradually got louder, the echo bouncing off the surrounding cliffs, until the front of an older-model pickup truck came into view.

"Colorado four seven seven boy Adam zebra. I can't tell the original color. Was that blue at one time?"

Bennett was silent for only a few seconds before saying, "1982 Ford F150, registered to Cobra Jones."

"Cold." Felicity peered through the binoculars, trying to see past the sun glare on the windshield to the driver and passenger inside. "They take his militia *and* his pickup? That's a country song just waiting to be written right there."

Bennett gave a cough of what sounded like laughter before saying in a serious tone, "We need to look more closely at what happened to Jones."

"Agreed." The truck was almost directly in front of their hiding spot, and she saw into the cab. "Clint Possible Murderer

Yarran's driving." His passenger turned his head to look out the side window, giving her a direct view of his face. Her heartbeat jumped in anticipation. "And none other than Dino Fletcher's riding shotgun."

As soon as the faded pickup passed their hidden parking spot, continuing toward the county road, Felicity started her car. Caution warred with the need to speed after her quarry as she eased the tires over the rocky stretch that connected their overlook to the logging road they came in on.

Bennett tapped on his phone. "This'll take us to Moose Peak Road, six miles southeast of where Clint and Dino will emerge."

"Whose road is shorter?" Felicity asked, resisting the urge to bounce her left leg up and down. She loved this—the chase, the potential of capturing her skip. Having Bennett there with her just seemed to enhance the adrenaline rush. "Any chance we'll catch up with them?"

"About the same." He flicked across his screen, and she saw various maps flash by. "Drive fast."

Felicity grinned. "Happily."

With a spray of gravel, she gunned the car around the first curve, rocketing between boulders and pine trees until she braked hard before a hairpin turn. The car swung around and took off again like a slingshot, and Felicity couldn't hold back an exultant laugh. She shot Bennett a sideways glance, expecting to see terror on his face—or at least a hint of fear—but he was fully immersed in the information on his phone. When the car slid on loose gravel as they took the next turn, sending them to the very edge of the cliff, he didn't even look up, just absently put one hand on the dash to steady himself. The amount of trust he had in her warmed her insides.

They raced downward, whipping around turns and bouncing over frequent ruts and loose rocks. Moose Peak Road came into view too soon, before Felicity was ready to quit her roller coaster of a drive.

"Left," Bennett said before she could even ask.

After a perfunctory check for traffic, she cranked the steering wheel to the left. The tires spun in the gravel for a moment before finding traction and shooting the car forward. The narrow dirt road stretched before them, empty of any traffic that Felicity could see. Noting the mileage on the odometer, she pressed down on the accelerator.

Five and a half miles flew by before she slowed to a more reasonable speed. "Since we didn't pass them, I'm assuming they turned the other way?"

Bennett gave an affirmative grunt.

"What are the next intersections coming up?" Her mind was working, trying to develop a plan without knowing where Dino was heading. So far, the bare bones of her plan were to find the pickup and then follow it until Clint stopped. At that point, she'd tackle Dino.

"A couple county roads and Highway Nine."

"Highway Nine." That was where they were headed, she knew in her gut.

"Probably," he said, sounding confident, like his gut was telling him the same thing as hers. He gestured to the left. "They came out here."

"Unless they haven't gotten here yet."

Bennett made a sour face. "Wish I'd gotten a tracker on that pickup."

"Wouldn't that be nice?" She couldn't count the number of times during the endless days of searching that she had wished she'd secretly microchipped her mom. No matter how many times she'd chased after a skip, trying to find a single soul hiding among the billions of people in the world often felt impossible. After her mom used their house as collateral for her bail, Felicity had felt like a bomb was ticking, counting down the seconds until her and her sisters' lives exploded. "What do you think? Continue or wait a few minutes to see if they're still on the compound road?"

"Continue."

Felicity relaxed a little as she pressed harder on the gas pedal. She would've considered stopping if Bennett had suggested it, but her leg was already bouncing. She much preferred chasing to lying in wait. Despite her impatience, she forced herself to stay within five miles of the speed limit.

That was why it was extra annoying when red and blue lights lit up her rearview mirror.

NINE

"WHERE DID THEY EVEN *COME* from?" Felicity grudgingly pulled to the side of the road until her right tires rolled over a few clumps of weeds. For a moment, she hoped that the squad car would speed right past her on its way to a different call, but instead it pulled in behind her.

Bennett made a displeased sound. Felicity had never felt such strong agreement with a grunt before.

She unlocked her phone and passed it to him. "Text Callum. See if he can make a call to get us out of this quickly. All these mountain people seem to know one another."

As she watched a sheriff's deputy approach in her side mirror, she felt Bennett take her phone. Time ticked away in her mind, and as the distance between them and her skip grew by the second, so did her annoyance with the delay. She rolled down her window, but even the crisp and clean mountain air wasn't enough to soothe her.

"Afternoon," drawled the deputy, whose name tag read

B. LITCHFIELD. Felicity instantly disliked him. He had a classically handsome face and a body that looked like he spent a lot of time in a gym, but his smirk and condescending tone ruined the whole picture.

Gritting her molars, she forced a smile that probably looked more like a baring of teeth. "Good afternoon, Deputy."

"Know why I stopped you today?"

Not this nonsense. Felicity resisted the urge to roll her eyes. *Sure, let me confess to all my traffic-law-violating sins.* "No."

"Hmm," the deputy hummed, studying her and then Bennett, who must've finished texting Callum, since her phone was nowhere in sight.

Bennett looked back with his best deadpan expression.

"License, registration, and proof of insurance, please." The deputy looked at Bennett again. "Let's see your ID too."

Bennett didn't move, his gaze still locked on the deputy.

"He's not the driver, so he's not required to show you ID," Felicity said with the same toothy smile as she held out her documents. "Why'd you pull me over?"

Litchfield studied her license intently. "Langston, huh? What are you doing so far from home?"

"Vacationing." It was getting harder to hold her smile. "Why did you stop me?"

He brought her license even closer to his eyes. "This a fake? You illegal?"

Bennett twitched, and a low growl came from him. Without looking at him, she reached over and squeezed his rock-hard forearm. "That is a real license, and you're not allowed to ask my status."

The deputy's gaze locked on to her, his eyes lighting up as if he had her cornered. Her smile got a little tighter as any hope of catching up to Clint and Dino slipped away. "That sounded like a confession."

Felicity sighed deeply, tired now that the adrenaline rush of the chase had faded. Before she could respond, Bennett spoke. "That was nothing even close to a confession, and you need to stop before you get sued and fired."

The deputy's head jerked at Bennett's words, and he took a step back before catching himself. "I'm legally allowed—no, *obligated*—to investigate suspicious behavior. No one's ever on this road except for—"

His eyes widened slightly as he caught himself, and a seed of suspicion took root in Felicity's mind. She briefly met Bennett's gaze, and from his knowing gaze, he was thinking exactly what she was.

After the smallest hesitation, the deputy carefully rephrased. "No one's ever on this road except for locals. When I see strangers—*city* strangers—slinking around the back roads, it's my duty to investigate."

"Mm-hmm." Felicity only had time to make the skeptical sound before the deputy's cell phone rang. He glanced at the screen and grimaced before stepping away from her door.

"Stay put," he said. "I'm going to check for warrants." He answered his phone as he hurried toward his squad car. "Hey, Sheriff. Can I call you back in a few? I'm in the middle of a traffic stop." He paused to listen, and when he spoke again, his voice was muted. "Yes, ma'am."

Felicity kept her window down, trying to overhear more of the deputy's side of his call with his boss, but he got in his squad and closed his door. Turning to Bennett, she raised an eyebrow. "On the militia's payroll, don't you think?"

"Yep." He passed her back her cell phone, and she glanced at the screen to see a two-word text from Callum: On it.

"Good. I was hoping the sheriff's interruption was…" She trailed off as she watched a second sheriff's department car roll up behind Litchfield's. "Seriously? More of them? They're going to have the SWAT team here in another minute."

"Think that's one of your soldiers," Bennett said, looking over his shoulder.

"Oh?" She couldn't see very well in the rearview mirror with Litchfield's squad car in the way, so she stuck her head out the window and craned her neck to see it was indeed Daisy's husband walking toward Litchfield's squad.

After a short conversation that was voiced too quietly for Felicity to overhear but that left Litchfield scowling, Chris made his way to Felicity's window.

"Deputy Chris," she said, very happy to see a—hopefully—sympathetic face. "Could you remind your coworker that he can't deport me?"

Chris blinked. "Aren't you Hawai'ian?"

"Half. How'd you know that?" Before he could answer beyond a slight wince, she'd already figured it out. "Ah, background check." She couldn't blame him, since she would've done the same if some stranger had wandered into her town and recruited her wife to her bounty-hunting army. Besides, she was feeling almost giddy that a reasonable person had arrived on scene, so it was hard to work up any righteous indignation. "Maybe he wants to send me back to Hawai'i? Because I wouldn't mind that."

He grinned and also winced. "Sorry about this. Boaz is new to the department and has some…unfortunate ideas. He'll have to learn, or the sheriff'll cut him loose."

"Hmm." Felicity watched as Litchfield got out of his squad and started their way. Lowering her voice, she quietly said, "You might want to check his loyalties."

Chris's eyes widened, but he shot a look at the approaching deputy and didn't ask any questions. Instead he gave her a tight nod.

Litchfield grudgingly passed back her license and cards. "No warrants, but you still shouldn't be wandering around this area." When Chris stiffened, Litchfield shot him a sideways look and added, "Lots of dangerous things out here—rockslides, bears—nothing city folk like you two want to get involved with."

"Thanks for the warning," she said sarcastically, putting her cards away.

With a scowl and abrupt nod, Litchfield stalked back to his squad car and peeled around them, sending a spray of gravel to ping off Felicity's car.

"Ass." Chris frowned at the departing deputy before turning back to Felicity. "What do you know?"

A pickup truck approached from behind, carefully skirting Chris's squad car and Felicity's sedan, the driver's gaze fixed on the road ahead while the passenger turned his face away from the window. Felicity watched, her mouth open with shock, as the faded blue pickup passed them and continued down the dirt road. She met Bennett's eyes and saw an answering gleam of excitement.

"Oop!" Felicity made a squeaky sound of excitement. "Gotta go, Deputy! That's my guy! Thanks for the intervention, and we'll get together soon to talk about your lovely coworker. I'll text you! Stay safe! See you!" Even as she was still talking, she was shifting into drive, pulling away from the shoulder as soon as a baffled-looking Chris stepped away from her window. She waved at him out her open window without looking back, her gaze fixed at the rear of the pickup already far ahead of them.

Wind whipped through the car, and she retracted her waving arm and closed her window. She didn't want to take her eyes off the distant truck in case it disappeared like a mirage, but she had to risk a quick glance at Bennett. When she saw he was full-out grinning at her, she could barely tear her eyes away.

"Can you believe it?" she asked, her voice awed. After all, they'd just witnessed a miracle.

"They were still on the compound drive."

She felt a grin take over her face. The awful Deputy Litchfield had actually done them a favor. "The bounty-hunting gods are with us today, Mr. Bennett Xavier Green."

"Yes, they are, Ms. Felicity Florence Pax."

Her nose wrinkled, but even her middle name—which she hated almost as much as her sisters' nickname for her—couldn't dampen her exuberant joy. "Now we just wait for them to get where they're going, and Dino is as good as tackled."

———

"They both must have bladders of steel," Felicity complained from the passenger seat over ten hours later.

"Or they're going in a bottle."

"Gross."

Except for quick, infrequent stops for gas, Clint and Dino had pushed the old pickup hard as the sun went down. They drove through the night, making it more difficult for Felicity and Bennett to keep the truck in sight without sitting right on their tail. Somehow, they'd managed it so far, taking lightning-fast pee breaks and swapping drivers during those few gas stops.

"They have to be going to Vegas, right?" Felicity asked. Ever since they'd gotten onto I-15, the signs for Vegas with ever-shrinking mileage had gotten more and more frequent.

Bennett passed an SUV as he shrugged. "Or Los Angeles."

With a groan, Felicity let the back of her head bump the seat. "Oh, please no. You're a very pleasant road trip companion—especially compared to Charlie—but I'd love to stop and shower and sleep in a real bed and eat something that's not half the protein bar I'd forgotten in the glove compartment months ago." When he shot her a strange look, she mirrored it back at him. "What?" she asked.

"Charlie?"

"Charlotte, my sister?" She smirked at him. "Didn't get to nicknames when you did your background check, did you?"

"No." He made the face that she knew meant he was making a mental amendment to his notes.

"Speaking of nicknames, I never asked if you prefer Ben to Bennett."

"No," he said quickly. "Bennett's fine."

"Yes, he is," Felicity couldn't resist muttering under her breath.

"What?" he asked.

"Nothing. So no nicknames for you? Even when you were a kid?"

He paused long enough to catch her attention, and she studied his profile, eerily lit by the dash lights. "My mom called me Benny sometimes."

"That's adorable." She smiled at the thought of a tiny Bennett but sobered when she remembered that his only parent had died when he'd been just a teenager. "What was she like?"

His silence seemed thoughtful this time. "She was a little flustered and overwhelmed by life, but she tried hard. I knew she loved me, although we never said the words to each other. When she got sick…" He swallowed and trailed off, staying silent long enough that Felicity started thinking of conversational segues. "When she got sick," he said again abruptly enough to make her jump, "it was fast. She hated doctors, didn't go in until things were…advanced. She was fine, then she wasn't, then she was gone."

"I'm sorry," Felicity said, hating how useless the trite phrase was but not knowing what else to say. "What were your foster parents like?"

He smiled a little at the question, and she felt like she'd won something. "They're great. I was—am—really lucky."

"What are their names again?" she asked, eager to know more about Bennett, especially now that she was out of the earlier emotional minefield.

"Zena and Dean Roman. They're still in Fort Collins."

"So you get to see them a lot," she said approvingly.

He dipped his chin in a nod.

"I'm always a little envious of people with good parents," she admitted, the darkness of the car and her overtired brain allowing her to be more open than usual.

"I know your mom isn't the best," he said, obviously picking his words carefully and making Felicity snort at the understatement, "but what's your dad like?"

It was her turn to consider the question. "Lono's a good guy," she finally said, "as long as he's not around Jane. He loved her too much, and she's very charismatic when she wants to be. Now that he's back in Hawai'i with his kind new wife and two little girls, he's great. It's just too bad he's so far away now."

He grunted as he took in the information. "They were married twice?"

"Yeah," she answered. "Jane's first and fourth marriages. Molly and I are full sisters, even though she's the oldest and I'm the youngest." Although Felicity knew that he'd found all this out in his background check on Jane, she still enjoyed sharing bits of herself with him.

"Do you... Hang on."

Whatever he'd been about to ask was forgotten as the pickup carrying Clint and Dino exited off the interstate. Felicity cheered. Even Bennett gave one of his little half smiles, so she knew he was also ecstatic they'd get to stop soon. He accelerated down the exit ramp, getting a bit closer to their quarry before the pickup merged into traffic.

"Things are really hopping for three in the morning," she said, leaning against her window. There was so much to look at, and everything was lit up like it was the middle of the day. All the visual stimulation was overwhelming.

"Vegas." Bennett's grunt had a whole heap of resignation in it, making Felicity laugh.

"I've been here a few times," she admitted, "but never for long, and I've never been to the Strip. It's…a lot."

"They're turning."

Felicity refocused on the old pickup as it took a right to stop in front of a slightly shabby-looking hotel. Bennett kept driving. Although she expected him to circle around, he continued for a couple of miles and pulled in front of a casino. A valet rushed to open her door, and she paused long enough to give Bennett a look before allowing the valet to help her out. Her joints and muscles complained about the long stretch in her car, although her ankle seemed to have improved a bit from the long rest. She wondered how Bennett—who was about two and a half of her—managed the drive without bursting out of the car in western Colorado and refusing to get back inside.

She stretched surreptitiously while looking at the entrance to the casino, trying to hide her awe at the grandeur of the place. From Bennett's arched brow, she didn't succeed very well.

"Everything's just so *sparkly*," she muttered under her breath, leaning toward him so only he would hear.

One corner of his mouth twitched up, and the look he directed at her was so soft and affectionate that her breath caught. She shook her head, dismissing the idea. Her Bennett-reading skills were just glitchy. That had to be it.

Two people in uniform opened the doors, and Bennett rested his hand on her lower back to usher her inside. Her stomach fizzed with excitement, and her heart beat faster, two things that usually only happened when she was close to bringing in a skip. She bit the inside of her lower lip, trying to bring back her reason and common sense. When that didn't work and a thrill still swept through her at the warm press of his palm on her back, she decided it was lack of sleep that was making her irrational. Once she got a good night's rest, her brain would reset, and all these ridiculous feelings would disappear.

"Is Ronan around?" Bennett asked after they passed through the sumptuous lobby to reach the desk.

"I'll check," the woman behind the desk said. "And your name?"

"PI Green."

As the woman stepped away, Felicity faced Bennett. "Any reason we didn't circle around and tackle Dino at that other hotel? We could've been back in Simpson by midafternoon."

"You need food and a real bed," he said.

She did, but it felt wrong to leave the skip they'd just trailed for half a day through four states. "What if they leave? Vegas is huge. We'll never find them."

He shrugged. "Doubt they're going anywhere tonight. They've got to be as tired as we are. Besides, we're running on fumes. No sense in coming all this way and then fumbling the takedown."

As much as she hated to admit it, he was right. Her ankle was better but still not a hundred percent, she was stiff from the car ride, and her blood sugar had to be bottoming out. "Okay. Sure you don't want to stay at the same hotel as Clint and Dino though? That way, we can keep an eye on them."

He looked like he smelled something bad. "That place is a pit."

As tired as she was, Felicity still had to laugh. "You're a terrible snob."

"I am not." Despite his words, the way he lifted his chin and looked down his nose at her in the most offended way just proved her accusation to be true. He was one step away from clutching his pearls. Her laugh gained strength, and she had to take a few deep breaths in order to keep from losing it in a complete belly-hurting, pig-snorting, exhaustion-fueled bout of laughter.

"Green!" a male voice called from across the lobby. A tall, urbane man in a gorgeous suit with flaming red hair and neatly trimmed beard strode over to Bennett, his hand extended. "Good to see you! I thought you'd never take me up on my offer."

Bennett shook the other man's hand, and although he didn't smile, Felicity had a feeling that Bennett liked the man she assumed was Ronan.

"And who is this beauty?" Ronan asked, taking her hand and holding it gently, like it was a precious baby bird, rather than shaking it.

"Felicity Pax," Bennett said, moving a little closer to her. "Ronan Fitzgerald."

"Felicity Pax," Ronan repeated, turning her name into a purr. Although she was pretty sure his greeting would've melted the panties off most women, Felicity just wanted to snort-laugh again.

Keeping a straight face with a great deal of effort, she nodded at Ronan and retrieved her hand. "Nice to meet you."

Ronan didn't look put off by her polite brush-off. In fact, his eyes lit up with gleeful interest. "I'm so happy for you, Green, that you've found such a delightful partner."

Bennett just answered with one of his neutral, could-mean-anything grunts, and Felicity felt for a moment that she should correct Ronan's misinterpretation of their relationship, but she was tired. Dead tired. The thought of explaining that she was his superior officer in their bounty-hunting army and that she was the daughter of Bennett's target was just exhausting and confusing, even to her, so she simply smiled.

"You have a room?" Bennett asked. He didn't seem annoyed, so Felicity assumed he was leaving out more words than usual because of exhaustion.

"For you, my favorite private investigator," Ronan said, sweeping his arms out in a grand gesture, "only the best." He moved to have a quiet conversation with the woman behind the counter, and Felicity took the opportunity to give Bennett a sideways look.

"I thought your background check reported that you didn't have friends."

"Not a friend," he muttered, too low for anyone but her to hear. "Did some work for him. That's all."

"Seems pretty friendly for a not-friend."

Bennett actually looked flustered. "He's like that with everyone. I found out who was stealing from the casino, so he's just grateful."

"Mm-hmm." She had a feeling that he had a lot of not-friends out there who considered themselves to be his actual friends, even if Bennett thought he was alone in the world. Before she could say anything else, Ronan brandished two key cards with a huge smile.

"If my hotel was gauche enough to have a honeymoon suite, this would be it," Ronan said, looking quite proud of himself as he held out the cards. "Room 1842. Enjoy, my old friend and my new friend."

Felicity cleared her throat, regretting her decision not to correct him about her and Bennett's relationship earlier. Now it would be even more awkward to attempt an explanation, so she reached for one of the cards with a glance at Bennett. He, she saw, was looking straight ahead, avoiding any eye contact with her. He'd also gone completely silent, so she dredged up a smile for Ronan.

"Thank you," she said with honest gratitude. It didn't matter if the bed was a honeymoon bed used to all sorts of just-married sex. It was guaranteed to be more comfortable than trying to catch a few minutes' rest in a car. "This is very kind of you."

Ronan waved his hand dismissively. "Like I said, only the best for Green." He slapped Bennett on the shoulder.

Bennett, although he'd also accepted a key card, still stared straight ahead as if he was frozen in a block of awkwardness, unable to move a muscle.

A suited older man hovered behind Ronan. "Excuse me, Mr. Fitzgerald? There's a minor situation on the floor that needs your attention."

"I'll be right there, Timothy." Ronan offered them an apologetic grimace before giving Bennett a quick, back-slapping hug and then kissing each of Felicity's cheeks. She'd always hated the double-cheek kiss, since she worried about going the wrong direction and ending up with full lip action with a near stranger, so she just stood still and let Ronan do his thing. "Very nice to see you, Green, and wonderful to meet you, Felicity Pax. Come see me if you need anything."

With a final wave, Ronan left the lobby with a stressed-looking Timothy, leaving Felicity feeling a bit shell-shocked and more tired than she'd ever been in her life. She didn't even know if she'd make it to the elevator.

"I feel like asking a bellhop if they can push me to our room on a luggage rack," she said wistfully, thinking of all the lucky luggage that got a wheeled ride to the hotel room.

Bennett gave a choke of laughter that sounded a bit strangled, but Felicity figured he was still working on coming out of his awkwardness paralysis. Dredging up all her last energy reserves, she turned toward the elevators, catching his hand on the way.

"C'mon." She tugged until his feet unstuck from the floor. "Let's go before I curl up under the reception counter and sleep there."

"Waste of a hon—uh...waste of a bed."

Bennett's utter mortification made her laugh huskily as she hauled him onto the elevator just opening its door. She stabbed the button for the eighteenth floor and then leaned back against the elevator wall.

"Everything here is gorgeous and lavish and worth goggling over," she sighed, her eyes closing of their own volition. "I just can't do it right now though. Too tired. We'll have to come back sometime we're not chasing a skip across the country."

Bennett's grunt had a surprised overtone, and Felicity opened one eye to look at him.

"Oh sorry." For a second, she'd forgotten that they weren't dating, weren't even friends really—even less than Bennett and Ronan were not-friends. "Didn't mean to imply...whatever I just implied." Honestly, she was too tired to be tactful.

He gave a tight shake of his head, which could mean anything, so Felicity took it as forgiveness for her—as Ronan put it—gaucheness and closed her eyes again.

"Felicity." His deep voice brought her out of her daze. "Wake up. We're almost to the room."

Drowsily, she followed him off the elevator and into what was much too fancy to be called a hallway. A foyer, maybe? It was Bennett's turn to grab her hand and tow her to a door. He touched his key card to the reader, opening the door when a green light flashed.

The final bit of consciousness still functioning in Felicity's brain was awed by the suite. It was enormous and open, the sitting and sleeping areas defined by the furniture rather than walls. The high ceiling arched above them, giving the room cathedral vibes. Everything was beautiful and lush and screamed expensive taste, making her small suitcase someone had brought up along with Bennett's look a bit tattered. The bed was over-whelming because there was only one of it, but it was so oversize Felicity felt fairly confident they could both sleep in it without ever making contact that might lead to awkwardness.

"Shower," Bennett said in an abrupt way that she would've taken as an insult to her state of personal hygiene if she hadn't known him. "I'll order room service. Want anything special?"

"Get me anything with lean protein and lots of veggies, and I'll love you forever."

Ignoring the fact that her comment had refrozen Bennett in his block of awkwardness, she grabbed a tank and shorts from her suitcase to use for pajamas and hurried into the bathroom. It was bigger than the bedroom she shared with Molly at home and had the same feel of over-the-top opulence the main section of the suite had. It took her a few minutes to figure out the controls for the multiple showerheads, but soon she was sighing with relief as hot water pounded down on her shoulders and head.

She could've easily fallen asleep standing up in the steamy warmth, but she forced herself to wash up efficiently. The knowledge that food was coming was a great motivator too. Even though she moved quickly, the food had already been brought to their room by the time she emerged from the bathroom.

"Want to clean up before we eat?" she asked, although her starved gaze was fixed on the food.

With a huff of laughter, he said, "No. Eat."

"Okay, Tarzan." When she saw he'd gotten her a salad with chicken that looked amazing, she had to resist the urge to hug him in gratitude. The thought of how he'd gone stiff at the mere mention of a honeymoon suite made her reconsider. A hug might leave him frozen for days. She downgraded to a simple "Thank you."

He ate his pasta with efficient quickness, finishing well before her and disappearing into the bathroom. The food revived her slightly, but she firmly kept her mind off the night—or early morning, more accurately—ahead on that plush, honeymoon-esque bed.

Bennett emerged soon after she'd finished her salad, shirt-less and damp in a cloud of steam. Felicity made a small sound that she really hoped he hadn't heard. It wasn't her fault though. His chest was a work of art—not chiseled like a body builder's but strong and bulging with muscle under his chest hair. Those arms though… She swallowed and forced her eyes down to her empty plate, and she started stacking the dirty dishes with more care than was strictly necessary.

Using the excuse to turn away from his distractingly gorgeous bare torso, she carried the tray toward the door. Her plan backfired, because Bennett followed to open the door for her, which required him to lean close enough that she was immersed in his clean, masculine scent.

Clearing her throat, she placed the tray on the floor outside the door and then retreated back into the suite, carefully keeping her eyes on things that weren't so tempting—like the bed.

No! Don't look at the bed! It was too late. Scenes rolled through her head like a movie, the two of them, naked, kissing, touching…

"Ack!" she squawked, finally ripping her gaze from the bed. "Just going to…ah, get ready for"—*don't say bed, don't say bed*—"bed." *Damn it.*

He didn't respond, but for once she didn't check his face for nonverbal clues about what he was thinking. Instead, she hurried back to the bathroom and closed herself inside. Leaning back against the door, she breathed in that warm, clean smell, that addictive scent that was distinctively Bennett. She huffed out a semihysterical laugh. Apparently, there'd be no escape from the temptation that was PI B. Green.

As she brushed her teeth and got ready for bed, fully appreciating the indoor plumbing, her exhaustion returned with a vengeance. By the time she left the bathroom, all worries about awkwardness or resisting temptation had fled her mind, leaving only the desire to sleep.

She didn't even look around the suite to see where Bennett was. Instead, she made a straight line to the bed, her eyes open only enough to keep her from walking into walls. Her knees hit the side of the bed, and she let herself fall forward, anticipating the soft give of an expensive mattress underneath her. When she landed, however, it was disappointingly hard and strangely lumpy.

It also let out a grunt.

"Did I just land on you?" she asked, not able to move despite the potential for enormous embarrassment.

"Yeah."

"Oh. Sorry." The Bennett mattress wasn't as uncomfortable as she'd first thought. In fact, once it adjusted to the points and curves of her shape, he almost felt as if he'd been contoured to fit against her body. Her eyes began to sink closed.

Bennett shifted underneath her, but instead of rolling her off onto the other side of the bed, he just moved her up so she could tuck her head beneath his chin, which, she found, was extraordinarily comfortable. Nestling closer and letting out a hum of contentment, she fell asleep.

TEN

MORNING LIGHT WAS PEEKING AROUND the curtains when she woke with a start in exactly the same position she'd fallen asleep. Bennett breathed underneath her in heavy exhales that were not quite snores. Moving carefully so as not to disturb him, she turned her head to look at the clock next to the bed and saw it was a little before eight in the morning. She'd only slept for a handful of hours, and her body felt heavy with the need for more rest.

Dino popped into her brain, though, and she knew it'd be impossible to sleep again. If Dino and Clint disappeared into the crowds of Vegas, she'd kick herself the whole long drive home. Bennett had been right though. She felt sharper and almost back to normal after a good meal, a shower, and some sleep in a comfortable bed.

Well, she thought, feeling the rasp of chest hair against her cheek, *some sleep on a comfortable man.*

She eased off him—or she tried to at least. His arms wrapped around her, holding her tight to his chest like he was five and she was his precious stuffed animal. Tempted to sink back into his warm embrace, she made herself move. Scooting down toward his feet, she tried to escape his hold that way, but his grip tightened, and she could feel his disgruntled sleepy mumble vibrate against her. Her predicament made her laugh, and she felt him start as he awakened.

His arms instantly released her, dropping her to the bed so suddenly she almost tipped sideways. Catching herself, she pushed off him and scrambled from the bed.

Telling herself to stop acting like an awkward teenager, she met his eyes. "Good morning."

His grunt questioned the accuracy of her statement, making her smile.

"Ready for a stakeout?"

"Not really." His bass voice was scratchy and rumbly in the morning, and she felt her grin getting wider.

"We might get to tackle some guys," she said in a wheedling tone, as if offering him a treat. When the corner of his mouth kicked up in a partial smile, she felt like she'd won a prize.

"Fine." He reached above his head in a full-body stretch, and she allowed herself to stare for a solid second before forcing her feet to move to the bathroom. Whoever invented the term "eye candy" had to have been thinking of a shirtless Bennett.

An hour later, Felicity sipped her take-out coffee and groaned. "We might as well have stayed in bed longer."

He gave her a sideways look, the one that lately she was finding much too endearing.

Hiding her smile against the lip of her coffee cup, she eyed the old pickup parked several rows in front of them. They'd paid for a day of parking in the tattered hotel's ramp and spent the first forty-five minutes searching for their skip's pickup. Now, they stared at the parked Ford and waited.

"Stupid security cameras," Felicity mumbled, glaring at the ceiling-mounted electronics. She would've loved to break into the pickup to search it, but that was guaranteed to send security running, and staking out Clint and Dino would be hard to do from the inside of a Vegas jail cell. Still, the windowless hard-shell topper had a beast of a lock on it, which meant it was almost guaranteed to contain something interesting.

The minutes ticked by, turning into hours. They took turns watching while the other one went on foot to get snacks and use the bathroom at the diner next door to the hotel. Seeing Clint and Dino's hotel and the scruffy area around it made her appreciate their wonderful not-honeymoon suite at Ronan's. As afternoon faded into evening, Felicity started to wonder if Clint and Dino had dumped the pickup here. She cringed at the thought.

"How long ago did you work for Ronan?" she asked between chewing carrot sticks, trying to distract herself from all the possible ways this stakeout could go wrong.

One shoulder lifted in a half shrug. "About two years ago."

"You investigated his casino employees?"

He gave a short nod.

"Did you go undercover?" She bit a carrot stick in half with relish as she thought about how fun investigating in a casino could be. "Maybe as a high roller who likes blackjack?"

This time, he combined his sideways look with a slight eye roll, making her grin around her carrot.

"Just saying. You could've had some fun with it."

He just shrugged, as if he didn't understand the concept of fun.

"Who was the thief?" When he paused, she clarified, "Not their name, just the position. I'm writing the screenplay in my head. It's a blockbuster."

"Wasn't an employee," he said, just when she thought he was going to keep her hanging. "His partner."

She felt her eyes widen. "Business partner or romantic partner?"

"Both."

"Nooooo." Her head fell back against the seat. "Ronan's a sweetheart. He deserves so much better, and I'm not just saying that because he's letting us stay in his not-honeymoon suite."

Although she expected Bennett to stiffen up, he actually gave her a half smile and said, "He does deserve better."

Something about the way he looked at her made Felicity's face warm. She mentally scolded her traitorous cheeks, telling them that there was absolutely no reason to be getting all flustered by a considerate, caring Bennett, but it didn't do any good.

To her great relief, the elevator opened, and the very men they wanted to see strode toward their pickup. Felicity went still, impatiently waiting as she watched Clint and Dino walk across the parking ramp. Once they turned toward their pickup, showing her their backs, Felicity put a hand on her door handle.

"Ready?" she whispered, her heart rate kicking up enough to make her bare her teeth in an anticipatory grin.

He gave her a full-on smile back. "Let's do some tackling."

She slipped out of the car, soundlessly closing the door most of the way. Catching Bennett's gaze, she tipped her head toward a concrete pillar standing between them and their quarry. He gave a slight nod, and they both made their way to it, concealing themselves from the two men.

Felicity peeked around the column. The men were at the pickup, Clint manually unlocking the driver's door with a key as Dino waited to be let in. Felicity's leg muscles bunched as she watched for her moment. They'd have to be fast, before security came running and muddled things up. As soon as Dino went to get into the truck, she decided, she'd sprint across the remaining distance and pull him back out and down on the ground.

She poked Bennett, who was peering around the opposite side of the pillar. When he turned to her, eyebrows raised in question, she mouthed, "I'll grab Dino. You handle Clint." He nodded again before returning to his surveillance.

Felicity followed suit, watching Clint reach across the cab and pop Dino's door lock. Just as she burst into a run, the elevator dinged, and Dino whirled to his right to face the opening doors, pulling a black handgun from his waistband that'd been hidden beneath his loose T-shirt.

Although Dino was still facing away from them, the sight of the gun made Felicity instantly put on the brakes. She stopped abruptly, barely keeping herself from hurtling forward and land-ing chin-first on the concrete. Her head whipped around to find Bennett a few steps away. Reaching out, she grabbed a handful of his shirt and backtracked, pulling him with her until they were behind the column again without being spotted by Dino or Clint.

Loud, rowdy laughter rang through the parking garage, echoing off the concrete, contrasting strangely with the grimly serious expression on Bennett's face—the same look Felicity was sure was on hers as well. Taking a deep breath to steady her nerves, she risked a glance around the column, seeing that Dino had lowered the gun but kept it out, tucked behind his left leg so the newcomers couldn't see it.

She and Bennett stayed in place as four people—the source of the raucous laughter and loud voices—made their way to their Jeep. Felicity made a face. For some reason, she'd always loathed Jeeps.

Bennett must've noticed her reaction, because he gave her a questioning look, but she just shook her head. Her odd aversion wasn't a priority right now, not while Dino's gaze scanned the parking area, the gun still in his hand. Finally, with one last look around, he tucked the gun in his back waistband and yanked his T-shirt down over it. Climbing into the truck, he pulled the door closed behind him with a loud slam.

The pickup backed out of the space as frustration filled Felicity. She'd taken down some armed skips before, but she wasn't about to run right into the barrel of a loaded pistol. As Clint gunned the pickup, sending it shooting toward the exit, she headed back to the car.

Automatically, she went for the driver's side, but Bennett gave her a look so full of hope and pleading that she almost laughed despite the situation.

"Fine," she said quietly, even though there was no way Clint and Dino could hear her on the other side of the parking garage. "But you'll owe me." Reversing direction, she hurried to climb into the passenger seat. Her reward was a sweet smile from Bennett before he sped after their escaping skip.

Night had fallen during their last stretch of waiting, but the multitude of lights made it feel more like daytime. The heavy traffic forced Bennett to stick close to the rear of the pickup, with only a half dozen or so cars separating them. Clint left the Strip and wove his way through the city, finally pulling into the small parking lot of a seedy-looking bar that reminded Felicity of Dutch's back in Langston.

Bennett drove slowly around the block, only turning in and parking after Clint and Dino had gone inside.

"What's the plan?" he asked, turning off her car.

"My plans haven't been working so well lately," she said a little sourly but shook off her spurt of ill temper. They hadn't lost Dino yet, and here was another chance to bring him in. "Let's play this by ear. We'll go in, take a look around, and then come up with a plan. I'd rather not try to tackle Dino in the middle of a bunch of Vegas militia members."

"We could just wait out here for them to come back out."

Although Bennett's suggestion was reasonable, she was about to crawl out of her skin with boredom at the thought of spending any more time sitting in her car, waiting for the skip to come to her. "No harm in having a quick look around. We'll make sure Dino doesn't get a glimpse of us." When Bennett eyed her askance, she sighed and gave him her best pleading puppy-dog eyes. "Pleeeeeease? Just for a minute? I'm so sick of this car. My butt groove is already imprinted on this seat. I'm going to meld with it soon, and then I'll never be able to leave it. I'll be like a weird cyborg Transformer."

With a huff of laughter, he gave an exaggerated sigh and opened his door. "C'mon then."

"Thank you!" She hurried to get out before reason took over and she talked herself out of going inside. The chilly desert night air slapped *some* sense into her, but it was just enough to get her to grab her jacket from the back seat. The long drive to Vegas and their extended stakeout had worn down her usual practical nature, and the adrenaline junkie was in the driver's seat now.

Almost giddy at the idea of an adventure—as tame as going into a dive bar promised to be—she caught up to Bennett and linked her arm though his. When he gave her one of his patented raised-eyebrow looks, she just snickered and pinched his side, making him jump and stare down at her. It was hard to tell in the spotty lighting of the parking lot, but she was pretty sure he was blushing.

Feeling a tiny bit bad for embarrassing him, she returned her hand to his ridiculously large biceps. "Sorry. I'll be good."

His quiet grunt sounded skeptical, and she grinned at him. Although they'd only met each other a short time ago, he already knew her so well.

The bouncer looked them up and down, glowered more

fiercely, and then jerked his head toward the door in an indica-tion to go inside. Felicity, who'd been about to pull her ID from her pocket, gave a mental shrug and walked through the door-way, Bennett so close behind her that she thought she could feel his body heat.

The noise hit them like a wall. The bar was crowded, every-one competing for who could talk the loudest. An old-school country song played but was almost drowned out by the voices and laughter. For some reason, Felicity half expected a clichéd record scratch leading to complete silence and staring when she and Bennett entered, but no one even looked at them.

She scanned the crowd, searching for Clint and Dino, but the low lighting and large number of people made it impossible to pick them out. Glancing over her shoulder, she gave Bennett a questioning look, and he shook his head. Apparently, even with his greater height, he hadn't spotted them either.

As she worked her way toward the bar, Bennett followed closely, one hand on her waist. Her attention wanted to drift to the electrified skin under his touch, but she forced herself to keep scanning for any glimpse of Dino or Clint. It would be bad if one of the two men spotted them first. She'd never met Dino before she started her search, but she assumed he'd seen at least a picture of her, since his militia friends were after her.

They made it to the bar without seeing any sign of either of the two men. Although she knew she should be disappointed, since that was the entire point of coming into the bar, she was secretly, guiltily relieved. Felicity felt like she'd been working constantly since Jane took off. Being in a bar, as seedy as it was, was a welcome change of pace. She just wanted to relax and enjoy herself for five minutes, and then she'd go back into bounty-hunter mode.

A man slid off his barstool and moved away, and Felicity claimed the seat with an inelegant pounce. Bennett slid in half next to her and half behind her where he could guard her back and keep an eye on the crowd at the same time. The guy on the next barstool made an irritated sound as he turned to confront the person who'd gotten in his space. When he laid eyes on Bennett, he deflated and turned his attention back to the drink in front of him.

Felicity watched the byplay with appreciation. Having someone Bennett's size at her side was a benefit—plus a time-saver. Normally, being small and delicate-looking, she had to prove that she couldn't be pushed around. With Bennett around, the bullies didn't even try.

The bartender, a tall, scarecrow-looking white man with greased-back hair, stopped in front of them. "What can I get you?"

Despite her desire for a normal night out, she wasn't feeling reckless—or stupid—enough to actually drink. "Orange juice, please."

"Water," Bennett grunted, obviously being of the same mind as she was. They had to bring the skip in, and *then* they could get stinking drunk. The idea of partying with Bennett held a strong appeal, so strong that her cheeks flushed with anticipation at the idea. She could let her guard down, have fun without worrying about what her wilder sister was doing or what bad things could happen to her. Bennett would be there. He'd protect her.

She dropped her eyes and studied the battered wood of the bar. Her thoughts seemed like a betrayal—to Charlie, to her job, to her feminist ideals. She did love her sister and working as a bounty hunter, but sometimes she got tired. The idea of someone else looking out for her for a change was oddly tempting.

Two glasses—one with juice and one with water—slid into view, breaking into her thoughts. Before she could pull out some of the cash she'd stashed in her pocket that morning, Bennett was already handing over a bill. When the bartender held out the considerable amount of change, Bennett waved him off. With a nod of thanks, the bartender stuffed the bills in his tip jar and turned to the next customer.

After taking a sip of her drink, Felicity rotated on her stool to survey the crowd again. After her earlier thoughts, she felt guilty enough to redirect her attention to their original goal— bringing in Dino. People were thick by the bar, though, and her seated position made it even harder to see over everyone's heads. Customers crowded in on both sides and even behind her, trying to get the bartender's attention. Even more grateful for the buffer of Bennett, she leaned into his enveloping warmth.

In turn, he placed an arm around her, tucking her closer to him. Giving up on looking for Dino and Clint for a moment, she allowed herself to enjoy his closeness, closing her eyes and tipping her head against a chest that was too hard to be comfortable, but she still didn't ever want to move.

Shouting made Bennett tense, and Felicity lifted her head, scanning the crowd as well as she could until her gaze landed on the source. A fight had broken out at the end of the bar, four guys who were pounding on one another in an apparently indiscriminate way.

"I don't get it," Felicity said, craning her neck to see better. "Who's on whose side? Or are they all on their own sides?"

"Think they're too drunk to know whose side they're on." Bennett shifted so his body was between her and the fight. When she raised an eyebrow at him, he pretended he didn't see it.

"Unless they have go-go-gadget arms, I'm not getting hit by a stray punch all the way over here."

He set his jaw, although a flush crept up to his cheekbones. "Someone might throw something or pull a weapon."

"That's true, I suppose." The bouncer hadn't even looked at their IDs, much less checked them for weapons. A good chunk of the crowd had to be packing.

She leaned around Bennett so she could see the fight. Two bouncers fought their way through the gawking crowd, and each grabbed two of the men by the backs of their necks or their shirts, pulling them away from each other. Once separated, the men were quickly marched toward the exit.

"That was a Vegas bar fight?" Felicity asked, slightly disappointed as she turned back to her drink. "I've seen worse at the grocery store in Langston when they're having a sale on avocados."

Bennett's chest shook with laughter, and she leaned into him again, idly people watching as she finished her drink. Although she'd always kept an eye out for Dino, the people within her view had stayed blessedly skip-free. The fight, as pathetic as it'd been, had been the most excitement she was going to get, and the crowd provided little entertainment. Glancing at Bennett's glass, she saw his water was gone. Time to get back to work. With a sigh, she made herself slide off her barstool.

"Better get to it...oh." Her feet hit the ground, and her knees folded, wanting to drop her on the sticky floor. Stiffening her legs, she grabbed the edge of the bar with one hand and Bennett's arm with the other. She looked up at him, and he matched her grim expression with one of his own. Her eyes darted back to where their empty glasses had sat just a second ago, but they'd already been swept away by a bar back. "You too?"

Bennett dipped his head in a short nod. "Let's go."

The sibilant sound of his *s* was drawn out an extra fraction of a second, and her heart began to beat faster. They'd both been drugged, and things could get really bad, really fast. She released her grip on the bar and his arm, instead taking his hand. Although she'd just been daydreaming about having some drinks with Bennett, that was some vague time in the future, when everything was wrapped up and they'd be safe. Now was not the time to be vulnerable.

She looked over at the bartender, her number one suspect, but a woman had taken his place serving drinks. Felicity's suspicions increased, but Bennett tugged at her hand, reminding her that they had other priorities right now. Bringing whoever spiked their drinks to justice could wait until the drug had made its way out of her and Bennett's systems and their brains and bodies were working normally again.

The floor felt wavy under her feet, but she gritted her teeth and charged through the crowd. When she stumbled, Bennett took the lead, and that was easier. She moved in his wake as he barged through the crowd, using his body like a snowplow to make a path through the mass of people. It felt like forever before the door loomed before them.

Felicity felt the back of her neck prickle, and she turned her head to look behind her while clinging to Bennett's hand to keep her balance. In the shifting crowd, a familiar face smirked at her.

"Dino," she said as Bennett pulled her through the doorway into the blessedly cool outside air. "B, we need to go back. Dino's right there."

"Can't get him now." Bennett looked furious, but she knew it wasn't directed at her.

The logic of what he'd said took a few seconds to sink in, but when it did, a burst of fear detonated in her chest. She and Bennett had turned from the hunters to the hunted after being dosed. "We have to get out of here."

The bouncer watched them leave, sneering, and her paranoid drugged mind wondered if he was in on it. Then his face blurred, and she doubted everything she was seeing, not sure what was imagination and what was reality. Bennett tugged on her hand, and she hurried to keep up, fighting to keep her too-soft knees from folding underneath her and dumping her on asphalt that smelled of pee, gasoline, and vomit.

It wasn't until they reached her car that their predicament really dawned on her. There was no way either of them could drive right now. They'd kill someone—and themselves. Felicity pulled out her phone with numb fingers. "I'll get a Lyft."

"No time."

Felicity followed his gaze, trying to turn her head but forgetting how, so she ended up rotating her whole body. Once her spinning vision settled slightly, she saw Dino emerging from the bar with Clint close behind him. "We should run, shouldn't we? Yes, let's run." Without waiting for a response, she took off as fast as her rubbery knees would carry her.

She was still holding Bennett's hand—or maybe she'd never let him go—and she was glad for the connection. Her balance felt precarious, so she didn't want to try to turn her head to look at him. Instead, she relied on the firm press of his fingers to let her know he was right there with her.

Behind them, she heard a shout, and she knew they were being pursued. The cars on the road flew by in blinding streaks of headlights, and Felicity had enough presence of mind to not attempt to cross the road in her current state. Instead, she locked her eyes on the neon sign a few buildings down on the same side of the street as the bar they'd just left. The curly letters read *Dinner*—no, *Diner*, she corrected herself. Clutching Bennett's hand, she ran with everything she had.

There was a *crack* just as a line of fire burned across the side of her calf. A mental image of Dino's gun flashed in her mind, and Felicity dodged sideways, crashing through a sand sagebrush into a laundromat's parking lot. She wasn't sure if she'd dragged Bennett through the shrub or if he pulled her, but it didn't matter. They were both still upright and running and alive...for now.

Bennett pulled out in front of her, and she was vaguely

offended by that. *It's the roofie*, she told herself, even as her brain was screaming at her to stop obsessing about their relative running speeds and focus on getting away. The competitive part of her mind wouldn't shut up though. Once she was no longer drugged, she decided, she'd challenge him to a trail race. *Let's see who's faster in my territory*, she thought smugly, just before her toe caught on the pavement and she headed for the ground, face-first.

Somehow, the running-while-roofied gods were with her, and she managed to get her feet under her again before she ate asphalt. Once she regained her sprinting rhythm, she looked up to find the neon sign again and discovered it was right above their heads.

Bennett must've had the same plan as she did, because he yanked her right through the front door of the diner. The brightly lit interior made her squint a little, but she was happy to see that more than half of the red and white booths were filled, as were a handful of the shiny Formica tables. Surely their pursuers wouldn't walk barefaced into a place with dozens of witnesses and almost as many cell phone cameras to continue shooting at them.

Slowing to a walk—albeit a fast walk—they headed toward a booth in the far corner, next to the emergency exit and the door to the kitchen. Not wanting to let go of Bennett's hand, she stayed right next to him rather than moving to the other side of the booth. He didn't seem to mind, ushering her into the seat before he lowered his considerable bulk onto the bench. Shifting his captive hand into her lap, she grabbed their linked fingers with her other hand. She felt overheated from their run, but she still wanted to touch as much of Bennett as she could reach.

With his free hand, he placed his phone in front of him and then reached over to grab one of the laminated menus standing behind the syrup containers. Clutching his other hand in both of hers, she watched, fascinated, as he used a stick-straight pointer finger to poke out a text to Ronan.

Pleas com get uss

Then he sent a picture of the address on the back of the menu, and Felicity gave a nod of approval.

"Ronan will rescue us." Her words were blurry, slurred but comprehensible. At least she was pretty sure Bennett could understand them.

His nod confirmed it. "Ronan's a good guy." He also drew his words out too long, as if they were sticky taffy that he played with before putting in his mouth.

The server—young and doe-eyed, with smooth brown skin and a red-and-white-striped uniform that matched the decor almost too well—stifled a yawn before asking, "Coffee?"

That seemed like a good idea, even though Felicity normally hated coffee. Maybe the caffeine would help counteract whatever drug they were given. "Please." She was proud that the word came out fairly decently.

The server placed a carafe on the table, and Bennett immediately reached for it. "What else can I get you?"

Felicity glanced at the menu, but the words wouldn't stay still, instead jumping around like little ants running across the laminated surface. Brushing her hand over the menu to check if she could feel the letters move, she searched her brain for diner food. "Pancakes!" Her voice came out too loudly and too proudly, as evidenced by the server's startled expression.

"Ooookay," the server said. "What kind?"

Her brain was swirling, making it impossible to hold on to her slippery thoughts. Unable to come up with an answer for a question she'd already forgotten, she looked to Bennett for help.

"Pancakes," he said solemnly, pointing at a picture on the menu as if the server needed help identifying what exactly pancakes were.

"What kiiind?" The server drew out the word in a different way, not like her tongue was suddenly uncooperative but like she was talking to someone who didn't understand her language. "Chocolate chip, banana nut, strawberry, boysenberry, or cream cheese? And do you want any sides? We have hash browns, bacon, sausage, ham, or eggs cooked however you want them."

They looked at each other and both shrugged.

"Just…pancakes," Felicity said, as if that were the answer. "With syrup."

Bennett gave a firm nod. "Definitely syrup."

Feeling a rush of affection, Felicity squeezed his hand with both of hers. "We think so much alike."

Bennett beamed at her.

With a deep sigh, the server turned away, muttering about drunk people being a pain in the ass.

Turning to look up at Bennett, Felicity was distracted by the way the fluorescent lighting highlighted his dark brown hair, bringing out glints of deep red and blond. Forgetting what she was about to say, she breathed, "You're so beautiful."

"You're the beautiful one." He used his free hand to trace over one of her brows and then pinch a small section of hair, pulling it gently through his fingers. "I want to touch you all the time."

"Same, obviously." She held up his captive hand with a laugh.

"Your hair is so soft." He kept stroking it. "And you're so smart and brave and beautiful."

Humming with contentment, she closed her eyes. Now that her adrenaline had faded, she felt the fogginess settling more firmly in her mind. "That why you stalked me?" The words came out more slurred than ever.

Surprisingly, he seemed to understand her question. "I tried not to, but ever since I first saw you, I couldn't focus on anyone else. Can I tell you a secret?"

Opening her eyes just a crack, she allowed a slow smile to stretch across her face. "I loooove secrets."

"I suspected I should've followed Charlotte."

Genuinely surprised, her eyes opened the rest of the way. "You did? But we were so sneaky. She even took Moo's weedmobile."

"I still knew she was more likely the one going after Jane." His hand left her hair and wrapped around the back of her neck. "Then once I got to Simpson and found out you were searching

for Dino, I couldn't leave you to chase him alone. Too dangerous. You might've gotten hurt. I had to stay and help you. I
called my client and told them I needed to deal with an urgent
personal matter before I could start work on their case again.
Told them if they didn't want to wait, they could get a different
PI, and I'd return their retainer."

"Really?" Felicity stared at him. "You gave up a job just to
help me bring in Dino?"

"I didn't really give it up. The client agreed to wait until my
personal business is finished." His lips curled up smugly, which
was almost as adorable on him as his pouty look. "I'm the best
at what I do."

"Still, you risked all that to help me?"

His lids lowered, and he peered at her through ridiculously
thick lashes. "I didn't want to leave you. I think I love you."

Her huff of laughter was more of a sigh. "You can't fall in
love in a week, silly."

"Can't you?"

The clatter of plates on the table caught their attention.

"Pancakes," Felicity breathed.

"Pancakes." Looking down at her, Bennett gifted her with
one of his gorgeous, full-faced smiles.

"Yeah, yeah, pancakes." Their server sounded equal parts
exasperated and ready to laugh. "In-love drunk people are even
more annoying than regular drunk people."

Turning to the server, Felicity asked curiously, "Do you
think someone can fall in love in a week?"

"A week?" The server looked skeptical, but then her

expression softened. "I don't know, but you look pretty gone for each other. If anyone can fall in love in a week, it's you two."

For some reason, this made excited sparkles fizz in Felicity's chest, and she looked up to smile at Bennett. He looked down at her with an expression so tender and gentle and utterly infatuated that her breath caught. Her heart started beating wildly, her blood rushing quickly through her veins.

"You make me feel like I'm chasing a skip," she said.

"Really?" He beamed even more brightly at her. "You make me feel like I just got video evidence of a husband cheating on his wife."

Warmth flooded her. "That's so sweet."

"You're both so weird," the server said, turning to walk away from their booth. "Let me know if you need anything else."

Felicity barely heard her, the words flowing unnoticed past her ears. All she could see was Bennett's wonderful face.

"What happened to you?" It was Ronan's voice that jerked them out of their little world of two.

Felicity clutched Bennett's hand, which she still hadn't let go, and leaned against him as she beamed up at her new friend, Ronan. "We fell in love!"

ELEVEN

As soon as Felicity woke, she wished she were still sleeping. Everything hurt, especially her head, and each beat of her heart seemed to send a pulse of dull pain to every corner of her body. She made a sound of misery but then broke off her groan halfway through because it made her hurt even more. Without opening her eyes, she lay very still, hoping if she didn't move, the pain would go away.

As she lay there unmoving, a deep groan filled the air around her, and her eyes flew open, her misery forgotten as her memory kicked in, reminding her why she was in a strange bed with Bennett Green.

They'd followed her skip to Las Vegas, spent most of the next day sitting in her car in a parking garage, staring at Clint and Dino's pickup truck, and then followed them to a dive bar.

Bennett rolled over onto his back. "Please shoot me."

"Me first."

He cautiously opened one eye. "You okay, Fifi?"

"Really?" She gave a huff, but it was a small one so it didn't move her aching head too much. "You too with the Fifis?" She reached over to pinch him—nothing too hard, just enough to remember it the next time he considered using her dreaded nickname.

He rolled off the bed in an effort to get away from her. As the sheets were pulled from his body during his fall, she was relieved to see that he still wore boxer briefs. He was partially naked, but at least he wasn't *fully* naked. She tried to convince herself that she wasn't the *tiniest* bit disappointed the important bits were covered.

Belatedly, she looked under the covers. With mixed feelings, she regarded the unfamiliar oversize T-shirt that went almost to her knees. When she checked, she found she did have her own underwear on. *There's that at least*, she thought before turning her attention back to Bennett. While she'd been distracted assessing her clothing situation, he'd found some pants and pulled them on. She felt that same pang of disappointment that his muscled legs were hidden, but she comforted herself with the thought that she could still ogle that gorgeous chest of his.

"To answer your question," she said, trying to get her brain off Bennett's pecs and back on how they'd ended up in this situation, "I'll live. Well, unless I chop off my own head to stop the pounding."

"Yeah, me too." He rubbed his face with both hands, his stubble rasping against his calluses.

"Any idea how we ended up here last night?" Felicity felt her face warm, but she pushed through the embarrassment, cleared her throat, and continued. "All I remember is the stakeout and following Dino into the dive bar." As she talked through it, more flashes of memories were returning. "We didn't see Dino or Clint, but there was a fight? Maybe?" That part seemed hazy. "Was I in the fight?"

"No." The line of his mouth was grim, and she had a feeling he was recalling even more than she was. "It was a distraction."

"Distraction for…?" Even as she asked, the memory of stumbling out of the bar came to her. "Someone drugged our drinks."

His nod was so stiff she thought his spine might shatter with the movement.

"Were Clint and Dino chasing us at one point?" she asked tentatively. The more she strained to remember details, the more they slipped out of her grasp. "And maybe…pancakes?"

His expression softened slightly. "Yes. To both."

Pushing herself up into a sitting position, she dropped her head on her knees and breathed through a fresh wave of nausea. "Guess that explains why I feel like overcooked meat loaf."

"Overcooked meat loaf?" The amusement in his tone made her look up, risking the movement in order to catch one of his rare smiles.

"Leave me alone," she said, trying and failing to sound stern. "I'm in no state to come up with good metaphors. At least we ended up here, generally intact. If the only consequence to our being roofied and chased by Clint and Dino is a hangover from hell, we got pretty lucky."

When he remained silent, she lifted her aching head and found him staring at the desk across the room.

"What is it?" she asked, unable to read his expression.

"That…" He cleared his throat. "That wasn't the *only* consequence."

Her stomach dropped. "What else?"

He gestured toward a small desk, but all she saw on it was a blush rose bouquet. "What's wrong? It's pretty, although a little too bridal for a not-honeymoon suite…"

He flinched at the word "bridal," and a terrible suspicion rose in her blurry mind.

"That's not… We didn't…" She didn't even want to say the words out loud, as if speaking them would make them true.

Giving her a hooded look, he strode over to the desk. Ignoring the too-bridal-for-a-not-honeymoon-suite bouquet, he examined the paper lying on the desk next to it. Unable to stand the suspense for another second—while also wanting to remain in blissful ignorance for as long as possible—she got out of bed.

Bennett's gaze immediately shot to her legs. Even though she was covered almost to her knees, she still blushed.

"This your shirt?" she asked, wanting to ignore whatever was causing that strange look on his face.

He looked at her too seriously for a question about a T-shirt and nodded solemnly. Swallowing hard, she moved closer to the desk and the answers it held. The first thing she saw was a five-by-seven photo. It was her and Bennett, and she was holding the too-bridal bouquet. Not only that, but what looked suspiciously like a *veil* was draped over her hair. The most incriminating part of the photo was the way Bennett had his arm wrapped around her, tucking her into his chest like he did when they slept together. She was cuddled up to him, carefully keeping the bouquet from getting squashed between them. They wore huge sappy smiles and huge blown-out pupils for the camera.

Felicity made a small sound, a sort of whimpering squeak, and looked at the other item on the desk. "A marriage license?" she said, as if Bennett couldn't see that documentation right in front of both of them. "Are we… We're *married*?"

Before Bennett could answer, a happy knock sounded on the door of their suite. They both jumped, whirling around to stare at the door as if a zombie were the one asking permission to enter. The knock came again, and Bennett was the first one to move, crossing the room to look through the peephole.

He grimaced but opened the door.

"My favorite newly married couple!" Ronan greeted, his voice much too loud for Felicity's current state. "Congratulations!"

"Um…thank you?" Felicity rubbed her forehead, wishing her headache would ease so she could absorb all this wild news that was tumbling over her like an avalanche. "You knew we got married last night?"

"Of course, my fabulous Felicity." Ronan swept over and gave her a side hug as Bennett swung the door closed with a little too much force. "I was honored to be your witness for the ceremony."

"Ceremony?" Her voice was a bare whisper, and she gave Bennett a frantic look. She was the one who needed to get pinched now. Everything seemed surreal, especially the fact that she now had a *husband*. PI B. Green, no less.

Bennett must've interpreted her look as the panicked plea for help it was. Crossing the room, he side hugged her from the other direction, gently detaching her from Ronan, who smirked and relinquished his grip. Her head spinning, she leaned gratefully against Bennett, borrowing his strength and warmth for a few moments. She just needed a little time to regroup and make a plan, and then she could stand on her own two feet again.

"What *exactly* happened last night?" Felicity asked, sick of getting spare bits of information and brief flashes of memory.

Ronan's eyes went wide. "You don't remember? I knew you were intoxicated, but I didn't realize you were blackout drunk."

"If you knew we weren't in our right minds," Felicity said, putting the whole spiked-drinks situation on the back burner for the moment, "why did you let us go through with it?"

To her surprise, Ronan laughed. "As if I could've stopped you. I don't know if you've noticed, but Green could bench press a Subaru, and I have a feeling you're a tough little scrapper yourself, as harmless as you look."

Felicity couldn't argue with that.

"Once you got the idea in your heads, you were determined to get married. If I hadn't driven you to the Clark County building to get your license, you would've walked—or stolen a car or hijacked a bus or who knows? You were both blissfully in love."

"Wait." Felicity held up a hand, trying to wrap her brain around what Ronan was telling them. "It would've been too late last night. The license bureau wouldn't have been open." A rush of relief flooded her as she picked up what must be a fake marriage license and waved it at Ronan. "We're not actually legally married." Even as she said it, though, a hollowness opened up in her middle. She couldn't be…*disappointed*, could she?

Her inner turmoil distracted her, so it took a moment to realize that Ronan was shaking his head. "This is Vegas. They're open until midnight. We got there just in time." He was beaming at them, looking so proud to be part of their sudden marriage. "The chapels are open twenty-four hours, of course."

"Of course," she echoed faintly.

"Your wedding was just beautiful. You went with the romantic package, had a unity ceremony where you lit each other's candles…"

"We lit each other's candles." Felicity felt unable to do anything but repeat Ronan's words as the fog around her memories slowly began to clear. She recalled their exasperated server at the diner and how Bennett admitted he dropped his case to help her chase after Dino. The clerk at the license bureau had been surprisingly jolly, presenting them with their official marriage license with the glee of a successful matchmaker. Everything had seemed to shine at their tiny wedding: the blush-pink flowers, the woman who'd officiated—*not* dressed like Elvis, thank goodness—and Bennett. Bennett hadn't taken his eyes off her the whole night, and happiness had radiated from him.

The drugs. It had to be the drugs.

A polite rap on the door made her jump, and Bennett wrapped an arm around her again. She let him, telling herself she'd lean on him for just another few minutes. Then they could start talking about unpleasant things, like annulments.

"That'll be our mimosas," Ronan said, heading for the door,

seemingly unaware of the bomb he'd dropped on them. "It's a bit early for a straight champagne toast, but mix some orange juice in there? Perfect."

Still a bit shell-shocked, Felicity accepted her mimosa, lifted it for Ronan's lengthy toast to their happiness and long marriage, and automatically took a sip. The touch of the juice on her tongue brought her raging thirst to her immediate attention, and she slammed back the rest of her mimosa.

"Okay," she said as Ronan blinked at her, his glass halfway to his lips. "We have a drug-dealing, drink-spiking, bail-jumping militia member to run to ground. Thank you so much for your hospitality, Ronan. It was a pleasure to meet one of Bennett's friends, and I hope next time we stay here, it'll be for pleasure, not for work."

Ronan stared at her for another moment before he barked out a laugh and knocked back his drink. "Have I mentioned how much I adore your new bride?" he said to Bennett, who must've finished his drink as well, since he placed the empty glass down next to Felicity's. "Best of luck on your search, happy hunting, and all that." He dug in his pocket and pulled out a set of familiar-looking keys, handing them to Felicity. "I had a couple of the valets retrieve your car from that unpleasant bar's parking lot. Come see me again soon. We'll have dinner, and you can tell me all about your adventures."

He shook Bennett's hand, gave Felicity one of those double-cheek kisses that she hated but didn't mind so much when it was Ronan, and swept out of the room.

Realizing that she hadn't looked at Bennett during Ronan's

entire description of their wedding, Felicity braced herself and turned, her gaze finding his. His expression was one of the rare ones she still couldn't decipher, and that made her worry.

"Are you okay?" she asked, annoyed with herself for her selfishness. All this had happened to Bennett too, and she'd been so wrapped up in her emotions that she hadn't even checked how he was feeling.

That inscrutable look went soft, and he stroked her cheek with his thumb. "I'm good. Ready to get Dino?"

Shaking off the daze that look and tiny touch had caused, she shoved all the wedding stuff into a corner of her brain and nodded. "So ready. Give me five minutes, and then I'll be physically ready too." She gave him a grin that she hoped wasn't too wobbly around the edges and then went into the bathroom.

As she guzzled glass after glass of water straight from the tap, she stared at her cell phone on the side of the counter. She knew she needed to check in soon, or Charlie and Molly would send in the cavalry. The last time she'd texted them was during the stakeout the day before, and in her drunken haze, she'd forgotten to charge her phone overnight. She almost didn't want to plug it in, since she had no clue what she was going to tell her sisters.

Mentally dumping that worry into the soon-but-not-right-now bin, she took a shower. The side of her calf stung, and she saw a shallow graze her hazy memories told her was from one of Dino's bullets. After scrubbing the small wound, she allowed herself to think only about how amazing the hot water felt and how indulgently luxurious the whole bathroom was. She and Bennett really had to come back for a real vacation soon.

When the thought registered, she gave a laugh that was a little too close to a sob for comfort. *Bennett. My* husband. *How wild is that?*

And why does the thought make me so weirdly happy?

———

By the time they'd both showered and packed their few possessions, Ronan sent up a huge breakfast of eggs Benedict, fruit, and incredible, melt-in-her-mouth sticky buns. Felicity's earlier nausea was gone, and she stuffed her face as if she hadn't eaten a whole stack of pancakes the night before. Bennett ate even more than she did and then watched her hungrily after his plate was empty, so she didn't feel self-conscious about her gluttony.

The food and all the water she'd drank earlier banished the last of her brain fog and most of her headache. Some ibuprofen took care of the rest—as well as the renewed ache in her ankle from all the running the night before. As they climbed into her car, she was feeling surprisingly perky for someone who'd unknowingly drank a spiked beverage, been shot at, and gained a husband the night before.

Settling in the driver's seat, Felicity reached to start the car but then dropped her hand and turned to Bennett. "What's the plan?"

"Let's check their hotel, see if they returned last night."

She doubted that Clint and Dino would do that, but Bennett was right—they should check, just in case. "Okay. Then back to that dive bar, so I can punch that bartender in the throat?"

"Balls, maybe?" Bennett suggested, looking doubtful. "Throat punch makes it hard to answer questions."

"Good point, but the throat is extra satisfying." She considered her options with grim satisfaction. "I'll decide when I see him. Either way, we'll see if he knows where the two drink-spiking jokers headed."

"If we don't find them here, we know where they live."

Felicity grinned at him. "I love how casually brutal you can be."

He actually blushed, sending her a bashful look from beneath those thick lashes, and her smile faded as she studied him. "What?" he asked, fully focused on her again.

"Nothing." With a shake of her head, she paid more attention than was necessary to starting the car. "I just thought of something."

About how we probably kissed last night...and I don't remember it.

He gave a skeptical grunt so Bennett-like that it made her smile again, the unexpected sting of their forgotten first—no *second*, although the first didn't really count because it'd just been a ruse to get out of a trespassing charge—kiss fading. Instead she focused on finding her skip. She'd allowed herself to get distracted, but that was done. Everything—her unexpected marriage, her felonious mom, her longing for a pause to just *relax*—was put aside until the job was successfully finished.

"Watch out, Dino," she said as she shifted into drive. "We're coming for you."

———

"I'm sorry," Felicity said half a day later, after a long, silent length of I-70 had disappeared under her car wheels.

Bennett gave her a questioning look.

"If we'd just stayed in the car last night like you wanted to, we would be back in Colorado by now, a cuffed Dino in the back seat." *And unmarried*, she thought but didn't say out loud.

"Maybe."

It was her turn to give him a look.

"They knew we were following them."

"Right," she said, "but we still could've taken them by surprise—if we hadn't been drugged."

"Maybe." This time, the word sounded even more skeptical as he studied the desert landscape around them. "They were armed and knew we were there. More likely we just would've gotten shot."

"I did."

"What?" He whipped his head to stare at her, his gaze raking up and down her body as if he could see through her clothes to wherever the gunshot wound was.

"Minor." She patted the air in a soothing gesture, although he didn't seem very soothed. In fact, he looked positively frantic. "It barely broke the skin."

"Where?"

"I can't remember all the details, but we were running toward the diner, Dino and Clint were chasing us, and then there was a *clunk* sound and the side of my calf burned. I cleaned it in the shower, and it's barely a graze."

He faced forward again, his jaw muscles working. "I want to see it when we stop next."

"Uhh…" She looked down at her skinny jeans. "Not sure that'll work. I'm not stripping down to my underwear at a rest stop. I'll show you tonight."

Although he gave a tight nod, he didn't look happy. Felicity decided it'd be a good idea for his stomach lining if she changed the subject.

"How much do *you* remember about last night?"

He didn't answer.

She kicked herself for mentioning the bullet wound. It was so minor, he wouldn't have ever needed to know, and now she had to entertain herself for the rest of the drive. It had been an especially frustrating last few hours in Vegas. There was no sign of the old pickup in the parking ramp of the hotel where Clint and Dino had stayed the first night, and all the front desk attendant could tell Felicity—when she pretended to be a friend of Dino's looking to meet up with him—was that they'd checked out that morning.

They didn't have any better luck at the dive bar. The greasy bartender from the night before had walked off the job, according to the bar owner, who wouldn't give them their main suspect's name or any information about him. The owner hadn't been in the night before, and he claimed to not know Dino Fletcher or Clint Yarran.

Which meant that they were driving back to Simpson, Colorado, with nothing to show for their trip to Vegas… well, nothing except a brand-new marriage license. Her brain wouldn't stop running and rerunning all her mistakes from the previous night until she pulled into a gas station and parked.

"Everything," Bennett said as he got out of the car.

"What?" Felicity got out as well, looking curiously at him over the vehicle's roof. They hadn't said a word for almost an hour, but now he was talking like they were midconversation.

"I remember everything." Turning away, he walked into the gas station, leaving her open-mouthed next to the car.

TWELVE

FELICITY COULDN'T THINK OF A way to bring up his comment once they got back on the road, Bennett driving this time. She couldn't stop thinking about it though. If he remembered everything, did that mean he hadn't been as affected by whatever their drinks had been spiked with? If the skeezy bartender had given them the same dose, that would make sense, since Bennett was so much bigger than her. But did that also mean he'd been thinking semi-rationally when they'd gone through with everything—the declarations of love, the license, the marriage?

She remembered at the diner, when he told her how beautiful she was, how smart and brave, and she wondered if he'd meant that. Could his inhibitions have been lowered but his true feelings not changed by his spiked drink? That line of thinking made her emotions go haywire—hope and wariness and worry that she was being naive, that she was inventing things to make herself feel better.

Tired of the thoughts rolling over and over in her head,

she turned to Bennett as much as her seat belt would allow. She saw him glance at her from the corner of his eye, his body stiffening, as if he was bracing for whatever she was going to say. That reaction made her relax, strangely enough. The idea that he was more worried about that conversation than she was made her brave…although not brave enough to actually *have* that conversation.

"Where are we going to stay?" she asked instead.

He blinked twice, as if he was mentally adjusting to a topic he wasn't expecting.

"Once we get back to Simpson," she continued, still too wound up to risk any awkward silences. "Since we've been banned from their only motel. Lou said we could stay with her and Callum, but I don't know them well enough to sleep down the hall from them."

From Bennett's expression, he strongly agreed with that. "What else's close by?"

"Um…" She opened a travel app and did a quick search. "Nothing within ten miles…or fifteen…" As she broadened the search, she shivered. She hadn't realized how very isolated Simpson was. What happened in the winter, when the highways closed because of a blizzard? Was the choice either rooming with strangers or staying in her car? A few more options popped up once she expanded her search to twenty miles and even more when she went to thirty. "Here we go. There's a so-called bed-and-breakfast in Liverton, which is south of Simpson, but the pictures make it look like a murder cabin. We'd be better off in the car, I think. Connor Springs is about twenty miles west, and it has a few places. Rosehill is thirty miles away, but it's an upscale ski town, so we'll be paying a lot more."

"The second one."

Felicity clicked on the first Connor Springs option, a decent chain hotel, but they were full. She tried the next place, a more run-down-looking motel, and that one was closed for repairs. "Or to clean up after the last serial killer went through," she muttered.

He made an inquiring grunt.

"Sorry. My imagination is still stuck on the murder cabin." She started checking the Rosehill listings, but everything was booked. "There's not even any snow yet. Why are people packing the place now?"

"Trees."

"What about them?"

"The aspens."

"*Pbtt.*" She blew a raspberry, even while ignoring the fact that she'd been excited to come to the mountains for that very reason. "They're aspens. All they do is turn yellow. Maybe some of these hotel-room hoarders should try the East Coast. They have all sorts of leaf colors there." Her grumping was interrupted when an available room at a Rosehill boutique hotel popped up. She eagerly read the details as her finger hovered over the *Book* button. "Oh, for Pete's sake."

"What?"

She tapped the button to book anyway and started entering her credit card information. "There was one room open in Rosehill. I'm grabbing it now."

He paused as if waiting for her to continue and then finally asked, "What's wrong with it?"

"Nothing." Her voice came out a touch sullen, even as amusement at the situation rippled through her, easing her sour mood. "It's beautiful. It costs an arm and a leg, but according to the reviews, it's worth every penny."

He huffed, and she could *feel* him waiting for the rest of her answer.

"Fine. It's the honeymoon suite."

After a moment of silence, a laugh ripped from his chest, so loud and booming and unexpected that it was irresistibly infectious. Felicity joined in, and every time another bellow of laughter came from him, she had to echo it. Uncontrollable Bennett laughter was the absolute best.

Once she finally settled and caught her breath, she asked, "Do you get the feeling we're cursed?"

"Nope." He paused before continuing. "Think the universe is trying to tell us something though."

She smirked at him. "The universe made us get married?"

"No. I blame Ronan for that."

"Me too!" She sat up straighter. "Who brings two people— both obviously off their asses—not only to get a marriage license but to the chapel? He helped us pick a *wedding package*! You saw our pupils in that picture. We looked like aliens!"

Bennett laughed again.

"I mean," she kept going, warming to her subject. With everything else happening, she never had a chance to really think about Ronan's part in their impulsive marriage. "We would've happily kept telling each other how beautiful we were while eating pancakes if Ronan hadn't come along and enabled us."

"I did text him," Bennett said, sounding a little guilty.

"True, but we'd just been shot at. We were feeling an immediate need for backup."

At the mention of being shot at, all the residual laughter left his expression.

"I'm *fine*," she stressed, guessing at what caused his quick switch from amused to stone-cold serious. "When you see the teeny-tiny mark on my leg, you're going to realize how ridiculous you're being. It barely touched me."

"But it was too close." He glanced at her for just a brief second, but the raw agony in his eyes took her aback. Needing to ease that pain, she reached over and squeezed his hard thigh.

"It was, but we survived." Even though he was focused on the interstate in front of them, she still kept her gaze steady on his profile. "We watched each other's backs and called in backup— who might have gotten us married, but that's better than shot, right?" When he just gave her a sideways smirk, she moved her hand off his leg and whacked him on the shoulder. "*Right?*"

He laughed. "Much better."

"Humph," she grunted, sitting back in her seat. "You better say that, buster, or you're getting locked out of the honeymoon suite tonight."

His laugh rang out again, and she smiled at the beautiful sound, proud she was able to draw that humor out of him. "I'm really good at breaking in to locked hotel rooms," he said.

Grinning, she met his gaze. "Me too."

———

As much as she wanted to stop and spy on the militia for a bit, see if Dino had made it home yet, it was dark by the time they got to Simpson. There was no way to drive to their hiding spot without headlights, and keeping the car's lights on during the drive up the logging trail to the copse they used as a spying point was just suicide. Even if they didn't drive off a cliff in the dark, the militia—and everyone within miles—would know where they were headed, and they'd probably guess why as well.

Instead, Felicity and Bennett stopped at Levi's for a late dinner. They'd just gotten their food when Bennett nudged her and lifted his chin toward the door. Felicity looked up and groaned. The murder club ladies and their assorted husbands were weaving through the tables directly toward them.

"But I'm so *tired*," she whined under her breath. "They're going to want all the details, and I'm going to have to admit that I let Dino slip through my fingers in Vegas. Why did I think it was a good idea to expand my bounty-hunting army?"

He snorted, shifting a little closer to her. "Should've just added your general and left it at that." He'd taken up what had become his usual spot plastered against her side, both their backs facing the wall.

"Captain," Felicity corrected absently. She saw the determined look on Lou's face as she led the murder-lady charge, and she took a huge bite of her brisket so she wouldn't be able to talk.

"Felicity! Felicity's stalker! It has been two days—*more* than two days—and none of us"—Lou made circle motions with her arms, indicating the group around her—"not a one has heard anything from you. Not a word. Not a peep. Not even a text. We were *worried*!"

Felicity instantly felt guilty. She hurried to chew and swallow the bite of food in her mouth while the group pulled chairs around their small table. When everyone was seated, they were pressed shoulder to shoulder, leaning in toward Felicity and Bennett.

Resisting the urge to draw back from all the curious eyes, Felicity braced herself and opened her mouth to say…something. She was exhausted and had no idea what information she should share and what should be held back. The memory of the motel owner finding out about Dino lingered in her mind, and she didn't want to give anything away in the middle of Levi's that would cause them problems later. She closed her mouth and tried to order her thoughts.

"We got married."

There was dead silence as Felicity turned her head to stare at the man who, yes, was technically her husband, but she didn't think they'd be spreading *that* news around. He lifted one eyebrow in a way that was both questioning and challenging, and the spark of humor in his eyes turned her bewilderment to amusement.

"Wait…what?" Lou was the first to speak. "Weren't you just stalker and stalkee a few days ago?"

"Inside joke?" Felicity offered weakly, but Lou still looked skeptical, so she tried again. "Aren't most husbands just legal benevolent stalkers anyway?"

The women looked at one another and shrugged.

"Fair enough," Daisy said.

"Hey," Chris protested, and Daisy gave his knee a reassuring squeeze, although Felicity noticed she didn't retract her statement.

"Congratulations!" Ellie cheered, which set off a round of well-wishing from everyone, even a guy she was pretty sure she'd never met who was sitting by Rory.

"Ian?" she guessed. "I'm Felicity, and this is Bennett."

The gorgeous man lifted his chin in greeting as Felicity wondered what was in the water around Simpson to produce so many attractive people. *Maybe they're all vampires*, she thought, punchy with exhaustion, and barely held back her giggles.

"Were you *planning* to get married?" Chris asked, leaning back and throwing an arm over the back of Daisy's chair. "Last I saw you, you were leaving me in your dust on Moose Peak Road. Thought you were chasing a skip?"

Felicity held up her fork in a shrug. "We followed him to Vegas, he disappeared, and we figured we'd get married." It was *technically* true, although the timeline was a bit wonky in this condensed version.

"No ring?" Ellie asked, eyeing their bare left hands.

"Nope." Felicity used the take-a-bite trick to give her a few seconds to think—plus she was actually hungry. "Too dangerous in our lines of work. We could lose that finger if we caught it on something." She wiggled the digit in question.

"Ian got me a panic room instead of a ring," Rory said, looking at her husband fondly. He grinned back at her, looking smug.

Behind her hand, Daisy mouthed *My idea* to Felicity, who took another bite to hide her laugh.

"Did you follow your skip back from Vegas?" Callum asked, apparently not that interested in the current ring conversation.

"Nope," Felicity said, feeling that pang of guilt again. Even though Bennett had made some good points about what might've happened if they'd stayed in the car rather than go inside the bar, it was still her fault they'd lost the skip's trail. She lowered her voice, even though no one was sitting at any of the nearby tables. "Clint was with him, so we're assuming they'll both come back home to roost."

"You know where he lives." Callum dipped his chin in what Felicity took as a gesture of approval of their actions.

She grinned up at Bennett. "That's what B said, but it sounded much more menacing."

Callum looked slightly offended. "I can do menacing."

Sharing an amused look with Felicity, Lou patted his forearm. "You're very menacing when you want to be, sweetie."

"What's the new plan?" Daisy asked, and everyone looked toward Felicity again. She went to put more food in her mouth to give her time to think, but her plate was empty. Laying her fork down mournfully, she delayed by wiping her mouth with her napkin instead.

"Back to surveillance," she said just a touch gloomily. They'd been so close to bringing Dino in, so it was hard to go back to square one. From the long faces of the murder ladies, they were hoping for more action as well.

"Wait." Lou sat up straight. "Do you have a place to stay? You can come home with us."

Felicity shook her head with a smile. "Thank you, but we've reserved at a place in Rosehill."

"Are you sure?" Lou looked a little disappointed. "We have plenty of room, and Callum makes a mean chili."

Chris coughed a laugh, and Lou looked at him, confused. "What?"

"They're honeymooners," he reminded her gently, although a smile still lurked in his eyes. "They probably want their privacy."

"Oh!" Rory said, sounding startled, as if she'd just had a revelation. "Because they'll want to—" She broke off and studied the checked tablecloth while Chris fought another laugh. Ian's eyes were fond when he looked at his wife, and he gave her a gentle side hug.

By this time, Felicity's face was flaming hot, so she knew it had to be bright red. She didn't dare look at Bennett, since he had to be just as embarrassed.

"Okay!" Felicity said too loudly as she stood. Bennett followed her up, quickly dropping money on the table to pay for their meal and tip, as if he was as eager to leave as she was. "Good to see all of you. I'll keep you updated. Chris, we still need to have that talk. Have a good night! Bye!" She spilled all the words out as quickly as possible, not giving them any time to respond as she grabbed Bennett's hand and left the table, quickly skirting the large group and making her way through the restaurant.

Once she was outside, she took a couple deep breaths of the bracingly cold mountain air and turned to Bennett, surprised to find him smirking at her.

"Zip it," she warned, and he laughed out loud.

———

This honeymoon suite was definitely not a *not*-honeymoon suite.

Everything about it screamed romance. It was one step away from having a heart-shaped bed. Felicity stared at the complimentary bottle of champagne and told herself to stop freaking out. She'd spent two nights with Bennett in a different honeymoon suite and one night on the floor of his car, and both of them had survived. Her gaze shifted to the bathroom door, which was currently blocking her view of Bennett, and then she moved to retrieve her phone charger from her bag.

Very carefully not looking at the painting of an embracing couple hung on the lace-patterned wall, she plugged in her phone, deciding to deal with a different uncomfortable situation to take her mind off this one. As soon as the battery was charged enough, a series of beeps made her cringe.

"Forty-nine texts and thirteen calls," she said under her breath as she looked at the screen. "That's not so bad." Honestly, she'd expected more.

Without listening to her voicemails or doing more than glancing over the unread texts, she called Charlie's number.

"You're not dead."

"If I am, I'm a zombie."

"You'd hate being a zombie," Charlie said in a hushed voice.

"I'll come chop off your head as soon as I get my hands on Mom."

"Deal." Felicity really would hate being a zombie. "You need me to call back later?"

"No, I'm—hang on." Charlie went silent for several seconds. "Yep, I'll call you later. Wish me luck."

"Good luck!" Felicity whispered, even though she wasn't the one who needed to keep her voice down. She had a moment of regret that she wasn't there to watch her sister's back, but she was even more determined to bring Dino in after what had happened in Vegas.

Next, she dialed Molly.

"If you're not dead, I'm going to kill you myself."

Felicity grinned. "Not dead, but I have a *very* good reason I haven't contacted you in two days."

"Mmm-hmm." Molly didn't sound like she believed her. "And what's that?"

"Charlie stole my phone charger last week, and we had to chase Dino to Vegas."

"We?"

Felicity winced. Of course her sister picked up on that. "Me and Bennett."

"Bennett Green?" Molly didn't sound too much happier than she had when she'd first answered her phone. "He's still hanging around?"

"Yeah, but he's been very helpful."

"Mmm-hmm." She sounded even more doubtful that time. "Did you get Dino?"

"No." Felicity was annoyed by that fact all over again. "After a full day of surveillance, he disappeared on us."

"So why didn't you call me last night?"

Felicity let out a huff. There was no way around it. Her sister would never be satisfied with the short, semiaccurate summary she'd given the murder ladies. "Dino had someone spike our drinks, so we were kind of out of it last night."

There was an echoing silence on the other end of the call before Molly screeched, "*What?*"

Wincing, Felicity held the phone away from her.

"Are you okay?" Molly was still talking—although at a less ear-piercing volume—when Felicity put the phone back to her ear. "What happened? What'd they drug you with? Did you go to the ER?"

"Yes, still working on that, not sure, no," she answered.

Molly must've figured out which answer went to which question, since she asked, "What do you know so far?"

"Bennett and I were at the bar when a fight broke out—a very *pathetic* fight that I was not a part of," Felicity quickly added before her sister could ask. "We think it was a distraction so that someone could slip something in our drinks without us noticing. Our main suspect is—"

"Your stalker?"

"No," Felicity said with absolute certainty. "The bartender. I'm guessing he was paid by Dino, because the bar owner said he walked off the job when we went in there this morning to punch our main suspect in the throat—or the balls. We hadn't come to a consensus on the location yet."

"Are you *sure* it wasn't Green?" Molly asked. "The number one suspect is always the stalker."

Felicity rolled her eyes at the empty room. "The number one suspect is always the *husband*. I learned that from old reruns of *Murder, She Wrote*."

Bennett chose that moment to emerge in a cloud of steam from the bathroom, a towel wrapped around his middle. His eyebrows shot up at her last statement, and she waved a hand in an I'll-explain-later gesture. Tearing her eyes from his once-again-naked chest, she unfortunately ended up staring at the painting of the embracing couple. With a heavy sigh, she closed her eyes and tipped her head back.

"Just because he acted drugged too doesn't mean he was," Molly continued as Felicity fought sleep. "It could've been just to throw you off."

Felicity was too tired to keep defending Bennett without letting him know what they were talking about, so she continued her tale, hoping Molly would drop the issue. "Dino ran after us, possibly with a gun."

"Definitely with a gun," Bennett muttered, just loud enough for Felicity to hear, with a pointed glance at her still-covered calf.

Ignoring Bennett's comment, she grimly plunged ahead, wanting to get the call over with so she could climb into the very comfortable-looking bed. "We made it to a well-lit and populated diner and ate pancakes, and then Bennett's friend Ronan picked us up and drove us back to our hotel." *After helping us get married.* "The next morning, the bartender had quit, the bar owner wouldn't give us his name or location, plus Dino and Clint had checked out of their hotel, so we gave up and drove back to Simpson."

"Hmm…" Molly's hum was so skeptical that it basically accused Felicity of leaving out huge chunks of her story. "So what's your plan?"

"We're going to stay and see if Dino returns to his militia's compound. I'm extra determined to bring him in now."

"Okay. Be careful—of *everyone*—and keep me updated… *daily*. Buy another phone charger."

"Charlie'll just steal that one too." Felicity wasn't even mad about it anymore, it happened so often.

"At least you'll have it while you're in the mountainous boonies. What's it like there?"

"Beautiful." Especially her current view of Bennett's chest. "Weird. There's an unusually high percentage of very attractive people here."

"Huh. Maybe I should go visit to see for myself," Molly teased. "Need backup?"

"Oh please," Felicity scoffed. "As if you'd look at anyone who's not John."

"I look at other guys," Molly protested, and Felicity heard John object in the background. "Fine, I never look at other guys. Happy now?"

Felicity was pretty sure that last bit wasn't directed at her, so she stayed quiet.

"Okay, John's here now, so neither of us is going to get a word in edgewise." More male grumbling on Molly's end of the call proved her point. "Stay safe, I love you, and remember what I said about cute guys in stalker clothes."

Felicity didn't want to hear more about that subject, so she resisted calling out Molly's nonsensical metaphor. "Love you too."

Once she'd ended the call, she instantly felt the tension of the room press down on her, making her skin heat and prickle. Without letting her gaze wander over to the mostly naked man sharing the honeymoon suite with her, she unzipped her bag, hoping to find something to use for pajamas. The slightly wilted bouquet of blush roses lay on top where she'd carefully placed it that morning, unable to leave it in Vegas. After all, it was her *wedding bouquet.* She may never have another one.

Gently placing it to the side, she dug through her clothes. Wrinkling her nose, she sniff-tested a few tanks. Her trip to the mountains was stretching longer than she expected. Soon she was going to have to find out if Simpson or Rosehill had a laundromat.

"Here."

Startled out of her gloomy thoughts, she looked up to see a folded T-shirt inches from her face. She kept looking up, up, up from her crouched position to see that Bennett had lost the towel but had gained a shirt and shorts. Since he was still holding his T-shirt extended toward her, she accepted it with a "Thanks? What's this for?"

"You. To wear." He gestured at her body without looking squarely at her, the edge of his cheekbones splashed red. "To bed."

"Thank you," she said again, accepting the shirt, humor creeping back at the sight of Bennett, awkward and tongue-tied from that short discussion about her pajamas.

He glanced at her suitcase, his gaze catching on the bouquet, and his lips curled up in a tiny, pleased smile. As sappy as it was, his expression made her extra glad she hadn't abandoned the flowers in Vegas.

THIRTEEN

ONCE INSIDE THE BATHROOM, SHE gave in to the urge to sniff his shirt. She could smell the light scent of his laundry detergent and—although she wondered if it was just wishful thinking— the faintest hint of Bennett. Shaking off her silly thoughts, she blamed her mushy mind on her lack of sleep and set the shirt on the counter.

After her shower, she took a bracing breath and stepped into the main room, trying to ignore all the wedding-inspired decorations and romantic paintings. Instead, she focused on the bed and the man stretched out on top of it, doing something with his phone.

Bennett glanced up as she walked toward him, his eyes darting over her quickly before a pleased smile touched his mouth. She wondered if that look was because he liked seeing her in his shirt, but she dismissed the thought as another symptom of sleep deprivation.

"I'm so tired," she sighed, allowing herself to fall like a tree and crash into the mattress next to him. It felt strangely domestic, sharing a room and a bed with a man—a very attractive man. Not allowing herself to dwell on the idea, since it would only make her stiffen up again, she let her brain drift.

"Let me see," he ordered, and her eyes popped open.

Rolling onto her back, she sat up using her stomach muscles. She was dying for a good workout and promised herself she'd check out the hotel's fitness room the next morning. "Let you see what?"

"Your bullet wound."

"Oh, right. Although 'bullet wound' sounds so dramatic. This is like a 'bullet scrape' or a 'bullet touch.' Actually, let's just drop the 'bullet' part, because I think that's what makes it sound so life-threatening." She wasn't sure what she'd expected him to say, but she'd forgotten about the small divot in her skin already. "Here." She swung her leg over his, rotating it slightly so he could see the scabbed-over groove.

He traced it with a gentle finger, barely touching it, making her shiver.

"Cold?" he asked, wrapping his large, warm hand around her calf. It covered a good portion of her lower leg, and the sight of his skin against hers made her breath catch. Her gaze flashed to his, and it wasn't until she saw him looking at her inquiringly that she remembered he'd asked a question.

"A little." She used that as an excuse to gently pull her leg away and then wriggle under the covers. She told herself she wasn't hiding from him, but she knew that was a lie.

"How's the ankle?" Rolling onto his side to face her, he propped his head up on his hand.

It was very hard to have a conversation, she was discovering, when her obnoxiously hot bedmate had focused his smoldering brown eyes on her and his muscular body was within reach. "Um…oh, fine. Just a twinge now and then. It was a little swollen after our little jog last night, but I took some ibuprofen and that's gone down now."

He frowned, his gaze dropping to the approximate location of her ankle under the covers.

"Nope."

His eyes found hers again.

"You don't have to examine it." She pulled the covers up to her chin. "It's fine, just like I said."

He made a "humph" sound that made her laugh.

"What?" he asked, the tiniest bit of his weirdly attractive pout on display.

Smiling a little too fondly at him, she said, "You sounded like a grumpy old man." Giving in to temptation, she leaned over and smacked a kiss on his cheek. "It was funny, Grandpa." She realized his face—including his lips—was only an inch away, and she sucked in a breath and held it. They stared at each other, a string of attraction pulling tighter and tighter until finally, it snapped.

The tension that'd saturated the air for days suddenly ignited, like a gas-filled house exploding into flame. She didn't know if he closed the distance or she did, but either way, his mouth was on hers, and it was incredible. Relief coursed through her as she realized this *had* to be their first real kiss together. No matter what drug had been running through her system, no matter how fractured her memory of the previous night was, there was no way she could have forgotten the earth-shattering pleasure of his mouth on hers.

There was no gentle exploration, no careful pressing of closed lips. Their kiss was immediately deep and carnal, mouths open and tongues exploring, as if they wanted to devour each other. She'd never felt anything so all-consuming, and this was only a kiss.

He rolled her onto her back and moved on top of her without breaking the contact of their mouths. Clutching at his shoulders, running her fingers through the short strands of his dark hair, she wanted to touch him everywhere all at once. Every moment they'd spent together, every urge she had to run her hand over his back or feel the rough rasp of his morning stubble, everything was possible now, and the floodgates were open.

He yanked and pulled at the covers until they were no longer blocking him, and then he did the same with his clothes. Once he was bare, he reached for her. Feeling protective of her borrowed pajamas and not wanting them to tear in his haste, she lifted her arms, helping him pull his T-shirt from her body. He tossed it aside and sat back on his heels, staring at her as if she was the most beautiful thing he'd ever seen.

"You're incredible," he breathed, lifting a hand to touch her belly but then hesitating as he met her gaze. "This okay?"

"Oh yes." If she'd been any less frantic to feel his hands— and his lips and tongue and teeth—on her, she would've been embarrassed by the way the words rolled from her mouth, coming out as a purr of assent.

He smiled, just a quick flash, and then went serious as he focused on her naked skin.

Not wanting to miss out on the opportunity to explore him, she started at his wrists, running her fingers over his hairy forearms to his biceps, marveling at their size. He wasn't cut like a bodybuilder, but he was thick and strong, like a lumberjack from a previous century, able to fight and lift heavy furniture and maybe even gently toss her around a little. She bit her lip, confused by what was turning her on at the moment but too caught in the rush of lust to question her reactions.

Then he laid his hands on her stomach, and the rest of the world disappeared. His callused palms lightly plucked at her skin, leaving streaks of heat in their wake. The way he stared at her—as if she was something wonderful and precious, something he'd never thought he'd have a chance to see—was almost as intoxicating as his actual touch.

Her heart thundered in her chest, beating faster than it ever had pursuing a skip. Bennett Green was the ultimate adrenaline rush.

His hands brushed over the tips of her breasts, making her arch with pleasure. His skin was just rough enough to almost hurt, but instead his fingers caused the perfect peak of sensation, making her suck in a breath and let it escape on a low moan.

He gave a smug half smile at the sound.

"Why do I find that look so adorable on you?" she asked huskily.

His smirk disappeared as he frowned. "Adorable?"

Giving a breathless laugh, she stroked her hands over his

chest. The wiry but soft brush of his body hair distracted her almost enough to forget to respond. "Yeah, adorable. Your pout is cute too."

"Cute?" There was a world of offense in his tone, but a thread of laughter was there as well. The whole time they'd been talking, he hadn't stopped caressing her, finding sensitive spots that made her gasp and shiver. Now, his fingers moved to her sides, and his exploratory touches turned into something much more intentional.

"No!" She immediately burst out laughing, squirming to get away from his tickling fingers. The shock of going from making out to this just made her skin more sensitive, and she didn't last more than a few seconds under his torture. "Stop! Please! Uncle! I'm tapping out!" She actually did tap his arm, as if he had her pinned in a sparring match.

The tickling stopped, but he still kept her beneath him, his face temptingly close to hers. The mix of hunger and laughter in his eyes was too much to resist, and she yanked his head down so his mouth was on hers.

The slow, exploratory pace was gone, and all she knew was frantic need. They rolled across the bed—her on top, then him, then her again—lips devouring each other as their hands roamed wildly. Somehow, she'd lost her underwear, then he was on top again, poised to enter her.

"Condom," she managed to gasp, that practical portion of her brain still functioning just enough to remind her in time.

He froze, his expression shifting from agreement to realization to crushing disappointment. Dropping down onto his elbows, he tucked his face into her neck and exhaled a hard breath. From that reaction, Felicity was pretty sure he didn't have any condoms with him.

A thought occurred to her, and she grinned and poked him playfully. When he raised his head and looked at her, she said, "Two words. Honeymoon suite."

It took a second, but then hope lit his eyes, and he practically leapt off the bed. As he dug through the basket of complementary goodies on the desk, she turned onto her stomach and reached for the nightstand drawer.

"Found them!" they both called out at the same time, holding up their prizes.

Laughing, Bennett dove for the bed. With a playful squeal, Felicity tried to roll out of his path, but she ended up underneath him again. His expression was open and happy, and she went still, staring at him, entranced by that rare expression and overcome by the thought that she'd caused it.

He sobered as well, his eyes heating as he slowly closed the distance between them. After kissing her gently, he sat back, holding up the two packages of condoms as if presenting her with an offering.

Her amusement returning, she said, "That is a lot of condoms."

His grin started slow but then spread over his entire face until he was beaming down at her. "Let's use them all."

Her breath catching in her chest at the sight of his smile, Felicity could only nod. It was an excellent plan after all. Then they were kissing again and touching, and this time, there was nothing holding them back when he slowly slid into her.

Once they were joined, they both stilled. Felicity wrapped her arms and legs around him, wanting this moment to never end.

"You're amazing," he said quietly, and she could only stare into his eyes. It was impossible to be this close to him and not kiss him, however, so she pressed her mouth to his as he began to move inside her.

Their kisses started soft, almost tender, but the wild storm of need caught hold of them again. They crashed together almost violently, as if they were trying to merge into one being. Felicity clung to him, loving the slide and friction when they moved apart but *needing* the slam of their bodies coming together, the feeling of Bennett deep inside her.

She felt the tension inside her tighten, the pleasure increasing like steam in a kettle, building and building until it was finally too much for her skin to contain. Her body went taut, back arching under the onslaught of feeling, and she came in a way she'd never experienced before.

Almost scared by the intensity, she held on to Bennett as he groaned his own climax and clutched her back just as tightly.

I'm never letting him go, Felicity thought.

She woke slowly, contentment making her body feel weighted and warm. Her eyes reluctantly blinked open to a brightly lit room, her eyes focusing on the painting of the embracing pair that'd been torturing her the night before. Now she smiled at it, feeling happy for all couples in love.

Her thoughts screeched to a halt. *In love?* she thought in a mix of panic and attempted scorn. *You've known Bennett for a week, you married him accidentally, and now you're in love?*

Ignoring the tiny voice inside her that whispered *yes* to the last question, she sat up abruptly—or tried to. Bennett was still wrapped around her like an oversize octopus, and only the fact that his enveloping arms felt a little *too* good gave her the strength to wiggle out of his hold.

When she turned to look at him, she saw his eyes were open, sleepy but wary as he watched her. Unable to resist that hint of softness she saw in his expression, she gave him a smile. In response, he reared up off the bed and snatched her right off her feet, bringing her back to the mattress in a lunge that reminded her of a different kind of sea creature.

She shrieked with laughter as they landed with her underneath him, Bennett catching himself on his elbows to avoid crushing her into the bed. "You're not an octopus," she said between giggles. "You're a kraken."

Growling, he nuzzled his face into the side of her neck, making her laugh even more. He switched to kisses, little sucks and bites that made her shiver, and heat flooded her.

"How do you do that?" she asked breathlessly, tipping her chin up to give him better access.

His grunt was muffled against her skin, but she interpreted it as a "What?"

"Make me want you so badly so quickly."

His entire body stilled for a moment, and then his lips were on hers. She kissed him back, immediately as caught up in him as she'd been the night before. A beep wormed its way into her consciousness, though, an obnoxious reminder that they weren't the only two people in the universe and that a world existed outside this room.

With a groan, she pulled back, laughing softly when he followed her retreating lips. Knowing she couldn't give in or they'd spend the whole day in bed, Felicity half stepped, half rolled off the bed, sitting on the floor with a thump.

"There's a chair," Bennett said, sounding amused.

Grabbing her phone, she used it to wave off his suggestion. "The hard floor keeps me focused." *So I don't hop right back into bed with you.* She knew she couldn't say the last part, or he'd do his kraken thing again and scoop her right back up. Then they'd be in bed for a *month*, Dino would be free to do all sorts of nefarious drug-dealing militia stuff, her mom would never be found, she and her sisters would lose their childhood home, and then Bennett would probably lose interest in her after all that.

"What's wrong?" he asked.

"What?" She looked up at him.

"You looked really sad all of a sudden."

She started to reply but didn't think he'd appreciate her answer of "I thought about staying in bed with you for a month" was a satisfactory reason for why she was suddenly morose. She smiled at her silly thoughts, and he instantly mirrored her before leaning down to give her a quick upside-down kiss on the lips.

"That's better," he said with satisfaction as her smile grew at the sweet little peck.

Realizing that the hard floor wasn't doing much to keep

temptation at bay, she rolled to her feet and headed for the bathroom, checking her phone on the way.

It was Charlie, with a text that said she was alive and well but Jane had given her the slip again. Felicity groaned quietly, feeling like they'd never be able to bring her in. Maybe all the running around and chasing dead ends was futile. If after all this, they ended up losing their house, what was the point? Maybe she should just have lots of amazing sex with Bennett in the honeymoon suite of a boutique hotel rather than chase after skips and get drugged and shot at.

"Everything okay?" Bennett asked, glancing at her phone and then her face.

"Not really," she said, still feeling gloomy. "But no one's dead yet, so that's something?"

Before he could ask for details, the recounting of which would just depress her more, she gave him a quick smile and scooted into the bathroom. Shooting Charlie a quick I'm-glad-you're-not-dead response, she sent Molly her own everything's-fine text and then lost herself for a time in the huge shower.

———

Once she worked out in the fitness center and got some breakfast inside her at the hotel's very nice restaurant, Felicity's outlook grew a lot sunnier.

"Are you ready to find Dino and pull his lower intestine out through his nose?" she asked Bennett cheerfully.

He side-eyed her for a long moment, taking a final sip of his coffee before pushing his chair back and standing. "Let's do that."

Felicity bounced up, reenergized and ready to tackle some skips—and one drug-dealing ass in particular. Turning around, she almost ran into their server, who was frozen with a horrified stare fixed on her.

"Everything was wonderful, thank you," she said cheerily.

He didn't move except for a small twitch under his left eye.

Puzzled, Felicity gave him an awkward half wave and was out of the restaurant before she realized he'd overheard her earlier comment about her plan for Dino's lower intestine. "Oops."

"He thinks you're a serial killer," Bennett said casually, walking beside her, his gaze alert as he scanned the tourists milling around.

"He does." The words came out as a groan. "And an especially sadistic one too. How many places of lodging are we going to get kicked out of before we pick up Dino?"

Bennett scratched his nose—hiding a smile, she was sure. "We'll likely break a record. For this area at least."

Her groan turned into laughter, and she poked him in the side. Playful Bennett, she was finding, was a lot of fun.

"Think we're okay to use that same lookout?" she asked.

While Bennett thought, she marveled at how nice it was to have someone to bounce ideas off of and double-check things with. Charlie, as much as Felicity loved her, was too much of a wild child to be of much use in that regard. Her sister was more likely to jump in with both feet without a plan, surviving just on pure guts and her ability to think under pressure.

Plus Bennett had never stolen Felicity's phone charger.

"Think it's our best option," Bennett finally answered,

pulling her out of her thoughts. "Not many places that give us a view of the place, and no sense in breaking into the compound and trying to fight the lot of them."

It was like he could see into her brain. "What if we *snuck* inside the compound, nabbed Dino, and slipped back out without anyone else knowing?"

"Without schematics?" He sounded skeptical, which was fair. It wasn't one of her best ideas, but she was getting impatient. Another full day of surveillance did not appeal.

Felicity caught herself. This was how she'd gotten them into trouble two nights ago. Her impatience and boredom had led to her making a dumb decision, and she needed to learn from that and make better choices in the future.

Wondering when her inner practical voice had turned into Molly, she shook her head. "No, you're right. Let's go to the lookout." She tried to dredge up some enthusiasm. "It'll be fun. We'll run all the faces through the system, see how many felons are hanging out in the compound."

———

Her resolve to be more mature and less impatient lasted for two and three-quarter hours. This trip was a revelation for her. Felicity had always thought of herself as the practical one—not as practical as Molly, of course, but she figured she was at least on the sensible side of the spectrum. Now that she didn't have Charlie in tow, however, her impulsiveness was coming to the forefront.

"Sooo…" she began, carefully not looking at Bennett.

Instead, she peered through her binoculars at the compound driveway, where there hadn't been any movement since they'd gotten there. Apparently, the militia slept in.

His answering grunt was slightly suspicious.

"I know we're not going to invade the actual compound, but what if we explored just a teensy, tiny bit?" Holding her forefinger and thumb just a fraction of an inch apart, she turned to give Bennett her best puppy-dog eyes.

In return, he offered a crooked smile. "You know it's not up to me, right?"

"I know." Tucking her binoculars under the seat, she grinned impishly at him. "I'm just getting you to give final approval so that I can blame you when things go badly."

"Good to know." His voice was dry, but his eyes still danced with humor. "We can look around, but remember it was *your* idea."

"Fine," she mock pouted. Easing her car door open, she carefully placed her feet in a way that didn't rustle the light layer of leaves that were just beginning to drop off the trees. Although they were far enough away from the compound that no one should be able to hear, she knew that sound carried differently out here.

There wasn't any noise from Bennett's side of the car, but suddenly he was there next to her. She gave him an admiring look, thinking that she needed to get some stealth tips from him once all this Dino and Jane stuff was over.

She paused, caught on that last thought. Would they even be together after Dino and especially Jane were behind bars again? Sure, they were married, but it wasn't real, no matter how many honeymoon suites they stayed in.

That depressed her for some reason, so she concentrated on where she was placing her feet. The flat hilltop area in the copse where they'd parked dropped on all sides, gradually first and then more dramatically. There were barely there trails—either from wildlife or occasional hikers—that wove between rocks twice as tall as Bennett. She followed one of the trails down to a small flat section that looked over the valley below. Bennett stepped up behind her, so close she could almost imagine those metaphorical sparks jumping between them.

This spot provided a better view of the compound, but everything looked just as quiet as it'd seemed from inside the car. She examined what layout she could see of the main struc-ture and smaller outbuildings, counting doors and noting the location of windows. There weren't any guards outside that she could see, although she was careful to stay out of the tower's view, so she wasn't sure if someone lurked in the old fire lookout.

Felicity let her gaze wander from the compound to the area around it. The view—despite all the razor wire and utilitarian buildings—was still beautiful, rocks and cliffs shimmering red and gold in the noon sun. Unable to resist, she let herself lean back against Bennett. He instantly welcomed her in, standing strong so she could take a break, his arms wrapping tightly around her upper chest to keep her secure.

Glancing at the path that made its twisty way down to the flattest part of the plain, Felicity saw an off-white gleam that didn't seem to fit with the colors of the rocks and tough, semiarid vegetation. Curious, she stepped away from Bennett—who tightened his grip a half second longer before letting her go. Turning back to the path, she followed the twisty narrow trail until she reached the area where she'd spotted the anomaly in the landscape.

A gully cut between their rocky hill and the next, narrowing until it divided the two rises by only a few feet. Felicity headed for the wider part of the division. Although Bennett shot her a questioning look, he didn't protest or speak, just following her instead.

The small rocks under her feet shifted and slid, bringing her attention back to her footing. Leaving the trail, she cut across the rocky ledge and half climbed, half slid into the gully. Bennett followed much more gracefully, and Felicity promised herself she'd drag her sisters to the actual mountains for training. If they could take down a skip on a rocky, steep trail next to a cliff, they could do it anywhere. Chasing someone across the rooftops of Langston's industrial district would feel easy in comparison.

As she made her way to the lowest part of the gully, Bennett leaned close and whispered in her ear, "What did you see?"

"Not sure." Her answer was barely audible. "Probably a rock or something."

From the way he carefully scanned the area around them, she was pretty sure he didn't believe it was nothing. Either that or he was just watching out for stray militia members.

There! The splash of light brownish white caught her eye again, and she moved over to where she'd spotted it. Recent rain had washed out the dirt and debris from under a protruding part of the rock surface, leaving a hollow beneath. Crouching, Felicity crawled under the overhang, feeling a bit like she was entering a cave. Although she was a little unnerved by that, Bennett was muttering what sounded like prayers or curses under his breath.

This time, she was the one giving him a questioning look.

"Hate small spaces," he admitted in a low, growly voice.

Bennett, claustrophobic? For some strange reason, this confession made her like him even more, that tiny pocket of vulnerability hidden in his giant ice-block man-body. Reaching back, she took his hand and gave it a squeeze.

Toward the back of the shallow cave, she saw the dirty white she'd been following. Her stomach started churning the closer she got to the object, as what had been a vague suspicion turned more and more likely to be a grim reality.

"Um…random question?" Her voice was pitched a little higher than normal. "Do deer vertebrae look shocking similar to human vertebrae?"

"No."

She sighed, peering closer at the scattered bones. "These are too big to be from a deer, aren't they?"

"Yes. And too flat."

Deeper in the cave, right where the back wall met the rocky ground, was something a similar brownish white as the vertebrae, but this was larger and part of it had a suspiciously familiar curve. Forcing herself to move toward it, she crouched lower so she didn't bang her head on the rock overhang. The cave was shallow enough that sunlight flooded most of it, but the very back was shadowed, so she used her phone flashlight app to get a better look at the object. Her breath caught in her chest. There was no mistaking this for an animal's.

"Is that a human skull?" she whispered to Bennett, not wanting it to be true.

His jaw was tight, although whether that was because of the small space they were crammed in or because the skull was almost definitely human, she wasn't sure. A few more crouched, shuffling steps got them close enough for Felicity to confirm it.

"Yes," Bennett said quietly.

There were definitely human remains in this tiny cave with them.

FOURTEEN

THE SKULL WAS CRUSHED ON the side with several teeth missing, but Felicity wasn't sure if that was from being dragged around by predators after he was dead or if that was why he died. A piece of dirty cloth was half-buried in the rocks and dirt covering the shallow cave's floor, and Felicity set her phone down and reached toward it.

A tap on her shoulder made her look at Bennett, and he thrust a pair of latex gloves at her.

"Sure, now you have latex," she teased quietly, holding back a snort at the way his cheeks darkened with a blush.

"It worked out," he said close to her ear, and then it was her turn for her cheeks to get hot.

"It really did," she said almost inaudibly, but when his hand gave her hip a brief squeeze, she had a feeling he'd heard her. It felt surreal to be joking right now, but it was either that or run screaming, and all the second option would accomplish would be to get them killed by a militia guard.

Pulling on the gloves, she reached out again, tugging the scrap of fabric out of the dirt and holding it close to her face. "Red-and-white-plaid flannel?" she guessed.

Bending over her shoulder, Bennett peered at it for a moment before giving an affirmative grunt.

Returning the scrap to the spot she'd gotten it, Felicity did a quick scan of the rest of the area around the skull and scattered vertebrae. Although she knew she could probably find more clues if she dug around, she didn't want to disturb the crime scene any more than she already had. Besides, CSU techs tended to get cranky if you messed with their evidence, she'd found.

Shuffling backward, she gave Bennett a gentle shove so he moved out of the cave. Even though she usually didn't have any issues like he did with small spaces, small spaces with human bones in them were a little more claustrophobia-inducing, she was discovering.

Their walk back up the trail to their car was silent, and she was wary to the point of being paranoid. Every pebble shift, every bird cheep, every rustle of the wind in drying leaves made her suspect a militia member was following them. From his tense expression, Bennett felt the same way.

It wasn't until they were locked in her car that she felt like she could take a real breath.

"Okay." Despite the car's limited sound-muffling powers, she still spoke in a whisper. "No reception here, so we'll have to drive to Moose Peak Road. What's the plan down there? Should we call our new friend Deputy Daisy's Husband or use one of the burner phones I know you have to call it in as a clueless random hiker? Not to brag, but my stoner tourist impression is *stellar*."

"Chris," he said after barely a pause. "Cops'll waste our time, but nothing like if they find out we discovered the remains and lied about it."

"Good point," she admitted, although her nose wrinkled in distaste at the cops-wasting-their-time portion. "We might even be able to get some info from him about the case if we're ultra super cooperative."

This time, it was Bennett who made a face. "I'm not great at being cooperative, much less…"

"Ultra super cooperative?" She wanted to laugh but worried that she might not be able to stop once she started, so she swallowed her hysteria down. "Just do your usual silent thing, and I'll be good witness to your bad witness."

The skin between his eyebrows wrinkled.

"Like good cop and bad cop?" She was definitely a little shocky. "Good witness and bad witness?"

He gave her a long look, but even he couldn't completely hide his amusement. "Start the car."

"Yes, sir." After carefully turning around and starting down the logging trail, she shot him an innocent sideways look. "Remember, you approved that hike. This is all your fault."

"Isn't this the fault of whoever smashed that person's head in?"

"True." She slowed to take a hairpin turn, resisting the urge to fly recklessly down the hill, to escape the dead body and the militia members who very likely caused the person's death. "They're the most at fault, then you're next, and I'm last. Blameless."

His snort was amused. The sound of it was so Bennett-like that it was comforting, and her fingers relaxed their grip on the steering wheel. Bennett was here with her, so everything would turn out all right.

She almost laughed at the thought. *Nothing* had gone right since she'd partnered up with Bennett. Despite that, she was still happy to have him there.

Once they were parked on the side of Moose Peak Road, Felicity realized she didn't have Chris's direct number—well, except for 911—so she texted Callum for it. His response was quick, with the contact attached to a single word text: Problem?

She thought for a second, her fingers hovering above her screen, before she tapped out her response. Not urgent, but the murder ladies will be excited.

The ellipsis showing that he was typing flashed by as she saved Chris's contact information and called his number with her phone on speaker.

Great. Callum didn't even need to use the eye-rolling emoji for Felicity to hear the sarcasm in his short text, and she gave a bark of semihysterical laughter. When Bennett looked at her in question, she showed him the screen, and he gave an amused huff as Chris answered.

"Chris Jennings." His voice was clipped and formal.

"Chris, it's Felicity Pax and Bennett Green. Hope it's okay Callum gave us your direct number."

"Hey Felicity." His tone lightened dramatically, and he sounded like his usual friendly self. "I'm glad you called.

Would you be available this afternoon to have that talk we discussed?"

"Um…I'm not sure *you're* going to be available this afternoon," she said. "We made a bit of a discovery in the gully just northwest of the militia complex."

Chris muttered what might've been a curse. "Don't tell me you found a body."

After a surprised blink at the phone screen, she said, "Your guessing skills are on point."

This time, he definitely swore. "Just what we needed, another body."

"It's not a *whole* body." She wasn't sure if that was reassuring or not. From the choking sounds coming from her phone, it probably wasn't.

Chris's voice sounded strangled. "It better not be missing a head."

"It's not," she assured him, glad she could give him some good news. "It's pretty much *just* a head. Well, most of a skull at least. And some vertebrae."

"You sure it's human?"

Exchanging a glance with Bennett, Felicity said slowly, "It's a *skull*, Deputy. Unless it's from an alien, a human skull is pretty obviously, you know, *human*."

Heaving a deep sigh, he said, "Okay. I'll send the troops. Did you disturb the scene?"

"Just got close enough to make sure it was what we thought it was." She crossed her fingers at Bennett's mocking look. "It's pretty disturbed already though. I think animals got to it, and the bones look sun-bleached, so I doubt this was where the victim died—or even where they were originally dumped." There was a speaking silence, and she hurried to backtrack. "Not that they were dumped necessarily. They might've not been murdered, just happened to bite it right next to a militia compound."

Chris's sigh this time was even heavier and ended in a groan. "I can already tell this is going to be a mess, and the investigation hasn't even started yet. You still with the remains?"

"No reception up there," Felicity said. "We're parked on Moose Peak Road."

"Always comes back to Moose Peak Road, doesn't it?" Chris asked with a hint of his usual good humor. "Sit tight. I'll let the sheriff and the CSU know, and then we'll head your way."

"Got it. Bye, Deputy." She ended the call and looked up at Bennett. "Not really the way I expected to spend our afternoon. Here comes the time-wasting part."

There was a warm gleam to his eyes that made her wary and thrilled at the same time.

"What?"

That wicked half smile of his curled his lips. "I know a good way to kill some time."

Felicity mock-frowned at him. "Chris'll probably be here in five minutes."

"I can finish in four and three-quarters?" He looked at her with a sweetly hopeful expression, using those deadly eyelashes of his to full advantage.

A pulse of heat flared low in her belly, but she had to laugh. "Don't think that's a bragging point."

Still, his wicked smile stayed as he moved closer to her. "One little kiss then?"

By the time she realized she was leaning toward him, their lips were just inches apart. "Nope!" With a huge effort of will-power, she shifted as far as she could toward the door and away from Bennett's tempting mouth. "I know how wrapped up we get when we kiss. Elephants could stomp over the car, and we wouldn't even notice." Bennett gave a smug smile at that. "I'm not going to be caught by the local deputy making out in my car like a thirsty teenager."

"We'll crack a window so we hear him coming." Bennett was advancing again, and that teasing heat in his eyes was almost irresistible...*almost.*

"They're going to know we were making out," she warned, unable to retreat any farther and unsure if she even wanted to escape from him. "They're going to think we're creepy, since finding a dead body made us horny."

That stopped him. "It *is* a little creepy."

"Very." Although she tried to hold her stern glare, a laugh tickled her throat.

Retreating to his passenger seat, Bennett sighed. "Fine. We'll wait until we're back in the honeymoon suite." He gave the last two words an extra emphasis that sent a little jolt of electricity through her.

She opened her mouth to make some reply—she wasn't sure what, since his attempted kissing and all-around adorableness had melted her brain—when the faint wail of a siren caught her attention. "Really?" she asked, opening her window so she could hear it more clearly. "They're coming in hot to this? Those remains are pretty old. And do they really want to alert the militia that cops are in the area?"

"So much for doing any more surveillance today." Bennett didn't look too upset by that. "Told you we'd hear them coming."

Felicity gave a skeptical snort. "Doubt we would've noticed, even if they all had their sirens blaring and surrounded us."

"Maybe if they got out the bullhorn." Bennett had his deadpan expression back, but the line of his lips ticked up just slightly as she eyed him.

The first squad car rounded the curve in front of them, sliding on the loose gravel, and Felicity had a nasty suspicion. "That better not be our least favorite deputy."

Bennett grumbled inaudibly as the squad pulled up facing them. "Of course it is."

"You know," Felicity said as she watched Deputy Boaz Litchfield climb out of his car, adjusting his aviator sunglasses in a way that made her want to punch him even more than she already did. "Judging by the karmic evidence, I'm coming to the conclusion that I was a serial killer in my former life."

"Or maybe someone who scammed old people out of their life savings."

She grunted agreement.

"Or a murderous dictator of a small downtrodden country."

"Highly possible."

"Or maybe a magician."

"No." She turned her head slowly to glare at him. "That's just a step too far."

Despite her giving him the evil eye, he grinned, looking happy and easy, as if he wasn't usually a stiff, buttoned-up, socially awkward tower of silence. As usual, she couldn't resist his look—or him in general—so she shot him a quick grin before turning back to her least favorite deputy, her punishment for whatever terrible things she'd done in a former life.

"Deputy Litchfield!" she called out. "Are you here to help with traffic control?"

Bennett actually snickered, a sound she hadn't thought he was capable of making. It was, as so many facets of him were, super cute.

Litchfield wasn't amused. "Funny how you two keep getting involved in active cases."

"Mmm…not sure how active this one is, mate." She wasn't sure why she'd suddenly gone Australian with her mockery, but it just seemed right.

"He didn't look very active. Opposite of active, in fact."

Felicity held a straight face with an incredible effort. If Bennett was going to be her sidekick in tormenting the deputy, she wasn't sure if she could swallow her laughter much longer.

The deputy was already going red in the face. "A man is dead, and you're making jokes?"

"It's the shock." Felicity widened her eyes at him.

His mouth twisted into a sour sneer. "Shock my a—" Whatever body part he was going to reference disappeared in the crunch of tires as Chris rolled up behind Litchfield's squad.

"Is anyone else getting déjà vu?" Felicity asked. "Because I'm getting déjà vu."

Bennett raised his hand like he was an oversize first grader.

"That's it," Litchfield spat. "Out of the car, both of you."

"Boaz," Chris said in long-suffering tones as he approached. "For the last time, you can't arrest people for snarkiness."

"These two need to be interrogated about the remains they 'found,'" Litchfield said, making finger quotes.

"They need to be *questioned*," Chris said in the slow, careful, yet hopeless way someone would use to verbally explain house-training to a puppy. "They're not suspects. They're traumatized tourists."

"Traumatized," Litchfield scoffed under his breath. He looked like he was going to argue further, but yet another squad car, followed by a tan-colored van with *Field County Sheriff Crime Scene Unit* on the side, pulled up and parked, distracting him. A woman got out of the squad and made her way over to them.

"Sheriff," Chris said before Litchfield could start talking. "This is Felicity Pax and Bennett Green. They're the ones who found the remains. This is Sheriff Eva Summers."

"Like Buffy?" Felicity said before she could stop herself, and all eyes turned to hers. "And Cyclops?"

"Yes," the sheriff said with the long-suffering tone of some-one who'd been asked this question before. "Like Buffy and Cyclops. Can you clearly describe how to reach the remains, or will you need to lead us to them?"

Felicity glanced doubtfully at Bennett, and they had a silent conversation that ended with her turning to the others with a sigh. "We'll need to lead you there."

The sheriff gave a short nod. "Boaz, you block off traffic coming from that direction. I'll get Harvey out here to block the other side."

Litchfield looked crushed that he was, indeed, being stuck on traffic duty. It was with the greatest difficulty that Felicity swallowed her laugh.

"Chris, you get a quick statement from Mr. Green," the sheriff continued, "and I'll talk to…Ms. Pax, was it?"

Felicity had a feeling that the sheriff knew exactly what her name was even before Chris had introduced them, but she just nodded, climbing out of the car and joining the sheriff behind it. Bennett did the same, walking with Chris until all three cars separated them. He shot Felicity a speaking backward look that she wasn't sure how to interpret, although it gave her a warm, giddy feeling that she wasn't in this alone even though her sisters were hours away. She and Bennett had somehow become partners in all this chaos. She made a mental note to promote him to colonel in her bounty-hunting army.

"Congratulations," the sheriff said, her tone dry, drawing Felicity's attention away from Bennett. Although she had a sneaking suspicion what Summers was referring to, Felicity offered the sheriff her best blank expression. "On your recent marriage."

"Oh, right." Felicity smiled. "Thank you." She hadn't decided whether the sheriff was a potential ally or roadblock yet, so she was playing her cards close to her chest. Felicity would've been impressed by how quickly Summers had learned about their impromptu wedding except that she'd announced it in Levi's the night before, so it would've been more surprising if the small-town gossip pipeline had failed to spread the news to everybody in Field County.

Abruptly, Summers shifted to an all-business tone, turning on her voice recorder before collecting Felicity's personal information and getting a quick synopsis of how she and Bennett discovered the remains. Even though the sheriff's eyebrows shot up a few times during the statement, she didn't interrupt. Once Felicity finished, they eyed each other in silence for several minutes. Accustomed to this technique—one she used on skips as well as sisters guilty of borrowing her things without asking and then returning them broken—Felicity smiled genially and waited her out.

"After you," the sheriff finally said, waving an arm toward the logging road.

"We can drive to the start of the trail," Felicity said, turning to get into her car.

Bennett must've spotted her movement, because he started walking away from Chris. From the deputy's startled and slightly exasperated expression, the interview wasn't done.

"Ride with me," the sheriff commanded.

Felicity made a face before turning back around. Apparently, she wasn't going to escape the sheriff so easily. Hiding her feelings behind a breezy smile, she said, "Front seat, right?"

There was a pause before Summers smiled back, although it was more of a teeth-bared warning. "Of course."

Biting back an honest laugh, Felicity walked toward the sheriff's car.

Before they got far, one of the CSU techs intercepted Summers. The sheriff waved Felicity on. "Go ahead and wait in the car. I'll be there in a minute."

Hoping for a quick word with Bennett, Felicity hurried to where Chris was talking to him, appearing more aggravated than she'd ever seen the laid-back deputy look before. Unable to contain her amusement, she laughed out loud.

"Poor deputy," she commiserated, joining their small circle of two. Bennett immediately moved close to her side and rested one of his hands on the small of her back. The heat soaked in, relaxing her more than any massage could, even while it ramped up her heart rate. She gave him a smile before turning back to Chris. "Getting one-word answers, are you?"

"If that."

Taking pity on him, she asked, "What are you missing from his statement? Can I fill in the holes?"

"Sure. His birth date?"

Tsking at Bennett, Felicity scolded, "You didn't even tell him that? Why not? We like Chris."

Bennett twitched his shoulders in an irritated shrug. "He already has it. Why does he need to hear it again?"

Rolling her eyes at the stupid male posturing, she opened her mouth to answer the deputy's question but then closed it again when she realized she didn't know. "What's your birth date?" Her tone was more curious than anything.

Before he could answer, Chris barked a laugh. "You don't know? I thought you were married."

Unbothered, Felicity just shook her head, still waiting for

Bennett's answer. "We're still learning all the interesting things about each other. We haven't bothered with the boring details yet."

A slow smile dented Bennett's cheeks in a way that made her want to kiss him. "Exactly. And it's January third."

"Mine's a third too!" She wanted to roll her eyes at her sappiness, but she couldn't help the glee in her voice at the silly little coincidence. "The third of August."

The way he gazed at her, as if she was the most interesting person in the universe, made her forget the deputy was even there.

Chris reminded them of his presence. "Year?"

Before Bennett could answer—if he even *would* answer—the sheriff was there. "Let's go," she said, charging for the driver's door of her squad car.

"We'll finish later," Felicity promised, hurrying around to the passenger side door. She wasn't sure why she was rushing. If the sheriff left without her, that was fine with Felicity. She'd prefer to ride with Bennett anyway.

The sheriff had other ideas though. Through her open window, she ordered, "Chris, you and Mr. Green ride in the CSU van so we limit the number of vehicles going up. No reason to attract the attention of anyone at the compound."

"Um…pretty sure that cow's already escaped the barn," Felicity said. "Deputy D—ah…Litchfield arrived on scene with sirens at full blast." She had to watch that she didn't call him one of her and Bennett's pet names.

Sheriff Summers's head dropped back against her seat as she muttered to the ceiling, "Sweet baby Jesus, give me strength."

Felicity was fairly sure that the strength the sheriff was asking for was to resist killing Deputy Donkey-Face.

"We're still just taking the two vehicles," Summers said once she'd sucked in a long breath. "Donaldson, follow us." The last part was directed to the tech she'd been talking to, and the tall, middle-aged Black man gave a wave and got in the driver's seat of the van.

With a frown, Bennett headed that way as well, although when he glanced toward Felicity's car, she could almost read his mind. The two of them could be driving away from this whole mess right now rather than genially being held hostage by local law enforcement as they tromped all over the militia's territory looking for human remains.

The sheriff's amused snort brought Felicity's attention back to the woman next to her. "The two of you are newlyweds, that's for sure."

Fully aware that her googly eyes were bordering on ridiculous where Bennett was concerned, she just smiled. "Only two days ago."

Summers's grunt sounded unimpressed. "Where are we going?" the sheriff asked.

"Up the hill." Felicity gestured at the logging road. "There aren't any turnoffs. Just follow the two-track until it dead-ends in a cluster of trees."

With a short nod of acknowledgment, the sheriff followed her directions, and they rode silently until they arrived at what Felicity had been mentally calling the lookout. Summers turned the squad car around with some difficulty until she was facing back down the hill, and the CSU van did the same, although it took them a few extra points on their turn.

Bennett was out of the van and opening Felicity's car door almost before the van came to a complete stop.

"You know," she teased as she got out. "You look pretty natural coming out of that van. Every stalker needs one."

His only response was a light pinch to her side, right where she was the most ticklish. She twisted out of reach, not wanting to laugh when they were on such a grisly mission. He reached out toward her again but only to take her hand.

"Lead the way," the sheriff said once the two CSU techs—Donaldson, the man who'd spoken to Summers earlier, and a short blond white woman—had their packs adjusted on their backs.

Felicity went first, but Bennett stayed close behind, still holding on to her hand. As she reached the spot they'd used as a second lookout, dread began curling in her stomach, and she tightened her grip on Bennett's hand, searching for comfort. An answering squeeze did help soothe her nerves, although she still wished they could call off the search and return to Simpson, maybe have a nice smoothie and a chat with Lou at the coffee shop.

Tightening her jaw muscles, she pushed on. It was important that the bones be identified and the killer—if there was one—brought to justice. She just wasn't used to interacting with dead bodies, no matter how little remained. Earlier, she was able to shove it to the back of her mind and make jokes to distract from the horror of it, but now she was going to face the bones directly for a second time, and the memory of it loomed large in her mind.

A big hand rubbed her shoulder, giving her a long, reassuring squeeze before dropping away, and she managed a small smile. As unpleasant as their mission was, it was nice to have Bennett there.

When rocks stood around them during a particularly claustrophobic section of trail, she had a worried moment that she was headed in the wrong direction. Then she got a glimpse of the gully and relaxed slightly. The sun had shifted, and she wasn't seeing the gleams of white she'd noticed before.

The gully was an even better landmark, however, and she led her small group down to the narrowest section, where the washed-out area under a rock overhang created a shallow cave. Peering inside, she had the sudden fear that the bones wouldn't be there, that someone had moved them or—even worse—that she'd imagined them. But Bennett's bulk behind her reassured her that it wasn't just her imagination involved. He'd seen them as well.

Then she glimpsed one of the vertebrae, then another, and finally the dim lump of white that made up the skull was visible at the back of the cave. "There," she said, breaking a long silence they'd all held on the hike.

"Thank you." The sheriff shifted forward, nudging Felicity and Bennett to the side so that the CSU techs had access. Donaldson and the other tech crowded into the small space.

"Human," Donaldson soon announced, and Summers and Chris shared a grim, tired look.

"Definitely," the other tech agreed, her digital camera click-ing as she photographed the scene, and the sheriff silently sighed.

"Okay, go ahead and process this. I'll give the BCA a heads-up since we don't have the resources here to do the type of forensic analysis this is going to require." The sheriff looked at Felicity and Bennett. "Good find. Chris, can you give them a ride back to their car?"

"Sure," the deputy agreed easily.

Felicity blinked in surprise. She'd expected a great deal more time wasting before they'd be allowed to leave.

As if Summers had read her mind, she gave a wry smile. "No sense in you hanging around while the techs work. Appreciate your cooperation. Don't go anywhere for a few days, okay?" Without waiting for a response, she turned back to watch the two techs.

"Ah...Sheriff?" Felicity asked. "When you say 'don't go *anywhere*,' can you be a little more specific? We're staying in Rosehill."

"Just don't go back to Langston yet," the sheriff said absently without looking away from the bones. "And for the love of god, please don't return to Vegas until this mess is cleared."

"Got it." Felicity wondered how much more information the sheriff had on them, but she kept her mouth shut. There was no way she was going to sabotage their chance to get out of there.

To her surprise, Chris didn't question them on the foot trail or in the car on the way down the logging road. Instead, he talked lightly about Daisy and some of the other murder club ladies. When they pulled up next to her car, however, he turned toward them and fixed them with a serious look. "We still need to have that conversation."

"You have my number," Felicity said, scooting out of the passenger seat and opening the back door for Bennett. She felt bad he'd been stuck in the back, although he'd insisted, using his bigger bulk to gently nudge her out of the way and slide into the back seat before she could protest. He had to have been claustrophobic in there though. "We're not going anywhere, on orders of the sheriff, so we should have some free time."

"I'll text you," Chris promised, giving them a wave before turning around and heading back up the logging road.

Bennett and Felicity looked at each other.

"Coffee shop?"

He gave a decisive nod, so she tossed him her keys.

"Let's go, hubby."

"Yes, *wife*." His steamy look nearly melted her brain, and only her empty and complaining stomach kept her focused enough to get in the car and not stand there staring at him like a lovesick idiot.

FIFTEEN

"FINALLY!" LOU CROWED AS BENNETT and Felicity walked into the otherwise empty coffee shop. "I've been texted by no fewer than five—count them, *five*—firefighters saying that another body was found by a visiting private investigator, and who else could that be but the surprise husband of my new bestie, Felicity? So I've been stuck here making nonfat, decaf lattes while *dying* of curiosity." She winced. "Sorry. I didn't mean to make a dead person pun. I'll rephrase. I've been *very curious* whether the firefighters are actually right this time or if those gossipy little bunny rabbits are full of it as usual."

Felicity was a little offended. "You're getting credit for my dead body?" she asked Bennett, who held up his hands in a defensive gesture. "How much do you want to bet that the rumor came from Deputy Donkey-Face?"

"Deputy Donkey-Face?" Lou repeated with glee. "Is that Boaz? I thought Laurence was bad, but he quit, and the new guy they hired to replace him is like Laurence squared. Wait! You found the body? There *is* a body? Oh no, talk fast! A customer just pulled into the parking lot. Wait—it's just Rory. But still talk fast because I need to knoooooowww."

After meeting Bennett's amused gaze, Felicity turned back to Lou. "I'm not sure how much we're allowed to say?"

"You're not law enforcement or anyone's lawyer, so talk away." Lou waved a hand as if physically brushing off her concern.

"I don't know much." Felicity sat on one of the counter stools as Rory came inside.

"Hurry up, Ror," Lou said without taking her fascinated gaze off Felicity. "She's about to serve the tea."

"Isn't that your job?" Rory asked seriously as she settled onto the stool two down from Felicity.

"It's a euphemism." Lou sounded as if she was used to translating for Rory's literal outlook.

"We were watching the compound this morning," Felicity said, still feeling like she shouldn't be sharing the story. Even though she knew Lou was right, she still expected the sheriff to burst in to arrest her if she shared the details. "I got bored, so we walked around a bit. I saw something strange, and when we went to investigate, it turned out to be some human bones."

"How'd you know they were human?" Rory asked, not challengingly but like she was actually curious.

"Well, the skull was a skull," Felicity explained. "And the vertebrae were pretty obviously human—too big and flat to be a deer or elk or anything."

"There was a *skull*? A human skull?" Lou sounded equal parts horrified and fascinated.

"There was."

"Anything else?" Rory asked. She seemed unusually talkative today. Dead bodies apparently brought out the social butterfly in her. "Other bones?"

Felicity shook her head. "We didn't look too hard, although we did see a piece of fabric that looked like it came from a red-and-white flannel shirt."

"Just the head…" Lou turned to Rory. "Any chance it belonged to Willard Gray, do you think?"

"Could be." Rory pursed her lips in thought before turning to ask Felicity, "Were the vertebrae from the neck or lower on the spine?"

With a blank expression, Felicity stared at her. She was about to admit that she had no idea and ask who Willard Gray was when Bennett spoke. "Lumbar, probably. Possibly lower thoracic, but I doubt it."

"Oh." Lou looked a little disappointed. "Not Willard's then. His spine was intact except for the very top part."

Felicity wasn't sure who to question first—the women about Willard Gray or Bennett on his excessive spine-identification knowledge. Since her fascination for her new husband out-weighed her interest in some headless dead guy, she raised her eyebrows at Bennett. "Do you moonlight as a chiropractor?"

He shrugged. "I like anatomy."

Lou gave Bennett a stern look. "That's not a good, non-serial-killer thing to say at all."

Swallowing a giggle, Felicity said, "He's considering getting a van too."

"Oh, honey, no." Lou looked honestly horrified by this, and Rory nodded in serious agreement with her friend.

Unable to hold back, Felicity laughed out loud. Bennett gave her a chiding look that just made her giggle harder. He shook his head, but she could tell he was trying not to smile.

"You know," Lou said, making Felicity realize that she and Bennett had been doing that annoying stare-into-each-other's-eyes thing. "I wasn't originally on Team Felicity and Her Stalker, but I kind of get it now."

Rory eyed the two of them. "He's fine. Not even close to the weirdest guy I've met."

"That's a pretty low bar, with some of your gun shop customers and your strange hermit neighbors," Lou said, clucking her tongue, but then her irrepressible grin reappeared. "We got off track. Hurry and tell the rest of the dead-body details before the after-school crowd arrives." She and Rory leaned toward Felicity, their avid gazes fixed on her, and she instinctively leaned away from them until her back bumped into Bennett's chest. It was warm and comfortable, so she just stayed there.

"That's pretty much it," she said, holding out her hands in a shrug. "The bones looked sun-bleached, so I think animals dragged them from somewhere else, or maybe they got washed there in the spring snow melt runoff. I'm just guessing though. For all we know, that skull could be a hundred years old."

Bennett disagreed in a grunt, and Felicity craned her neck to look up at him.

"No? Why not?" she asked, honestly interested in his opinion.

He shook his head. "You'll just call me creepy," he pouted, although there was a thread of amusement in his words too.

"I'd promise not to call you creepy, but if you say something creepy, I'm calling you out on it." She shrugged, not really sorry.

With a dramatic sigh, he gave in. "One of the teeth had a composite filling. That wasn't used until the sixties."

"Dentistry facts, B? Really?" She did warn him after all.

"I remember facts and dates," he said a bit defensively. "And I like science. I'm not interested in dentistry *specifically*."

Lou was snickering. "Okay, I sort of get why you married him in Vegas. He grows on you, doesn't he?"

"He's adorable," Felicity said fondly, reaching up to pat his cheek. He looked down at her with a long-suffering expression, but that couldn't cover up the affection in his gaze.

"Puppies are adorable," Rory said, sounding confused. "I'm not seeing the adorable here." She gestured up and down Bennett's beefy form, and he frowned at her.

Felicity laughed. "Didn't you see his pout? There's no way to describe it except as adorable." From her angle, she could see a flush working its way up his neck, and she felt bad for embarrassing him. "Sorry, B. We'll focus on dead people again."

"Yes, please!" Lou's eyes lit up again. "Where exactly—" Her question was cut off by the door opening, and a trio of high-school girls entered the coffee shop, giggling and chatting as they approached the counter. "Out of time. Too many conversational detours," Lou muttered as she turned to help the girls.

Rory stood up. "Better get home. I have a shift tonight at the fire station."

"Oh?" Felicity asked. "Are you one of the gossipy firefighters?"

"Gossipy? No." Rory made a disgusted face. "Firefighter? I'm working on it. I still feel pretty clueless most of the time."

With a snort, Felicity said, "I still feel that way, and I've been working as a bounty hunter for years."

With a quick flash of a startlingly pretty smile, Rory turned and headed toward the door.

Bennett lowered himself onto the stool next to Felicity. "New plan?" he asked.

She groaned, stretching her arms out in front of her and resting her cheek on them, her head turned so she could see Bennett. "Forget Dino or dead bodies exist and enjoy our honeymoon suite?" She was thinking more on the lines of room service and sleeping in the soft bed, but the heat that flared in his eyes made her reconsider her phrasing. Clearing her throat, she sat up again. "First, food. Breakfast was forever and one human skull ago."

As if she were psychic, Lou darted over as soon as the last high schooler took her blended coffee drink. "I forgot to ask if you two wanted anything! I'm a terrible barista."

"You're fine," Felicity soothed. "There was a lot going on. Dead body trumps coffee after all."

Bennett made a skeptical grunt. "Sometimes."

Giving him a sideways look, Lou warned, "Setting off the creep-meter again, champ." Her sunny smile returned the next instant. "Now what can I get you?"

———

Once she'd finished a turkey and avocado sandwich, Felicity's brain started working better, and everything that was happening seemed a little bit more manageable.

"After all," she told Bennett, who'd inhaled several sandwiches and an almond croissant as well as a large coffee, "neither of us is dead or horribly injured yet."

"Been there," Lou said over her shoulder as she steamed milk for one of the after-school crowd she'd warned them about.

"You've been dead or horribly injured?" Felicity asked, needing clarification.

"Neither, but I've been in the spot where that's the only reason the glass is half-full."

"Gotcha." Felicity leaned on her elbow as she turned to look at Bennett sipping the last of his coffee. "Our only good lookout spot is now overrun by cops. What's the plan?"

His eyebrow arched as he set his cup down. "Are you trying to get me to say we should break into the compound?"

"No." Lacing her fingers together so they wouldn't give her away with their twitchiness, she wished she had her own cup to occupy her hands. Her sense of honesty quickly got the better of her though. "Maybe."

He snorted into his cup.

"I'm just saying that we shouldn't dismiss it completely," she explained. "Let's just keep it on the table as an option."

"What are some *options* less likely to get us killed?" he asked mildly.

Resting her elbow on the counter, she propped her chin in her palm. "If we can pick Dino up somewhere *out* of the compound, that'd be ideal. Who knows how many weapons they have in there, and the militia's going to be extra twitchy with the murder investigation."

As if *murder* was the word used to summon her, Lou was suddenly in front of them. "Murder investigation?" she repeated in a hushed whisper. "Is it definitely a homicide then?"

"Back to work." Felicity made shooing motions with her hands, urging Lou back to the line of cranky-looking customers. "You're going to have a revolt on your hands soon. Never stand between caffeine addicts and their drug of choice. You should know that." A couple of her sisters had taught her that. When Lou didn't move, just widened her pleading eyes, Felicity sighed heavily. "We have no new information. If we do, we'll immediately share it with you, customers or no customers."

It was Lou's turn to give an exaggerated sigh. "Fine." Once again, she plastered on her shiny customer-service smile. "Nancy! Good to see you. Your usual?"

Turning back to Bennett, Felicity paused, trying to remember where they'd been in their discussion before the interruption.

Bennett frowned. "Not sure how we're going to do that."

Right. Getting Dino out of the compound. Felicity felt a renewed surge of guilt. "If only we could've picked him up in Vegas. That was ideal."

"Not really."

When she gave him the raised-eyebrow look she'd learned from him, the corner of his mouth crooked up.

"We would've had to drive back with him," he finally elaborated. "Plus Yarran likely would've been a problem."

"Still can't believe the head of a militia doesn't have *any* active warrants." Bennett's points made her feel a little better about messing things up in Vegas, but it still seemed easier than somehow luring Dino out of the compound.

Wait. Luring... Her brain pinged with the start of an idea, and she sat up straight on her stool.

Bennett gave one of his "what?" grunts.

"Just thinking..." she said absently as she tried to tease through her thoughts to reach a workable plan.

Looking faintly alarmed, Bennett carefully placed his cup on the counter without taking his eyes off her.

"If we could lure Dino out somehow," she said slowly, the idea still forming in her brain, "the way that the sheriff's office at home sometimes sends out those fake 'You're a Winner!' letters to everyone with an active warrant and picks them up when they come to claim their prize."

"Doubt he'll believe he's won anything," Bennett said thoughtfully. "Not with us right here."

"True." Still, it was worth a shot. "Lou!"

The barista immediately turned around. "Is there new news?"

"Not yet." Some of the glow faded from Lou's face, and Felicity felt oddly guilty. "Mind sending me Rory's contact?"

"Sure." Lou already had her phone out and was swiping at the screen. "Just so you know, Rory's texts are quite abrupt."

"I won't be offended," Felicity promised, amused, as she rattled off her number. Why Lou thought she'd expect Rory's texts to be sunny and chatty when the woman wasn't either of those things was a mystery. Her phone dinged with the contact. "Thanks."

> Hi Rory, it's Felicity. Quick question—has Clint Yarran ever come into your shop?

It only took a few seconds for a response to pop up. At the *beep*, Bennett leaned close to see her screen. She moved her phone a little so he could better read the text.

> No

Felicity revised her rough plan in her head.

> Any contact info for Cobra Jones?

> I don't give out customer info

With a grimace, Felicity studied Rory's last text for a moment before sending another. She didn't want to state her growing suspicion as fact, but she had a feeling the cops would be coming back with an ID on the skull soon anyway.

> Does it make a difference if he's almost certainly dead?

It was Rory's turn to pause, and several seconds went by before a new text popped onto Felicity's phone screen.

Why do you want a dead guy's contact info?

For some reason, the question struck her as funny, and she huffed a short laugh before responding.

I'm hoping the killer is monitoring his emails

The ellipsis repeated over and over for a solid minute, and then an email appeared on her screen.

cobra@freedomsurvivors.org

"Hang on," Felicity muttered, turning her phone so Bennett could get a straight-on view of Rory's latest text. "Don't tell me the militia is a 501(c)(3)."

"What?" Lou called over after obviously overhearing. "The Freedom Survivors don't even have to pay any taxes? There's something extra wrong about that."

"Very wrong," Felicity muttered under her breath, quickly sending a thank-you text to Rory. Opening a new email to Cobra's address, she hesitated, looking at Bennett. "Should we send it to Cobra's or directly to Dino? Even if Clint is monitoring Cobra's emails, we don't want to catch Clint in our trap. He doesn't have any outstanding warrants, so it'd be a waste of a good sting."

"Dino's," Bennett agreed. "Probably has a similar email format."

"That's what I was thinking. Where should we have him go

to collect his 'prize'?" Her breath caught as an even better idea occurred to her. "Hang on."

Returning to her texting app, she sent another message to Rory.

Want to help us with a sting operation?

Almost immediately, Rory sent a one-word response.

Sure

"Yes!" Lou cheered, almost directly in Felicity's ear, making her jump. "I *knew* you'd bring some excitement to this sleepy town, Felicity Pax."

The thought of being responsible for her enthusiastic but amateur bounty-hunting army recruits made her panic a little. It must've shown on her face, because Bennett grinned at her.

"See if you're still smiling if I accidently kill off an innocent Simpsonite," she muttered at him, which only made his smile widen. Looking back over at Lou, who was looking much too excited, Felicity forced a weak smile. "Yay?"

SIXTEEN

FELICITY WAS NORMALLY RELUCTANT TO involve anyone except her sisters—and now Bennett—in any skip-hunting plan, since civilians could be wild cards, but she had to admit that using the gun store in the fake contest win was genius. The whole murder club joined them there early that evening, and Felicity had a hard time pulling herself away from the displays in order to put together the fake-winning email. Rory didn't just have currently popular pistols and long guns in stock, she had everything from antique guns to bear spray to an array of Tasers to—Felicity's favorite—a tiny little revolver displayed in a place of honor and listed as not for sale.

Bennett was also distracted by Rory's two dogs—Jack, a big German shepherd, and Kiwi, the cutest little Yorkie Felicity had ever seen. Immediately after they'd arrived, both dogs had made a beeline to Bennett, and he was soon crouched down with two canines—one large and one tiny—licking his face as he scratched them both behind the ears, a huge grin on his face.

Felicity was then distracted staring at her favorite Bennett—happy Bennett—but she eventually managed to focus on planning Dino's takedown.

"I think we should go with Cobra's email," Daisy said. She was still wearing workout clothes after a shift at her gym, with Ellie's toddler, Mila—as adorably serious and watchful as usual—perched on her hip. "How would Rory have gotten Dino's email—or even his *name*—to enter him in the drawing?" She grinned down at Mila while bouncing her a little, earning a tiny smile.

"One of the other Freedom Survivors?" Ellie suggested, but her tone was doubtful.

"Someone else entered him in the drawing?" Felicity didn't think that was very likely. She was leaning toward agreeing with Daisy. "I don't know if the other militia guys are that magnanimous."

"But if it goes to Cobra, that's so uncertain," Lou argued. "What if Clint isn't monitoring his emails? And why would he bring Dino with him? Or what if Cobra's still getting his emails in his RV in Texas, and he comes here to collect his winnings?"

"I'm not actually giving anyone a free Browning rifle," Rory stated flatly.

All Lou's points were good ones. "I think we're going to have to direct the email to Dino," Felicity said. "Hopefully it's the right address and he won't think too hard about how he was entered."

"He's just jumped bail. Of course he's going to be suspicious."

Felicity gave Bennett a stern look. "No criticizing without suggesting solutions."

"You let Lou do it," he said, looking offended. When she

kept her pointed gaze on him, he heaved a dramatic sigh. "Fine. Sending the email to Dino is still the best option."

His proud sideways glance at her, as if he was waiting for praise, made her melt a little. He was having one of his obnoxiously adorable moments, especially since he was cuddling Kiwi in his arms. She did her best to ignore the tempting distraction and said, "Dino's email it is."

"Shouldn't we vote on it?" Lou asked.

"This is a benevolent dictatorship, not a democracy." Felicity borrowed the line Molly always used on her younger sisters when she wanted to get her way. Without waiting for argument—because whenever Molly used it, plenty of arguing followed—she turned to Rory, who was sitting at her shop computer. "Let's see the certificate."

Rory turned the screen so they could all see.

"Very nice," Ellie said approvingly. "It looks very official and not at all shady or sting-like."

"What are you saying in the email?" Lou asked, peering at the screen as Rory brought it up. "That looks good, but I think we need more exclamation points after the 'Congratulations.'"

"We want it to be believable," Rory said without adding any extra punctuation to the email. "If it's from me, exclamation-point overload would not be believable."

The women looked at one another and nodded, conceding the point.

"When is he supposed to come in?" Daisy asked, leaning in as close as she could with a toddler on her hip. "Make sure it's when we can all be here. I don't want to miss the excitement."

"We had to keep it broad so he wouldn't get suspicious—well, more suspicious," Felicity said. "Anytime tomorrow during open hours—ten to six." Several of the women groaned with disappointment, and Felicity had to agree. It was going to be a long day hiding in Rory's back room.

"Okay, go ahead and send it." As Rory hit Send, anticipation built in Felicity, amping her up and making her feel like doing laps around the shop.

The door opened, and they all jumped. As Felicity turned toward the newcomer, she illogically expected it to be Dino, as if sending the email had magically conjured him. Instead, Deputy Chris walked in, and the tension suddenly released in the shop like an untied balloon.

"Hey, Dais." He made a direct line to his wife, as if he couldn't wait another second to be near her. Placing a quick kiss on her lips, he looked down and smiled at her for a long moment, until Mila grabbed a handful of his uniform shirt. Chris shifted his attention to the toddler. "Hey, Mila." He blew raspberries in her neck, drawing a giggle from her that made everyone else in the room smile.

"Sometimes I worry that her expectations will be unreasonably high when she starts dating," Ellie said. "She's constantly held and kissed by extraordinarily attractive men. It's going to skew her perspective."

Chris looked smug.

"Okay, Deputy Chris, that's really cute and all," Lou said, "but we're dying to know the latest."

His good-natured smile was tired as he wrapped his arm around Daisy. "Not much I can share, Lou. You know that."

"Any ID? I know no dead body is a good dead body, but at least this one has some teeth to check dental records on, right?" Lou didn't let Chris's refusal to share bother her.

He just shook his head. "Time to return the baby, Dais. I'm asleep on my feet."

After several kisses, Daisy relinquished Mila to her mom's arms. "I have to work at the gym until noon tomorrow, but I'll be here in the afternoon. Fingers crossed Dino's not an early riser."

"He's not," Felicity and Bennett said in unison and then smirked at each other.

"Park in the pole barn," Rory suggested. "That way, he won't see your car in the lot."

"Good idea. See you tomorrow for the sting! I'll bring cookies!" Daisy waved to them as Chris swept her out of the shop.

Before the door closed behind them, Felicity heard Chris ask in a long-suffering voice, "What sting? I'm an actual law enforcement officer. Why do you always get to do more stings than I do?"

Too antsy from anticipation for tomorrow to sit around chatting any longer, Felicity turned to Bennett. "Ready to go?"

He nodded even before she finished speaking.

"Bye, everyone." Felicity headed toward the door. "Thank you for all your help, especially you, Rory. Hopefully, we'll wrap this thing up tomorrow and let your murder club focus on the latest dead body."

They left after a chorus of goodbyes and see-you-tomorrows.

As they walked to her car, Felicity asked, "Any word on your SUV?"

"Should be ready tomorrow afternoon."

"Bet you'll be glad to no longer be crammed into my car all the time."

He gave an affirmative grunt and a playful sideways glance. "Don't mind being crammed up next to you."

"Aww…" She grabbed his hand and tugged, trying to get him to bend low enough for her to kiss his cheek. Instead, he used their clasped hands to haul her toward him until she bumped into his chest. Tipping her head back, she met his smoldering gaze and promptly melted into a gooey, boneless blob of lust. She could only lean against his hard chest, waiting, as he bent, bringing his lips closer and closer until—

"Evening."

The greeting yanked her out of her lustful haze as effectively as if someone had emptied a bucket of cold water over her head. She turned to look at the speaker, knowing that murder was in her eyes.

The hot fireman—Rory's husband—didn't seemed bothered by her homicidal eye lasers. Rather, he looked amused. Ellie's husband—George, the one all the murder club ladies were calling Bennett's long-lost twin—was standing there as well, but he looked more discomfited by the hot guy's interruption than entertained, so Felicity decided to spare him.

"Your Mila's adorable," she said, meaning every word.

An enormous smile lit up his face for just a second before disappearing again, and she decided that George and Bennett might indeed share a parent or two.

"What was the murder club meeting about?" asked the hot

firefighter who she still wanted to kill—*Ian*, Felicity remembered belatedly. His smile was still lurking, flashing an occasional dimple. Although the man was shockingly attractive, she was mildly surprised to realize that she was completely unaffected. *Maybe it's because I'm an old married woman now*, she thought.

She realized Ian was still waiting for an answer and gave him a sunny smile that just had a hint of teeth. "Oh, that? Nothing really." Still holding Bennett's hand, she headed for the car. "Just planning a sting." She waved at him over her shoulder.

"Sting?" Ian called out after them, but Felicity just sent him another wave before closing the car door. She started up the engine and drove out of the lot with Ian and George still staring after them as she snickered to herself.

"You know their wives are going to spill everything."

"I know." Despite that, she was still satisfied. "Just my tiny bit of petty revenge for his interruption."

The corner of Bennett's mouth curled up.

———

They'd eaten at the murder club meeting—Callum had dropped off a big pot of chili before heading back to the station to prep for dive team training later that evening—so Felicity drove straight to their cute little boutique hotel. As they walked into the honeymoon suite, the simmering tension hit a full boil before the door even closed behind them.

Bennett pulled her tight against him as if they'd never been interrupted in the gun shop parking lot. While that had been teasing, this was direct—his mouth landed on hers as soon as her chest pressed against his. They didn't break the kiss as they yanked and pulled on each other's clothes, not even hearing the occasional rip of popping seams or lost buttons. All they were focused on was finding and touching the other's naked skin.

In what felt like just a few breaths, they were both bare and stretched out on the bed, their mouths still locked together as Felicity reveled in the slide of his lightly furred skin on hers. She roamed his body with eager hands, needing to know every part of him as well as she knew herself.

Bennett broke the kiss, ignoring her small sound of protest, and began nibbling along the line of her jaw. Finding this an appropriate substitution, she tilted her chin to allow him more access as she explored the hard planes of his back. Just when she was about to dig in the nightstand drawer, Bennett beat her to it, and she smiled dreamily as she grabbed a handful of his shaggy hair.

He groaned as she lightly pulled, scratched at his scalp, and then gently yanked again. When he tilted his head back, she took the opportunity to kiss and take tiny bites of his throat, causing him to moan even louder.

His pleasured sounds made her feel powerful and gorgeous. She reached for the condom packet forgotten in his fist, but before she could grab it, her phone rang.

With a groan that had more to do with exasperation than pleasure, Felicity dropped flat to the mattress and closed her eyes for a moment. Even though she wasn't even close to pulling herself together enough to answer, she still reached for her phone. If she didn't answer, her sisters would very likely send in the cavalry or—even more frightening—come themselves. Although they'd probably have the Dino situation sorted in minutes, Felicity wanted to bring this one skip in on her own. She'd worked with Charlie so much that it felt like they were a melded-together pair, and she'd started to wonder if she could even bring skips in on her own anymore.

Although she did have Bennett to help, he didn't count, since he was hers. Glancing at him, she saw that he'd tipped off her to the side and was mirroring her position, flat on his back with his eyes closed. She gave him a peck on the nose, and he smiled without opening his eyes.

Her phone stopped ringing, and she remembered why she'd called a halt to fun times. Charlie's name was on the display, and Felicity quickly called her sister back.

"Bad time?" Charlie asked as soon as she answered.

Yes, Felicity immediately thought but didn't say that out loud, because then she'd have to explain *why* it was a bad time, and that'd just be awkward. "Nope, just didn't have an extra hand available to answer my phone," she answered truthfully. When she glanced at Bennett, she saw he was giving her that smoldering look again, and she flushed with heat, looking away so she could concentrate on what Charlie was saying.

"Any luck with Dino?"

"Not yet, but we have a plan. A good old-fashioned fake contest win."

"Ooh, I love those," Charlie enthused. "An oldie but goodie that works shockingly often. Is the 'we' part your PI?"

Glad that her sister didn't call Bennett her stalker, as usual,

Felicity said, "Yes, although the 'we' also includes four ladies in the local murder club."

There was a beat of silence before Charlie spoke, and Felicity mentally gave herself five points in the shock-Charlie game. "Murder club? Do I need to visit this town? Because I think I'd like it."

"You'd fit right in," Felicity said, meaning every word. "Plus the murder club members are enthusiastic, helpful, and surprisingly practical."

"I want a murder club," Charlie moaned dramatically. "Or a bounty-hunting club, actually. Mom's running me in circles again."

A spark of guilt lit in Felicity's chest. "You need help? Because I don't think Dino's going anywhere. We can plan our sting for next week."

"Nope," Charlie said. "No sense in you being stuck driving through Nebraska too."

"Oh, Charlie, no," Felicity said with true sympathy. "Not *Nebraska*. What happened to hanging out in Colorado Springs?"

"That was my fault." Charlie sounded abashed. "Zach spotted me surveilling them because I got bored and sloppy."

"Done that." It made Felicity feel a little better that her sister wasn't a perfect bounty hunter either. "So they ran?"

"They ran." Charlie sighed. "Straight through Nebraska."

"Where're they headed? East Coast?" Although she mentally flipped through all her mom's connections, Felicity couldn't think of any on the east side of the Mississippi River.

"Who knows?" Charlie said gloomily. "East Coast, Iowa. Maybe she'll circle around through Dakota again."

Charlie's insistence on combining the two states into one generic Dakota made Felicity smile. As many phone chargers as Charlie lost, Felicity still loved her sister.

"Good luck," Felicity said warmly. "Let me know if you need backup. Love you."

"Same, same, Fifi."

Once she ended the call, Felicity put her phone on the nightstand and then leaned over Bennett. Although he stayed on his back, his arms crossed behind his head, every muscle in his body was taut as he met her hungry gaze. Reaching up, she pulled off the band holding her hair coiled in a bun at her nape, and the heavy strands tumbled over her shoulders, the feathery tips brushing his chest.

When she turned her head, sliding her hair over his skin, he grunted low as if she'd punched him in the gut. Smiling, she moved her head again. Scooting down, she allowed her hair to trail across his belly and lower. He tensed even more, his muscles standing out in bold relief, his skin almost quivering with anticipation.

Her phone rang again.

All the air rushing out of her lungs, Felicity crumpled forward, resting her forehead against his chest. His big hand swept over her bare back, testing her resolve.

"I have to get it," she groaned more to herself than Bennett. She knew that he understood, but her needful body sure didn't.

Reaching over with his long arm, he nabbed her ringing phone and held it out to her, his eyes still burning with need but also wryly affectionate.

"Thanks," she said flatly, making him smile.

"Molly!" she answered with grim enthusiasm. "What's up?"

———

Bennett's mouth on her belly woke Felicity.

When she lifted her head to look at him, he gave her a wicked smile before wedging his head between her thighs. He kissed and licked, obviously paying close attention to when her breath caught or goose bumps rose on her skin. His complete focus on her pleasure, as if his life depended on how hard he made her come, sent her flying quickly, her fingers gripping fistfuls of the sheet beneath her.

Afterward, her body went limp as she sucked in air, trying to orient herself in time and space. Bennett lazily kissed her thighs as she recovered before making his way over her belly and to her breasts, where he lingered, keeping everything light enough to not overwhelm her overstimulated skin.

"Good morning." Her voice was husky as she ran her fingers through his mop of silky hair.

Resting his chin between her breasts, he smiled at her so sweetly that she felt her heart squeeze. Cupping his raspy cheeks, she pulled up for a lingering kiss, mouth to mouth this time.

"That was a nice way to wake up," she said when he pulled back slightly.

A crease formed between his eyebrows. "Nice?"

She laughed. "Spectacular? Is that better?"

"Only if you mean it." He kissed the tip of her nose and then her mouth again, as if he couldn't keep his lips off her.

"Oh, I mean it." She used her hands, still on his cheeks, to tip his face so she could kiss him properly. As always, it was as if someone struck a match in a room full of gas fumes. As soon as their lips and tongues met, she was primed for him, her earlier orgasm a distant memory as her body cried out for more of Bennett.

He pushed her knees up and wide as he sank into her heat, fitting so well that she had the whimsical thought that they were made to come together. Then he was moving, and all her thoughts scattered as she clung to him and rode out the storm of another mind-blasting orgasm.

Still mostly hard, he rocked in her afterward, small movements, as if he didn't want to leave the heat of her body. When he finally did withdraw, she gave a disappointed sigh, which made him grin.

"Yeah," he said, and she realized he really did know how she felt—that empty loneliness when they weren't locked together.

As he disposed of the condom in the trash can next to the bed, Felicity blinked. "I'm glad you remembered protection," she said, "because I wasn't thinking straight."

"You were thinking straight the first time," he said, bending to give her another kiss that started light but deepened quickly, until she was panting with renewed need by the time he pulled back. "We'll take turns."

Since she'd already forgotten what they were discussing the second his lips touched hers, she doubted she'd be much use in remembering next time. "Maybe there's an app that'll remind us."

His low chuckle drew a shiver down her spine in the best way. "I bet there is."

Felicity did a full-body stretch, feeling pretty amazing, considering their intense schedule over the past week. "What time is it?"

"Six. That's why I woke you. Figured you'd want to work out before breakfast."

She beamed at him, both for his consideration and the way he'd chosen to wake her up. "You're rather spectacular."

His proud grin was quickly hidden. "That the word of the day then?"

"Spectacular?" Stretching again, she felt like a pampered cat who'd found a patch of sunshine. "Yes, that works. I believe it's going to be a truly *spectacular* day."

————

That promise held true through breakfast. As she popped a perfectly ripe strawberry into her mouth, she felt strangely like she really was a carefree woman on her honeymoon in a beautiful place with a gorgeous partner, well satisfied in every way and ridiculously in love.

Wait.

In love?

The words made her instantly panic, and she darted a look at Bennett.

He tensed, half standing, his gaze scanning the room. "What's wrong?"

"Nothing, sorry, absolutely nothing." She wasn't normally

a babbler, but right now she was definitely babbling. "Sorry I scared you. I just had a thought, but it's not even real, so there's nothing to worry about."

He stared at her, his gaze piercing, but her reassurances must've done the trick, because he relaxed slightly, settling back in his chair. "Everything okay in your head then?"

The wording made her laugh. "As okay as it ever is."

He smiled back at her. "Ready?"

Immediately brought back to reality and the sting they needed to pull off, Felicity sucked in a bracing breath and then blew it out, expelling all the weirdness her random thought had stirred up in her mind. "Ready."

SEVENTEEN

HER CAR AND RORY'S PICKUP were the only vehicles parked in the pole barn, so Felicity was surprised to see Lou in the gun shop, wiping down the display cases with vinegar water.

"Hi! I swapped shifts with another barista so I could spend all day here," Lou announced before Felicity could get a word out. "Callum dropped me off. He's going to join our back-room party later, if that's okay with you?"

"The more, the merrier," Felicity said with a shrug. "I know he knows how to be quiet."

Lou laughed. "Unlike me?"

Waving off the concern, Felicity said, "I have a feeling you wouldn't be president of the Simpson Murder Club if you couldn't zip it when you need to."

"Simpson Murder Club?" Rory repeated. "I didn't know it had an official name."

"It doesn't, that I know of." Moving a couple waiting area chairs so that the backs were to a wall and they faced the entry with the back-room door on their left, Felicity sat. With an approving tilt of his head, Bennett took the other chair. "I just made that up."

"I don't know how you can sit," Lou admitted, spraying another glass display case. "I have so much nervous energy, I can't stay still. I drove Rory batty in about five seconds, so she handed me these and pointed at the nearest shiny surface."

"Worked out for an hour this morning." Felicity gave Bennett a pat on his knee as another thank you for thinking of it. "Otherwise, I'd be cleaning right next to you—or maybe doing laps around the store."

Rory finished filling out whatever form she'd been working on and stood. "I'll show you around the back," she offered, heading toward that door, and Felicity followed, Bennett right behind her.

"I'll hold down the fort out here," Lou called after them. "I know you're not officially open yet, and you have a monster of a gate with razor wire and everything that's still closed, keeping people out, but I'll still…well, keep cleaning, I sup—"

The door closed, cutting off Lou's nervous chatter midword.

"Soundproof?" Felicity asked, impressed as she looked around the roomy space. There was a deep sink, lots of counter area, and even a centrifuge, which she figured was used somehow for cleaning guns.

Rory tipped her chin in a nod.

"How will we know if Dino comes in?" Felicity wandered around looking at everything, her hands tucked behind her back like a kid at a museum. There were a couple of dismantled guns, the pieces laid out neatly on towels, waiting to be fixed or cleaned, she assumed.

In answer, Rory lifted a remote and turned on a bank of TVs set in the wall across from the sink. The interior and exterior of the store were revealed in crisp definition from multiple angles, so every corner of the space could be seen. Even the woods and open areas around the shop were covered, all the way to Rory's very impressive fence bordering her property.

"Sound too—but just in the shop." Rory pushed a button, and Felicity could hear Lou humming tunelessly to herself.

"Nice," Felicity said, glancing at Bennett, who looked impressed.

"There's an exterior exit." Rory pointed to a door with numerous dead bolts on it.

Felicity wondered if she and her sisters should consult with Rory about treasure-hunter-proofing their home.

"Everyone involved in this will enter and leave through the back. If you hear a knock, check this camera"—Rory pointed to one that looked out on a small porch and lots of trees beyond— "and then you can let them in if you recognize them. If you don't, text me."

"Got it." The gun store was ideal for a sting. Felicity wished they could transport it to Langston. "Thank you, Rory. This is perfect."

Rory gave a stiff nod. "I'm about to open, so I'll send Lou back. Sorry."

Felicity laughed. "No problem. Her chattering doesn't bother me. She's fun."

"A good ally too. Make sure to lock this door behind her." With another tight dip of her chin, Rory went into the front area of the store. As promised, Lou came through the door a few seconds later, turning the dead bolt before Felicity had to remind her.

"Ready for this?" Lou asked, obviously excited.

Her enthusiasm was catching, and Felicity grinned back. "Let's do this."

———

Then they waited.

And waited.

The day was broken up by the arrival and departure of the various murder club ladies, and they all came bearing food. Felicity and Bennett made sure they had everyone's contacts in their phones as they snacked and watched the camera feeds. Lou stayed for a few hours but then had to help with the lunch rush at the coffee shop. Ellie stopped by just to drop off doughnuts before leaving to pick up Mila from a playdate and promising to return later that afternoon. Daisy arrived around twelve thirty with cookies and—thankfully, since Felicity was starving but already buzzing from all the sugar in the doughnuts—mini quiches.

They all switched off watching the monitors, and Felicity even took a few outside breaks, just to breathe fresh air for a few moments. She stayed close to the door, not wanting any stray customers—especially Dino or any of his buddies—to get a glimpse of her.

Rory's shop had a steady flow of customers of all types, but there was no sign of Dino's tall form as the hours slowly rolled past.

By five o'clock, Felicity was starting to resign herself to another failed plan. All the murder ladies were there, along with Callum. Ian and Chris wanted to come, but both had shifts at work, and George had Mila at home. "We thought she was a little young for her first sting operation," Ellie had said when she'd arrived without her child in tow.

Felicity watched the monitors idly while her brain attempted to work out the next step in capturing Dino. Hopefully, he'd never gotten the email. If he'd seen it and was too suspicious to come, that would make any other attempt to bring him out into the open that much harder.

There was a small rush at the store, the after-work crowd, Felicity guessed. A family with two teenage kids, a pair of women probably in their thirties, and two separate men roamed the store and gradually left, until only one of the men remained. He eventually bought two boxes of ammunition and then exited.

Felicity glanced at her phone—ten minutes until Rory closed the shop at six. "Guess we're coming up with a new plan," she said, stretching her arms above her head. Although she'd sat or stood around for most of the day, her body ached like she'd been bouldering the entire time.

"We could burn their compound down?" Ellie suggested, making Felicity choke before she realized Ellie was joking. At least she *hoped* Ellie was joking.

"If we could get ahold of some building plans, we could

break in," Felicity suggested, ignoring Bennett's soft groan. "The problem is that the militia don't usually get building permits when they renovate their compound."

"What about plans for the original structure?" Callum asked.

"According to the Field County Building Department, they're 'lost.'"

"That's annoyingly coincidental," Daisy said to murmurs of agreement. "How would—" She broke off as someone entered the store.

Her mind busy coming up with a plan for breaking into the compound, Felicity sent the new customer a distracted glance. Her eyes widened as she leaned closer to screen, completely focused now on the tall man. "That's him."

"That's him?" Lou repeated, shifting to get a better look at the monitors. "*Him* him?"

"Dino Fletcher, in the flesh. All six four of him." Felicity grinned at Bennett with fierce satisfaction. "It actually worked."

Just then, all their phones dinged from a group text. Felicity glanced at hers to see a text from Rory. He's here. Come get him before I have to give him a free gun.

Felicity snorted at her text and hurried to the door into the store. Bennett was already out the back door. With her hand on the doorknob, she turned around and fixed the murder club ladies—and man—with a stern look, one she learned from Molly, so she knew it was effective.

"Unless we're about to die, do not engage," she said. "Even if we're about to die, only engage if you can do it safely."

"We know, we know!" Lou scolded, waving her hands at Felicity like she was shooing away a chicken. "We've already discussed this and agreed. Go get him before he leaves! Hurry!"

Taking a steadying breath, Felicity yanked open the door and burst into the store.

Dino's head whipped around from where he'd been studying the Browning rifle while Rory scowled at him. Felicity sprinted toward him as his eyes darted around like a trapped badger, his fingers tightening on the rifle in his grip. She was suddenly very glad that none of the guns in the store were loaded.

Still clutching the gun, he pivoted to face the exit and darted for the door. Felicity saw a flash of movement from the other side and slowed her run, a smile stretching across her face as she predicted what was about to happen. Sure enough, Dino yanked open the door and ran through the opening—only to bounce off Bennett's broad chest and stumble right back into the store, tripping and landing on his ass.

With a laugh of delight, Felicity pounced, grabbing the rifle and passing it to Bennett in one move. She caught Dino's arm, twisting it as she turned him over before he even realized what was happening. Pulling out her handcuffs, she secured them around his wrists and then double-locked them so they wouldn't tighten any more.

From her position on her knees, straddling her still shocked skip, she grinned up at Bennett.

"You let him run into me," he rumbled.

"I did, and it was so much fun to watch!"

It was his turn to laugh as he offered her a hand up, which

she accepted. The two of them helped a cuffed Dino to his feet, and Felicity kept a secure grip on her skip's arm. She'd expected more yelling and flailing and definitely more cursing from him, but he was surprisingly subdued. Felicity wondered if he was still stunned from his full-body collision with her mountain of a husband. Bennett walked the rifle back to Rory, who was still by the register, talking on her cell phone. She took the gun with careful hands and tucked it fondly under the counter.

"Clear," Felicity called out to the group waiting in the back, and they all streamed into the store, chattering with excitement.

"That was beautiful," Daisy said admiringly. "The way you just let him bounce off your big guy there. Way to incorporate a husband into your bounty-hunting toolbox."

"Thank you." Felicity could only laugh again, feeling giddy at accomplishing her mission—at least this one. Her mom had led them on such a frustrating chase that she needed a win to get her confidence and love of the game back. "Speaking of husbands, we should give yours a call, get him to pick this one up."

"Already done," Rory called out as she ended her call. "ETA twenty-five minutes."

"Twenty-five?" Felicity blinked at her.

Rory lifted one shoulder in a half shrug. "It's a big county."

Still, that seemed…not ideal. In Langston, the average police response time was six minutes. "Don't a lot of people… you know, die?"

"Yes," Rory said. "That's why I have all this." She gestured toward the back room, indicating the cameras and extensive security system that Felicity was sure she had, but her answering nod was a little uneasy. It was hard to wrap her head around such a do-it-yourself emergency-response system, like the Wild West still existed.

"This feels almost anticlimactic," Ellie said. "Is it always this easy?"

Easy? Felicity thought back to their eventful chase to Vegas and the consequences of that trip that they hadn't even started talking about yet, much less dealing with. "This was actually one of the tougher ones. A lot of bail jumpers just aren't that smart."

Everyone's eyes turned to Dino, who scowled at the room.

"Don't be talking about things being too easy, El," Lou scolded teasingly. "That's a good way to jinx us."

Ellie's hand slapped over her mouth as if to hold back words that'd already escaped, and her eyes rounded with remorse.

Felicity laughed along with everyone else, opening her mouth to comment when she glanced out the still-open door at the gathering dusk. A flicker of orange caught her attention. It looked almost like a tiny flame, like from a match, and her first thought was that someone was lighting a cigarette, but it was too close to the ground for that. Then the flame stretched into a line, and she knew that wasn't a cigarette.

"Down!" was all she had time to yell before she yanked Dino to the floor and covered his head with one of her arms. A huge, heavy weight landed on her back, and it only took a fraction of a second for her to recognize the comforting bulk of her new husband. This time, the knowledge that he was stretched over her didn't lead to a safe, content feeling, since he was vulnerable in his current position, and she hated that.

Felicity wrapped her free arm around Bennett's head, pulling him down until his face pressed into her neck. It wasn't much protection, but at least she felt like she was doing *something*.

A terrible, too-bright flash whited out her vision, followed by a *boom* that shook the floor underneath them. The tremors hadn't even stopped before Bennett and then Felicity were on their feet. Blinking the residual sparkles from her vision, she hauled Dino up with her, grimly determined he wouldn't escape in the chaos after the explosion.

"Felicity! You okay?" Bennett shouted, but his words were still muffled.

"I'm good. You?" She ran her eyes over him, overwhelmingly relieved to see him in one piece without any obvious blood.

"Fine. I'm going after them." Without waiting for a response, he turned toward the door.

"B!" she shouted, her voice echoing strangely in her head and raspy from the layer of smoke spreading through the store. Bennett was almost out the door, but he turned at her call. "Handcuffs?"

He pulled them from one of his many pants pockets and tossed them to her. Her eyes watered from the smoke, blurring her vision, but she managed to catch the cuffs in one hand.

"Thanks!" she called out before coughing. Rubbing her face against her upper arm, she wiped new tears out of her eyes and shoved down on Dino's shoulder. "Sit!" she ordered, feeling very uncharitable about him at the moment. When she'd nabbed a skip, he should have the courtesy to stay nabbed rather than have his friends try to steal him back, which was what she assumed was happening.

Dino resisted, trying to peer through the smoke, so she twisted his thumb and applied downward pressure.

"I'm sitting! I'm sitting!" he yelped, his knees sagging obediently.

"Hurry up!" she yelled, completely out of patience with him now. "I've got things to do, and I can't be hauling you around with me." First off, she had to check all of the murder club members, and then she needed to help Bennett chase down whoever thought they could blow up—literally—her successful mission.

Once Dino's recalcitrant butt was—finally—on the floor, she handcuffed his right wrist to the counter support, which looked to be a steel post set in concrete.

"Stay," she told him rather redundantly, since he shouldn't be able to go anywhere locked to the post like that. Still, it'd been a day, and she wasn't about to take anything for granted from this point on.

She turned to see that everyone in the murder club was on their feet and looked generally intact, and Rory and Lou were already heading for the back room. The room was filled with dust and haze, but except for the two-foot hole in the front wall and a few toppled display cases, the shop didn't appear too damaged.

"Everyone okay?" Felicity yelled and got verbal confirmation that they'd all escaped any major injuries.

Bennett was outside and already out of sight, but she had a feeling she'd be running into him soon. It was impossible to see anything through the hole in the wall beyond a few feet, since it was almost fully dark outside now. Running for the door, she did a quick scan of her surroundings before darting into the gravel parking lot.

No one was in sight, although the evidence of the militia members' visit was in plain view. The brick front of the store had taken the worst of the hit, a pile of blackened and smoldering rubble beneath the gaping hole in the wall. She felt a pang of guilt for being the cause of the damage to Rory's store, but she pushed it aside, figuring she'd make up for it later. She could bake Rory cookies or reload ammo for her or pay her insurance deductible or something.

Her phone buzzed in her hand, and she glanced down automatically at the text from Rory.

Bennett chasing two BGs 100yds due east

Felicity grimaced. In the dark in an unfamiliar place, she wasn't sure which way was which. Deciding to just guess, she turned to the right. Her phone buzzed again.

Wrong way

Turning around, she picked up a jog, trying to keep her footfalls quiet as she settled into stealth mode. Another buzz of her phone made her jump, and she glanced down to see Rory's latest message.

Change of plan. BG's van parked right outside gate.
Poke a few tires, then help Bennett.

Even though every part of her was straining with the need to find Bennett and protect his back from the bad guys—who she assumed Rory meant by BGs—the murder club's advice was good. Mentally grumbling, Felicity ran quickly down the driveway, slowing when she reached the open gate. Slipping from shadow to shadow, she peered through the darkness, looking for the van.

Of course they have a van, she thought, amused by that even after everything. *I'll have to mention that to Bennett.*

At the thought of him outnumbered and without backup, her sense of urgency increased. A pale gleam of one of Rory's security lights was reflected back at Felicity, revealing the bumper of a dark full-size van partially hidden in the trees next to the gate.

Right outside the gate, my ass, she thought, carefully making her way through the dry underbrush. Rory didn't mention anyone being inside the van, but Felicity knew better than to assume it was empty. The way it was parked in the shadows of the trees, it would've been almost impossible for anyone watching the feed to tell if there was an occupant, even with such high-quality cameras.

Making a cautiously wide circle around to the passenger side of the van, Felicity ignored the voice nagging at her to go help Bennett. *He can take care of himself*, she told the voice firmly and focused on the vehicle in front of her. The interior of the van was as black as night, and she resisted the temptation to press her nose against the glass to peer inside. Instead, she slipped her favorite folding knife out of her pocket and flipped it open as she crouched by the right rear tire.

Felicity knew that once she punctured the first one, she'd need to be quick with the others. If there was someone inside the van, they'd feel it list toward her corner—and they very likely would hear the escaping air. Taking a deep breath and releasing it slowly, she raised her hand, preparing to plunge the knife into the first tire.

Someone grabbed her wrist.

With a startled inward scream that burned her already smoke-roughened throat, Felicity straightened her legs with an upward thrust that would've made an elite gymnast proud. The back of her head smashed into something that felt smooshy and damp that she guessed was a face. The grunt behind her seemed to originate from there too, confirming her assumption.

The grip around her wrist loosened slightly, and she dropped her arm down hard and twisted it, popping it free from its hold. Immediately, she drove her elbow back into another smooshy part, although this one wasn't quite as damp as the first. *Belly*, her brain offered, and she nodded in agreement, ignoring in the chaotic moment the fact that she was agreeing with herself.

There was a snap of twigs as the person behind her took a step back, and a grin spread over her face as she whirled around to face her attacker. *Who drilled breaking holds over and over, long after my sisters wanted to pack it in and go home? Yeah, that was me, Felicity Florence Pax. It certainly wasn't you, Stumbly McStumbleson.*

In the faint ambient glow of Rory's security lights, Clint Yarran's bloody nose looked black, the heavy streaks beneath his nose making it appear as if he had a hole in his face, like a zombie or a skull.

That's way too many skulls to be encountering over two days, she decided, even as her hands came up automatically, curling lightly into loose fists that hovered in front of her face.

"Look who came exploring," Clint sneered, pausing to spit a wad of mucus and blood close to their feet. Felicity tried to focus on the upcoming fight that was almost guaranteed to happen, but she couldn't help giving a grossed-out shudder at that. "The bitch who thinks she's a bounty hunter."

"I *am* a bounty hunter," she said politely. "Want to see my license?" *And my knife?*

"Sure you are." He spat again.

"Please don't do that."

He ignored her request and continued talking. "Having a license doesn't make you less of a stupid bitch."

Felicity cocked her head, eyeing him. Why wasn't he coming after her? Although she'd gotten out of his initial hold and managed a few good hits, she knew perfectly well that he wasn't wary of her. This was the point where the skip always tried to go at her, and then she'd take them down. Clint didn't seem like a genius, so why wasn't he following the routine?

A twig cracked behind her just as realization hit her.

Clint was stalling.

Then her head exploded with pain, and the world went hazy gray.

Why didn't I learn after the last time this happened to me? she thought muzzily as she swayed, trying very hard not to pass out.

"You didn't hit her hard enough," Clint—that ass—was telling the person behind her.

"I didn't want to kill her." The voice was vaguely familiar, but her brain was incapable at the moment of sorting through her memories. It was all she could do to stand on her feet. "We need her for leverage. They still have Dino."

"Told him he shouldn't fall for that 'free gun' scam," Clint growled. "Hit her again."

Felicity let her knees soften so she fell to the ground. Even though she controlled the drop as much as possible, it still hurt. She was still dazed from the blow, but even the few working brain cells she had at the moment were enough to realize that she wasn't in any shape to fight off two attackers. If they hit her again, she'd really be unconscious, and she really, really didn't want to be vulnerable and helpless while being held captive by militia members in their van.

"See," the other guy said. "I hit hard enough. You need to trust me about things like that, Clint. I'm a professional after all."

A professional what? Felicity wondered, forcing herself to go limp as rough hands rolled her onto her front and yanked her arms behind her back. *Professional kidnapper?*

"Professional?" Clint scoffed. "You're an adrenaline junkie who likes to play with fire."

Fire. The connection clicked. He was one of the firefighters she'd met that first night at Levi's. Not the chief or the young, frowny one but the cheerful, middle-aged one—what was his name? Something Irish…Phineas or—*Finn.* Finn Byrne. She remembered the career-appropriate surname.

"Hurry up," Clint said. "Let's get out of here."

"What about Kelsey and Trey?"

"Deadweight." Clint's voice had a note of dark amusement. "Why do you think I chose them to set the bomb?"

Finn didn't respond except for an exhaled huff that could've meant anything.

A zip tie tightened around her wrists, digging into her skin and bringing her back to her rather dire current situation. Those same rough hands rolled her onto her back, and she struggled keeping her expression slack and her body limp when her weight painfully pressed her captive hands against the rocky ground. He pulled her phone from her pocket and must've tossed it, because she heard a distant *thunk* she assumed was her cell hitting a tree trunk. There was the familiar *rip* of duct tape being pulled off a roll before a piece was flattened over her mouth.

It was hard not to panic at that point, wondering if the next piece of tape would cover her closed eyes. Instead, she heard the side van door roll open, and she decided that *that* was the scariest sound, even worse than the duct tape. Felicity knew all the statistics, knew that once she was in the van, the chances of her surviving dropped off the cliff. As the men each grabbed one of her bound arms and heaved her inside, she fought to stay limp, every instinct in her screaming for her to fight back and run. Maybe there'd be a better opportunity later to take her captors by surprise and escape, but maybe there wouldn't be.

Maybe she'd die first.

EIGHTEEN

BENNETT SAW THE FLASH OF lighter skin the militia member had missed with the body paint. With a feral grin, Bennett ran toward that bare patch of neck, trying to stay as soundless as possible as he darted from tree to tree. His blood sang with the thrill of the chase, and he couldn't believe it was less than a month ago that he'd felt burned out and constantly numb.

Then he'd seen *her*, and his world had lit up.

Focusing on his quarry, he firmly reined in his thoughts. If he started thinking about Felicity, his concentration would be shot, and he'd be useless for anything except staring into space with a goofy smile.

The pale-necked militia member crouched next to an evergreen, breathing hard enough for Bennett to hear the wheezes twenty-five feet away. The way the bomber's gaze was frantically darting around made Bennett fairly certain that they hadn't spotted him.

Sticking to the blackest shadows, Bennett closed in. *Last*

time you'll try blowing up my wife, he thought with grim determination. His heart had almost stopped when she'd pulled Dino
to the floor and he realized what was about to happen. When
he tried to cover her with his body, she'd done her best to cover
him right back.

The goofy-smile thing was starting to happen again, and
Bennett quickly sobered. He didn't need a flash of his teeth to
catch the light and give him away at this point. Slowing his
pace, he crept up behind his quarry and then exploded into
action, grabbing the militia member from behind and shoving
them face-first to the ground.

"Get off me!" a feminine voice shrieked, but Bennett didn't
hesitate.

Pulling her hands behind her back, he had her secured with
his spare pair of cuffs within seconds. Zip ties worked to restrain
her ankles and then connect the two to finish the hog-tie.

"C'mon." Her tone had changed drastically, become coax-
ing, even flirtatious. She tried to toss her hair, but it didn't work
very well with it hidden in her beanie. "Untie me. I'll walk
back with you, turn myself in. You don't think I'll give you any
trouble, do you? Not when you're so big and strong."

Ignoring her pleas, he stood, noting the location to let the
sheriff know where he could find her, and then he went back
into hunting mode.

The bound woman on the ground was still trying to convince him to let her go, but her voice rose to a frustrated shriek
as he walked away.

"Kelsey?" a male voice shouted. "Are you okay?"

Bennett blinked. Apparently, his second quarry wasn't going to be much of a challenge. Slipping through the shadows once again, he made his way toward where the calls originated.

"He tied me up!" Kelsey yelled back. "You have to come rescue me, Trey!"

There was a long moment of silence that Bennett used to close the distance between him and Trey, followed by the sound of someone running while trying to keep it quiet. The snapping of twigs and scuffling of leaves were getting fainter, and Bennett held in a snort when he realized that rather than rescuing his partner, the second bomber was running away.

Kelsey seemed to realize this as well. "Trey! Don't you dare leave! Get back here right now and help me, or I swear to God, I will tell Clint you were the one who forgot to lock the armory that night. Trey!"

Bennett pursued the running man, moving faster now that silence wasn't required. Between the crashing sounds Trey was making as he plowed through the underbrush and his heaving breaths, there was no way he was hearing anything else.

When Trey broke through the trees into a clearing and sprinted for the perimeter fence, Bennett allowed himself to grin. This was it. He sped up, lengthening his strides until he was just a few feet behind Trey. Glancing over his shoulder, Trey gave a panicked yelp before sprinting faster, obviously hoping to reach the fence before Bennett could catch him.

A motion-sensor light flashed on, bright as the sun, and Trey put on the brakes, coming to a screeching halt. Momentarily blinded, Bennett didn't see the man in front of him had stopped until he crashed into him, sending both of them to the ground. Taking advantage of the situation, Bennett immediately grabbed Trey's wrists and secured them behind him with a zip tie, going more by feel than anything, since white spots still covered his vision. By the time he had Trey hog-tied just like Kelsey, his eyes had adjusted, and he was able to see clearly.

Straightening, he wondered where Felicity was. He'd half expected her to be right behind him after she'd secured Dino with his cuffs. As fast as she was, she would've had no problem catching up to these two slow yahoos. Pulling out his phone, he tried calling her, but it went to voicemail. Next, he tried Callum.

"Watched you take down the guy just now on the monitor—nice job. Got the other one secured?" Callum asked as soon as he answered.

"Yeah. Felicity?"

"Disabling the van, just in case you let one of them get past you."

Bennett grinned. Of course she was. "Rory got eyes on her?"

Callum relayed the question, and there was a muffled response. "Rory last saw a glimpse of her a minute ago at the gate, but—and this is a quote from Lou—'your wife is pretty sneaky.'"

The glow of pride he felt—both because she was indeed sneaky and because she was his wife—was doused by a pang of worry. "Where's the van?"

"In the trees next to the main gate."

"Quickest route?"

Callum again consulted Rory and then reported back.

"Follow the fence to the next gate. There's a golf cart parked there. Take it and keep following the fence to the main gate. We'll let you know if we spot her."

Bennett gave an acknowledging grunt, already running along the fence as he ended the call. A curdled feeling in his gut warned him that something was wrong. It would've only taken a few seconds for her to disable the van, and then she would've found Bennett. Despite the short length of their relationship, he knew his wife—his brave, beautiful, incredible wife. If she wasn't with him, watching his back, there was something preventing her from fighting by his side.

His fear for Felicity built as he swung into the golf cart. It wasn't the fastest mode of transport, but it was quiet—just an electric whir—and it did beat his best sprinting speed, especially when he pushed down on the accelerator and discovered that Rory had made a few alterations. Zipping along at a solid twenty-five miles an hour, the cart carried him toward the main gate as his apprehension grew. The night wind blew over him, whistling by his ears and making it hard to hear anything else. He pressed harder on the accelerator, even though he knew he'd already maxed out the speed.

The fence posts whipped by, and he finally saw the open main gate ahead. Peering through the trees, he searched for any sign of the van or Felicity, but the trees and brush were packed too closely together, and his vision was hampered by the lights on the security fence next to him.

Suddenly, a gas engine roared to life on the other side of the fence. Bennett's heart took off at a gallop as his lips tightened into a straight line and a pulse throbbed in his jaw. Immediately, he knew in his gut that she was in that van, and he tried to wring a bit more speed out of the straining golf cart.

Barely slowing as he reached the gate, he turned the cart, the small, fat wheels sending out a spray of gravel. It fishtailed as he fought to straighten it, the boxy body not made to go the speeds Rory had rigged it up for. The van shot forward, angling toward the driveway. Without headlights or any interior illumination, it looked like a dark beast, a blocky dragon bursting from the trees and barreling down the drive.

Wishing for his SUV—or any actual *car*—he grimly set his gaze on the back of the van and pushed the golf cart to its top speed.

———

Felicity was already regretting her decision not to fight back immediately, and the van hadn't even gone a block. Telling herself there was nothing she could do about it now, she carefully sat up to spare her poor bruised hands. After checking to make sure neither man in the front was watching her, she scooted her way closer to the back of Clint's seat, feet first.

"What's that?" Finn grumbled, looking in his side mirror.

"What?" Clint was instantly alert.

"Something's behind us, but it's too small to be a car. Deer, maybe?" Finn rolled down his window so he could crane his head out and look behind him. There was a loud *crack* of a gunshot, and Finn yanked his head back inside the van, swearing and flattening his hand over his ear. When he released it to

THE SCENIC ROUTE   287

pull a black handgun out of the glove compartment, Felicity saw the dark gleam she assumed was blood streaking down the right side of his neck.

"Deer don't shoot guns," Clint said grimly, and the van engine roared as it sped up.

"Slow down." Finn moved to lean out the window again, this time with the gun, but hesitated, making Felicity smirk. She wasn't sure who was following them, but her money was on Bennett. "He's dropping back too far behind us. I want to take him out." From his bitter tone, he'd been rather fond of his now-mutilated ear.

Not liking the idea of Finn shooting at Bennett, much less "taking him out," she carefully shifted until she was behind his seat. Despite the amount of adrenaline flowing through her, her head still throbbed with pain, making it hard to come up with a coherent plan.

The van slowed, and Finn leaned out the window, aiming behind them. In her new position, Felicity saw the moonlight reflect off his teeth as he smiled in anticipation. "Come closer, you asshole," he muttered, and Clint let the van slow even more. "Closer…" His smile widened as he braced his right elbow on the seat back, steadying his grip as his finger settled gently on the trigger.

Nope. Not on my watch. Felicity slid her leg between his seat and the door, using her heel to press the seat lever as she leaned back, ignoring the pain when her bound hands pressed against the van floor. The seat back reclined completely, almost smacking her in the face. A yelp from Finn made her hopeful, but then the gun fired, and she could only hope that her maneuver worked to throw off his aim.

Without pausing, she pushed off the base of the seat, ignoring the carpet burning her hands as she shoved herself clear of the reclined seat. Rolling to her feet but staying low, she saw Finn had recovered and was turning toward her, his teeth bared and the gun in his grip.

Hunched over so she didn't bump her already aching head on the ceiling, Felicity kicked him twice in quick succession—first his face and then, when his head was knocked back, the wrist of his right hand. The gun went off again as it flew from Finn's hand, and Clint roared, but Felicity was too focused on Finn to check whether he'd been hit or was just enraged that she was fighting back.

Finn's right wrist hung, limp and useless, but he grabbed at her with his left as she kicked again, catching her boot in his hand. She'd seen it coming but had already committed to the kick, so she used his grip to push off as she hammered him with her other boot heel, right in the bridge of his nose.

There was a loud crack of breaking bone as he dropped, releasing her right foot. Felicity fell back, cringing in anticipation of her full weight landing on her bound hands, crushing them. Pulling in her knees at the last moment, she managed to tuck her body and land on her shoulders and the back of her head. The additional thump on her skull didn't feel great, but at least she spared her hands.

Using her momentum, she finished her backward roll and popped into a crouch. The van floor lurched beneath her feet, and she thought her concussion was acting up for a second but then realized the uneven bumping was because one of the rear tires was flat. She grinned. Bennett had done her job for her—a little later than ideal, but she'd take it.

Clint swore as he struggled to steer the lurching van with his left hand, his right scrambling for the gun Finn had dropped by his seat. An unconscious Finn slumped sideways off his seat, blocking Clint's reach. Felicity launched herself toward the gun.

Abandoning the steering wheel completely, Clint shoved Finn out of the way and grabbed the gun just a fraction of a second before Felicity. She switched gears, scrambling back to get in a position to kick it out of his hands, but the van veered off the road and bumped over a large rock, the bounce knocking her off balance.

She managed not to fall, but the effort took time she didn't have, and Clint grabbed a handful of her shirt, yanking her toward him. Flipping her around, he ripped the tape from her mouth in one cruel motion while his other hand pressed the gun to her temple. Even though she went still, he wrapped his free arm around her throat.

"Interfering bitch," he snarled. "The trouble you've caused me… I'm going to enjoy hearing you scream as I kill you."

"What trouble?" It was hard to get the words out with the pressure he was putting on her trachea, especially with the van tossing them around as it slowly decelerated over the rough ground, but she was determined. She'd always really hated being blamed for things she didn't do. "I wasn't even after you. You don't have any warrants." *Yet. After tonight, he'll be racking up a whole slew of them.* "Why'd you even bring Dino with you to Vegas if you didn't want me coming after you?"

"The Vegas buyer likes him," he admitted before stiffening behind her. "None of your business. You're going to help me get away from your PI out there, and then I'm going to kill you… slowly."

"That's not a great motivator for me," she muttered, but he wasn't listening.

Releasing her throat, he reached over to open the driver's door without moving the gun from her head. The van hit an extra-big bump, and the jounce tossed Felicity forward. She caught the side of Finn's seat back with her shoulder, which kept her from landing on his unconscious body. Turning in the same motion, she hoped to take Clint down with a well-placed kick now that the gun wasn't pressed against her temple. He'd recovered too quickly, however, and was aiming the pistol at her face. Deciding a face shot wasn't any better than a temple shot, she reluctantly kept her feet on the ground.

With an annoyed grunt, Clint twisted so he could stomp on the brake, bringing the van to a lurching halt before he slammed it into park and turned off the ignition, keeping the gun pointed at her the whole time.

Fear twisted inside her, but she mashed it down, knowing it would take over if she let it. When fear was in charge, there was no making smart decisions, so she just told herself she'd gotten out of worse situations before, ignoring the tiny voice inside her brain that insisted *this* was probably the worst situation she'd been in.

So after I survive today, I'll use this *as my worst situation I've survived before*, she shot back, ignoring the fact that she was once again arguing with herself.

Clint pushed open the door and stepped out of the van, the gun continuously trained on her. "Get out."

She shot a quick glance at the dark form of a still-unmoving Finn. "Are you just leaving your buddy?"

"He was a traitor anyway."

"You're really good at tossing your own guys under the bus, aren't you?" she muttered.

"No, just the..." He caught himself. "None of your business. Get out. You should be glad anyway. He's the one who tipped me off about you, and he got his cousin to kick you out of her motel."

"Finn's cousin..." Her hazy thoughts were working against her again, and it took a moment for her to make the connections. "Marian?"

"Of course, Marian," he scoffed. "You get kicked out of some other motel too? Now move!"

It was a struggle to maneuver around the driver's seat without the use of her hands, but she somehow managed to get her feet on the ground. Immediately, Clint grabbed her again, turning her away from him so he could wrap one arm around her neck and rest the muzzle of his gun right above her ear.

There was full darkness now, only a hint of moonlight keeping the inky blackness from being impenetrable. Felicity looked around as well as she could without being able to move her head, but she didn't see any sign of Bennett, which sent a surge of relief through her. The wind had died down for a moment, so the only sounds were the ticking of the van engine as it cooled and the sigh of the breeze as it rippled softly through the trees' branches.

She realized in that moment that she was glad to be the one with the gun pointed at her head if it meant Bennett was safe. Felicity blinked, processing the thought. The only other people she'd ever felt that way about were her sisters.

So I guess I do love him?

She stiffened in Clint's hold, and his arm tightened around her neck.

"What? What is it? You see something?"

"I just realized I love my husband."

There was a long beat of silence before he asked, "You're married?"

"Is that really important right now?"

He huffed. "You started it! Never mind. Let's go." He started walking, but the position was too awkward to move quickly, and he soon released the hold around her throat. "Walk. You even think about acting up, and there'll be a bullet in the back of your head."

She led the way, scuffling her feet along the rough ground to both feel her way and also delay them. He'd already told her she was dead once they reached wherever he was taking her, so she wasn't in any hurry to reach it. With a huge effort of will, she kept herself from looking around for Bennett.

You don't need a knight in shining armor to rescue you, her brain scolded. *You're pretty good at rescuing yourself.*

Felicity raised a mental eyebrow at the voice. *Any ideas on how to accomplish that last part?*

The voice was silent.

"Faster," Clint ordered, giving her back a hard enough push to make her stumble forward.

"Watch it!" she snapped. If she fell, she'd land on her face without her hands to catch her and not enough forward momentum for a dive roll.

"Don't speak to me like that," Clint growled, grabbing her hair where it was coiled in a bun at the base of her neck and yanking back as he pressed the gun muzzle hard against her temple. "I have the power here. I can end you in a second—and will. So watch your mouth."

Felicity bit back the response she wanted to give him and gave a very short nod, all she could manage with his grip on her hair.

"Now walk." He shoved her forward as he released her.

It was very hard not to respond. When she was scared or stressed, snarky comebacks were what steadied her. She hated feeling helpless. *Hated* it. In her frustration—and also her fear of getting a bullet in the back—she strode forward, disregarding the footing. A firefly flashed in the darkness ahead of her, and then another, their presence oddly comforting.

A strange, quiet *whir* filled the air around them. It took Felicity a moment to recognize the sound, and when she did, she couldn't hold back her grin. *Here comes the cavalry.*

"What is that?" Clint asked, nerves showing in his voice.

"Fireflies," she improvised. The wind picked up just in time, the howling loud enough to cover any other sounds.

"There aren't any fireflies in Colorado," he scoffed, having to raise his voice to almost a shout for her to hear it over the wind. "Besides, they don't make any noise."

"Sure there are." She smiled wider as she snuck a peek to their right, getting just a glimpse of a faint white shape before she hurried to face forward, not wanting Clint to look that way. To keep his attention focused on her, she shouted over the noisy wind, "There's even a species *specific* to Colorado. Their wings make that sound."

"That's bull—"

A white golf cart sped out of the darkness to their right and slammed into Clint, sending him flying in the middle of his rebuttal.

NINETEEN

With a triumphant laugh, Felicity ran to where Clint was sprawled on his side. She kicked the gun next to his right hand, sending it flying into the darkness. Bennett hopped out of the golf cart he'd just used as a battering ram to check Clint's pulse and breathing before hog-tying him with an ease that made Felicity breathless with adoration.

"It's kind of fun to be rescued by a knight in shining armor," she said giddily. "Have a knife on you?"

"Why?" Bennett asked as he stood, immediately pulling a knife from his pocket. "Want to stab him a little before the cops get here?"

"Tempting," she said, turning her back to Bennett. "But I'll need the use of my hands first."

He stepped behind her, and with a *pop*, her hands were free. She groaned with both relief and pain.

"You okay?" Bennett's voice was deep with concern as he gently gripped her shoulders to turn her around.

"Fine." She shook out her hands, trying to speed the blood flow. "Just pins and needles."

"Hurt anywhere else?" His eyes were scanning over her, even though she knew he couldn't see much in the dark.

"I'm fine." Strangely enough, now that she was safe, her voice started to shake. "I realized something though."

He gave an inquiring grunt as he pulled her gently against his chest, wrapping his big arms around her in *the* best hug she'd ever gotten before in her life.

"I love you."

"Finally."

"What?" Her outrage was tempered by laughter as she tried to pull back to glare at him. His arms tightened, keeping her plastered against him, so she decided to subside against his chest and yell at him from there. It was extremely comfortable—and comforting—there after all. "What do you mean 'finally'? We met, like, a second ago!"

He snorted. "I knew I loved you the first time I saw you."

"That's not love," she scoffed, although her entire heart had melted at his declaration. "That's lust."

"Nope. Love." He said it with such certainty that she actually started to believe him, even though the idea was ridiculous. "I saw you, and it was like someone squeezed my heart really hard."

"Sounds painful. You sure you weren't having a small heart attack?"

A laugh rumbled through his chest, vibrating against her cheek. "I'm sure. It just got stronger the more I got to know you. If it were a heart attack, I'd be dead by now. It's definitely love."

"I'm glad you're not dead." She burrowed deeper into his chest, smelling his comforting Bennett scent and wishing she could stay like this forever—or at least for a solid peaceful week. When he stiffened, however, she knew her time was up.

Pulling free, she looked around the darkness to see two headlights speeding through the darkness toward them. "Any idea who that might be?" she asked.

His grunt was definitely a no.

"To the golf cart then," she sighed. "This night is never going to end, is it?"

Red and blue lights flashed on for a few seconds above the headlights, and Felicity paused before jumping into the passenger seat of the cart. "Good cop or bad cop?"

"Probably Chris."

"And possibly Deputy Donkey-Face?" She grimaced. "Think we can make it back to Rory's store before he catches up to us?"

Even in the near darkness, she knew exactly the look Bennett was giving her. "It's a golf cart."

"Fine," she sighed, sitting back, regretting kicking the gun away from Clint rather than grabbing it somehow—maybe with her mouth? If it was Donkey-Face, she and Bennett were in a very vulnerable position without any way to protect themselves except for a heavily dented golf cart. Her muscles tensed as the squad car got closer, the headlights brightening the scene in a way she could've used a few minutes ago when she was trying to stumble through the darkness without falling on her face or getting shot.

The squad turned alongside them so the headlights were no

longer shining directly in their eyes, and the driver's window lowered. When Chris stuck his head out, all the tension drained from her body, and it was all she could do to remain upright.

"You called?" he asked, smiling his usual good-natured grin. "I take it that Operation Free Gun worked like a charm?"

Felicity turned her head to meet Bennett's eyes before letting out a peal of laughter.

"Yeah," she said to Chris without looking away from her husband. "Like a charm."

Chris got out of his squad car and walked toward a hog-tied Clint. Felicity knew the moment he recognized the man on the ground, because his body jerked before he turned to look at them. "You know this isn't Dino Fletcher, right?"

Felicity, still feeling giddy from surviving and Bennett's confession of love, giggled. "Dino's at the store. A few things happened during your *twenty-five-minute* response time." She was still horrified by that.

He grimaced. "I was on a traffic stop on the other side of Liverton. I figured you could hang on to one skip while I convinced LeRoy Carson that he needs two functional headlights on his Buick. Want to explain why you have Clint—just the guy I wanted to talk to about his role in Cobra Jones's death—trussed up and waiting like an early birthday present for me?"

"The skull was Cobra's?"

He nodded. "DNA testing's not back yet, but dental records match."

She tried to take in this news, but it was a little too much on top of the evening's events, so she pushed it to the back of her mind to examine more closely later. Instead, she concentrated on summarizing everything else that'd just happened. "A couple of Clint's lackeys blew up Rory's store."

Chris stared at her. "Again?"

"Again?" Now she felt extra guilty. "This has happened before?"

"Not exactly this, but definitely the bomb in the store part. Everyone okay?" He rushed back toward his squad car while snapping out questions too quickly for her to fit in an answer. "Is Daisy hurt? Do I need to call for medical, or are they already on scene?"

"Everyone's fine," Felicity hurried to tell him before he zoomed off and left her and Bennett to deal with Clint who, by the sounds of his moans, was coming to. She really didn't want him in the back of their golf cart. "No one's hurt. There's just a hole in the front of the store. In fact..." She squinted through the surrounding darkness to see another set of headlights coming their way, this time from the direction of Rory's store. "I'm guessing you're going to see for yourself that Daisy's okay in just a minute."

Chris let out an audible breath, but at least he didn't jump in his squad car and tear off. "Explain, please." He still sounded terse though.

"The gun giveaway setup went just as planned. Then I had to say something about how well it worked, and two of Clint's militia minions—"

"Trey and Kelsey," Bennett interrupted. When she and Chris looked at him, he finally expanded on that. "Tied up outside Rory's store."

Pretty sure that was all the details they were getting out of Bennett for the moment, Felicity continued. "Trey and Kelsey set off an explosive device outside the store. The wall has a good-sized hole in it, but *no one was injured*." She emphasized this part, since Chris was starting to look tense again. "Bennett took off after those two, and Rory texted me that their van was outside her front gate, so I went there, planning to incapacitate it before helping Bennett."

Bennett's interest perked up at this part, which made sense, since he'd experienced the first part of her story firsthand.

"Clint grabbed me, and we tussled." She felt Bennett's thigh tense against hers, so she kept her voice light. "I would've won too, but Finn cheated and snuck up behind me to knock me on the head."

Bennett instantly started gently feeling her skull, looking for the lump, and she smiled up at him. When she looked back at the deputy, he was staring at her in disbelief. "Finn?"

"Finn Byrne." She gave a decisive nod and then winced as Bennett found the bump. He immediately lightened his touch, giving a displeased grunt at her injury. Despite her sore head, that made her smile.

"Wait—Finn Byrne, the firefighter? You're sure?"

"Wild, right?" She knew her expression was much too happy for this conversation, but she couldn't help it. Her husband loved her and hated when she was hurt. "Firefighters are never the bad guy." She remembered something and jumped a little in her seat. "Oh! He's still in the van. *He* probably does need medical." Wrinkling her nose in distaste, she pointed at where Clint was starting to stir. "Him too. He got run over by a golf cart."

Still looking shell-shocked, Chris radioed in that he needed medical and backup. Once he'd put his radio back, he looked at Felicity expectantly. She swayed a little, exhaustion suddenly hitting her hard, and Bennett wrapped his arm around her, steadying her.

"You okay?" he asked for the third—fourth, maybe?—time that night.

"Yeah." She leaned into him, soaking in his strength. "Just tired all of a sudden."

"You're going to let the EMTs take a look at you when they arrive."

Felicity opened her mouth to argue and then reconsidered. "Okay."

"Okay?" Bennett sounded surprised at her easy acquiescence.

"Probably a good idea after getting knocked over the head. Again."

"Can you finish your statement?" Chris asked sympathetically. "Then you can go back to the shop, have medical check you out, and give me a written statement in the morning."

"Sure." Bennett's warmth and coziness were making her a little too comfortable, and she was about to fall asleep, so she sat up straight. He kept his arm around her shoulders, however, and she was grateful for the support. "I wasn't knocked out by Finn's hit, but I was a bit wobbly, so I didn't fight back when they tied my hands and tossed me into the van. They took off, driving away from Rory's, and Bennett must've been following.

Finn was going to shoot him, so I kicked his seat lever to recline his seat, then kicked him a couple more times to make him drop the gun and then to knock him out." When she recounted what happened, it sounded a little more premeditated than it actually had been. She'd just kicked until the threat was mitigated. "Bennett must've shot out their tire?"

Glancing at Bennett, she raised her eyebrows at him, and he nodded, confirming her assumption.

"So the ride was pretty rough, especially when Clint let go of the wheel to grab the gun and then me. He got the van stopped, we got out, started walking—which is really hard in the pitch-black—all while he was talking about how much he was going to enjoy killing me." She didn't want to be whiny, but she felt pretty justified in complaining a little. Bennett's arm stiffened as he made an unhappy sound, so she gave him a reassuring pat on the leg. "Then there was a whirring sound, and I told Clint it was the sound of firefly wings, and Bennett ran him over with the golf cart while Clint was arguing with me about whether Colorado has fireflies. Bennett tied him up, and then you showed up, and we were really glad it was you and not Deputy Donkey-Face, since we think he's allied with the militia."

Chris stood there for a few moments before nodding and heading over to Clint, who'd opened his eyes but was still looking rather bleary. Cutting the zip ties, Chris replaced the one on Clint's wrists with handcuffs and then hauled him up onto his feet. Clint swayed, stumbling a little as the deputy led him over to his squad car and sat him in the back seat.

As Chris closed the back door, locking Clint inside, Rory's pickup came to an abrupt halt next to the squad car, and all four murder club women poured out.

"Felicity! Bennett! You okay?" Lou asked.

Giving her abbreviated statement had used up Felicity's last reserves of energy, so she just offered a little wave and smile. Chris immediately swept up Daisy in his arms, and they had a low-voiced, intense conversation that Felicity was glad she couldn't overhear. It was enough at the moment just to deal with all her own newfound feelings.

"Callum's babysitting Dino," Lou said as she, Rory, and Ellie gathered around the golf cart. "You were all out of camera range, so we came to check on you."

"The whining was unbearable," Rory said.

At Felicity's confused look, Lou translated. "Dino. He tried begging and threatening and had moved on to crying when we left. We were mainly concerned about you two, but I have to admit that it was very nice to get away from that. I feel bad for whatever deputy is stuck in a car with Dino when they bring him to jail."

"What happened?" Ellie asked. "All we saw was the van flying away from the gate and then Bennett pursuing in a golf cart."

"I made improvements," Rory said, stroking the front of the cart affectionately, "but even so, I didn't think you were going to catch up." She eyed the van huddled pathetically just outside the light from the two vehicles' headlights. "How'd you manage that?"

"Bennett is a good problem solver." Felicity followed Rory's gaze and was reminded again about Finn. "Oh! Deputy!"

Chris had already detached himself from Daisy and was walking toward the van. At her call, he turned around, but she waved him on.

"Just going to remind you of Finn, but you're already on it."

He gave a nod and continued toward the van.

"Finn?" Lou asked, and Felicity winced. She really didn't want to go through everything again, especially since Rory volunteered with the fire department. There was a good chance that she'd been friends with Finn. Felicity's eyes wanted to close, so she allowed them to sink down as she rested her head on Bennett's shoulder.

"She's tired," Bennett said firmly, starting the golf cart. "We're going to get her checked out and then go to the hotel."

When Felicity cracked her eyes open, she saw they were headed back toward the store—headlights on this time. She smiled and let her eyes sink closed again, burrowing into his side as his arm tightened around her.

Just this once, she'd let her knight sweep her off into the sunset on his trusty electric souped-up golf cart steed.

———

Bright light turned the insides of her eyelids orange, bringing her slowly awake. She was lying on her stomach in a cloud-soft bed, and a smile curved her lips as she stretched her arms out to either side, searching for her husband. When her reach only turned up crisp sheets, she frowned and opened her eyes.

Although the main room was empty, she could hear a low rumble of his voice in the bathroom. Assuming he was on his phone and didn't want to wake her, she stretched again, feeling the bruises and aches from the night before. Her hands were the worst, especially the rug burn, but they were still usable. A low-grade headache throbbed behind her temples, but she knew once she popped a couple of ibuprofen, she'd be right as rain.

Since Bennett didn't seem to be wrapping up his phone call anytime soon, she reached for her own cell. She was overdue in contacting Molly thanks to her sleep-in, and she didn't want her sister descending on their honeymoon suite, especially not knowing that it was an actual, literal honeymoon suite.

"Did the fake gun giveaway work?" Molly asked as she answered.

Felicity grinned. Despite everything that'd happened, that little trap had performed beautifully. "It did indeed. Walked right into our snare, the silly little skip."

Molly cheered, and she heard John in the background asking for more details.

"There were a few hiccups afterward with his militia buddies, but Bennett helped me out, and it all ended well."

"Want to elaborate on those 'hiccups'?"

"Nope." What Molly didn't know couldn't give her an ulcer, so Felicity breezed right by that. "Enough about that. I have news."

"Good news?" Molly asked eagerly. "Because I'd love some good news."

"It is." Despite her nerves about telling her sister, Felicity felt excitement bubbling up inside her. "Bennett and I got married."

The silence on the other side built until Molly screeched, "What??"

"We're married!" Nervous relief released in a happy laugh. "We didn't really plan it—long story—but we're really happy."

"I…what…married?"

Felicity giggled again at hearing her usually composed sister so discombobulated. "Married. And in love." She didn't mention that, for her, they happened in that exact order.

"Really?" Although Molly still sounded skeptical, there was an edge of hope in her voice. "You're really happy to be married? Because last I knew, he was stalking you."

"Yeah, he's supersmart and great at his job but horribly awkward socially." Now that the hardest part was over and her sister seemed to be taking the news semi-well, Felicity propped some pillows behind her and snuggled in, excited to be able to talk freely about her new husband. "He reminds me of Norah, actually."

"You know," Molly said thoughtfully, "I can actually imagine Norah stalking someone—just by accident." John's laugh boomed in the background.

"Exactly." Smiling, Felicity mentally replayed what he'd said to her the previous night. "I've even started liking his grunts, because only I know what he means, so it's like we have this private language."

"His grunts?" Molly started to laugh. "Now I *know* you're in love."

"Pax, put Fifi on speaker." John's voice came through more clearly, meaning he was trying to squish his head against Molly's so he could hear. "I'm just getting bits and pieces, and I'm dying here."

Molly's giggle turned into a squeal, and then there were some rustling noises and heavy breathing and more laughter from both of them, and Felicity pulled her phone down so she could give it a dubious look before putting it back to her ear.

"Fifi, it's John Carmondy."

Felicity could hear Molly's breathless voice in the background, demanding her phone back.

"Tell me *everything*."

Felicity couldn't help but laugh at her ridiculous boyfriend-in-law. "First off, I know who you are. Why did you tell me your last name like Molly has a stable of Johns running around the house?" She paused, since that came out a little differently than she'd planned. "Second, let me talk to Molly. I'm not going to gush over my new husband with you. That'd be weird."

"Fine," he huffed, and there was a slight pause before Molly's voice came through with a slight echo that told Felicity they were on speaker.

"Sorry, Fifi," Molly apologized. "Remember how you all liked him and I didn't because I thought he was stealing all my jobs and you told me how great he was?"

Felicity shrugged even though her sister couldn't see her. "I still like him," she said easily.

"Thanks, Fifi," John butted in, sounding smug. "You're my favorite after Pax."

"Mm-hmm." Felicity had a feeling he'd also told that same thing to Cara, Norah, *and* Charlie on different occasions.

Before she could say anything else, the bathroom door opened. She couldn't help the sappy smile that spread over her face at the sight of her husband, the one who loved her. He grinned back, the crease between his eyebrows smoothing out of existence.

"Moo, I have to go. We'll be back in a few days, so I'll tell you the rest in person, okay?"

"Only if I'm around to hear it too," John said.

"Hang on, Fifi." Molly's voice sobered. "Sorry to do this to you, but would there be any way you can give Charlie a hand? She's trying to pretend that everything is fine, but I think she's having a hard time. There's just a few weeks before Mom's next court date, and if we don't get her back in time for that…"

"She forfeits her bail and we lose the house," Felicity finished as her heart sank. She'd been hoping she and Bennett could actually have that real honeymoon they'd joked about, the one where they didn't leave the suite for days at a time. There was no way Felicity could let Charlie struggle alone, however, especially when their family home was at stake. Her sister needed her, so she'd be there. As much as she wanted it, a real honeymoon could wait. With a silent sigh, she forced a more cheerful tone. "Of course. Give me a day to wrap things up with the sheriff's department. Is Charlie still in Nebraska?" Her heart sank even more at the mention of her least-favorite state.

"Yep, Omaha, according to her last text. We'll fly you out and have Charlie pick you up at the airport—or both of you if Bennett's going too?"

Her gaze met his, and she couldn't help the wry edge to her words. "He'll be going. Won't be able to keep him away."

He gave her a puzzled look as she exchanged her usual I-love-yous and be-carefuls with Molly and John.

"Charlie needs help," she explained after she'd ended the call. "We'll be flying out tomorrow to meet her in Omaha—or Des Moines, maybe, if Mom keeps heading east."

His eyebrows knit again. "We?"

Her stomach gave another churn, but she forced a smile. "Sure. Now that you're back on the case, you can join us on our Mom-chasing adventures."

His expression blanked as he sat on the edge of the bed. She studied him curiously. He almost seemed…nervous?

"I'm not on the case," he said, studying his hands where they were braced on his knees. "I just called my client—my *former* client—and told them I'm off the case. Permanently."

"But why?" Felicity asked, her heart leaping with hope. "Aren't they your best client?"

He shrugged, catching her gaze. His eyes were hungry, making her mouth dry and her heart thump against her ribs. When he smiled, though, the heat shifted into such an intense love that she pressed her fist to her chest. "Conflict of interest. I'm married—and wildly in love—with Jane Pax's daughter. Plus I'm a general in her bounty-hunting army."

This time, when a smile curved her lips, she meant it with her whole heart. "And she's wildly in love with you—but you're a colonel. That's the highest I'll go."

"I'll take it." He lunged, making her squeal with laughter as he landed above her, caging her to the bed with his arms.

"We're staying married then?" She'd assumed they would,

with the love declarations and all, but she wanted it confirmed before she could stop that tiny niggle of worry.

His expression turned cautious. "Do you *want* to stay married?"

"I do." She grinned at her unintentional vow.

His face still serious, he gazed down at her, his eyes full of more love than she'd ever expected to receive from anyone. "I do too."

Looping her arms around his neck, she tugged him down toward her. "Then I proclaim us still married…forever."

"Forever." He said that as a vow before his lips met hers.

She kissed him for a long, sweet moment, her eyes closing, before pulling back. "You don't have to come with us. I mean, it's *Nebraska*. If you have another job to do, I'll totally understand if y—"

He cut her off with another kiss. "Where you go, I go."

She smiled fondly at him. "Stalker."

He grinned back. "You love your stalker."

"I do."

They were both still smiling when their lips met again.

TWENTY

FELICITY LOOKED AROUND WITH FONDNESS at the little coffee shop. Even in the short time she'd been in Simpson, she'd gotten attached to this weird little town and its inhabitants, especially Lou and the coffee shop.

"You can't go," Lou moaned. The cappuccino machine groaned as if agreeing with her. "You brought the excitement back to town. Who's going to stumble over bodies now?"

"I don't know." Felicity took a sip of her antioxidant smoothie. "I heard you're pretty good at that."

Lou huffed. "Did you hear that from a firefighter? Those gossipy hens."

"Nope. Deputy Chris told me himself when we went to the sheriff's department earlier to give our official written statements about last night."

Lou tsked. "Deputy Chris? I thought he was more tight-lipped than that."

"Can't really blame him," Felicity said. "Between the

militia's shenanigans, Cobra's remains, and Deputy Donk…ah, Litchfield being suspended while he's being investigated for his Freedom Survivors connections, I don't think Chris has slept more than an hour over the past three days, and most of the blame for that falls on us." She circled her finger, indicating herself, Bennett, and Lou.

"Me?" Lou gasped, touching her chest in a very fine imitation of someone clutching their pearls. "I would never…"

"Never kick a headless dead body?" Felicity smoothly interjected before taking another sip of her drink.

Lou couldn't maintain her offended expression any longer and looked sheepish. "Okay," she admitted. "I did kick a headless dead body—*once*."

"We're even then. One dead body each." Felicity held her drink up in a toast, felt weird about toasting the finding of dead bodies, and hurried to set her glass back down.

"Not really even," Bennett muttered. When both women looked at him, he gave one of his half shrugs. "Felicity didn't kick hers."

Lou clutched her imaginary pearls again as Felicity choked back a laugh. It seemed even worse to laugh about dead bodies than it was to toast the finding of them.

"When are you coming back?" Lou asked. "It better be soon, because I'm counting on both your signatures on the petition to change the Freedom Survivors' name."

It was Felicity's turn to wince. "Not sure how long there's going to be a militia in Simpson," she said honestly. "Their current leader is suspected of killing their previous leader, plus three of their members are in jail for attempted murder and kidnapping, in Finn's case. Oh, and what about Finn's son? What was his name?" Felicity thought back to that first meeting of the firefighters, but all she could remember was his cranky expression. "The surly one. Is he involved in the militia too?"

"Kieran?" Lou held up her hands in a shrug, looking sad. "Who knows? All the firefighters loved his dad. Finn fooled everyone." Letting out a breath, she smiled, although it looked a bit rough around the edges. "Back to you though. I need to know a return date."

"Soon, I hope." Felicity glanced at Bennett, finding him looking at her with that mix of love and wonder that never failed to turn her insides to mush. "Once we get things straightened out with my mom and the house, I want to come back to have a real honeymoon—without all the skulls and explosions and kidnapping and such."

Bennett caught her hand under the counter and squeezed it.

Lou nodded solemnly. "I get how that could put a damper on your honeymoon."

"How about a cabin in the woods this winter?" Felicity asked Bennett, getting excited about the idea. "Just you, me, a roaring fire, and a big bed." Realizing that Lou was still part of the conversation, she looked at her, blushing. "Sorry. Overshare."

"No problem, but as a former cabin owner, you might want to reconsider," Lou warned. "Even before my house was set on fire, cabin living wasn't all it's cracked up to be."

Felicity blinked. "This is a rather…violent area."

Lou waved a casual hand. "I mean, except for thin ice on

the reservoirs and the rockslides and avalanches and occasional arsonists and militia members and murderous sheriffs, it's pretty quiet around here. Oh, and bears."

"Murderous?" Feeling her eyes go wide, Felicity met Bennett's equally startled gaze. "Um…Sheriff Summers?"

"Oh no," Lou was quick to reassure her. "This was her predecessor. He's dead now." Her sad look returned, but she shook it off. "You'll need to bring your sisters next time. I'd love to meet them."

"Um…maybe?" Felicity was still stuck on the dangers Lou'd just listed.

Lou snorted a laugh. "Bad segue, right? Although something tells me that your sisters can handle themselves."

"Most of them," Felicity said, thinking about Norah. She was a little too naive and gentle for the dangerous world they inhabited, so Felicity and her other sisters all worried about her the most. "And they'd love you—plus all the murder club ladies."

"Told you," Lou said. "First time we met, I said we'd be best friends."

Glancing around the coffee shop again, Felicity knew they'd be back to this beautiful, quirky, strangely murderous town. She grinned at her new bestie. "You were right."

A customer drew Lou's attention, and Bennett gave Felicity's hand another squeeze.

"After your mom's preliminary hearing and before our… honeymoon"—Bennett's gaze heated as he said the word—"want to go to Fort Collins with me?"

"Sure?" The location seemed random until Felicity

remembered that Fort Collins was Bennett's hometown. "Oh! To meet your family?" A shot of terror darted through her at the thought. *What if they hate me?*

"Yeah. It's my foster dad's retirement party." Bennett's shoulders were stiff in the way they got when he was nervous. "I told him and Zena—my foster mom—about you. That you're my wife. They'd like us to stay with them for a few days so they can get to know you."

"Of course we can," she said, The way he'd said "wife," so reverent and adoring, muted Felicity's anxiety about meeting her in-laws. Even if they *did* hate her at first, she'd win them over. For Bennett, she'd do anything.

As if reading her mind, he gave her one of his rare, sweet smiles. "They're going to love you. How could they not?"

For that, she had to kiss him. How could she not?

EPILOGUE

NORAH PAX STARED AT THE door. It was fairly nondescript as doors went, but what was on the other side frankly terrified her. She paced the alley, five strides north and then five strides south, back and forth ten times until she was in front of the entrance again. She was relieved that there wasn't a window to see her strange behavior.

Just as she had that thought, the door to the neighboring business—a café—opened, and a man with a full garbage bag stepped into the alley. Giving her a curious but friendly look, he started to raise his free hand. The thought of having to make conversation with this stranger terrified her even more than what was behind the door. Ducking her head and pretending she didn't see the guy, she yanked open the door in front of her and stepped inside.

It was…quieter than she'd expected. No rock music blared, and no muscle-bound men tossed their weights noisily back on racks. There were only mats and a ring and equipment neatly stacked against the far wall. It even smelled nice, not like the mix of body odor and vinyl that most gyms had.

Only one person was there—a very large, muscular person— and he was staring right at her, scowling.

"What do you want?" he barked.

She didn't mind the directness. It was comforting, really, that he didn't hide his purpose in politeness. "I need to learn to fight."

"Why?"

"So I won't be useless next time someone tries to murder my sisters."

His glower didn't lighten as he studied her with eyes as dark as night. "Come in then," he finally snapped, and Norah started to smile.

This might just work out after all.

KEEP READING FOR THE FIRST CHAPTER OF KATIE'S

FISH OUT OF WATER

AVAILABLE NOW!

ONE

"Welcome to the Yodel Inn," said the stocky middle-age Black man. "Where there are *no dull* moments."

Dahlia tore her gaze away from her phone, blinking at him. She'd futilely hoped for a response from her sister, but only Dahlia's twenty-plus frantic outgoing texts filled the screen, the last of which was undelivered due to no cell service. After a night of no sleep, a delayed morning flight, and *hours* of wandering around the mountains looking for the teeny-tiny town of Howling Falls, she knew she wasn't at her sharpest, but the odd emphasis gave her pause. "I'm sorry. Did I miss a pun?"

He grimaced. "Yodel, no dull? Supposedly it rhymes."

"Oh!" Now she felt bad she hadn't caught it immediately. Normally, she was a huge word-play fan, but it'd been a stressful twentyish or so hours. "It does rhyme—clever!" She tried to make up for her initial lack of enthusiasm, but he still looked mopey.

"I wanted 'Welcome to Yodel Inn, where yo-delight is our delight,' but I was outvoted."

"I do like yours better," she said, finally taking a moment to glance around the small motel office. It looked like a tiny fake log cabin, but it actually *smelled* like freshly cut pine, which made her wonder if it wasn't fake or if they just used a really authentic air freshener. The pun-master and front desk clerk was wearing a red plaid flannel shirt with a name tag proclaiming his name was Bob, and the whole scene made her feel like she'd wandered onto the set of a maple syrup commercial.

"Thank you." Bob looked a little brighter at her approbation. "Do you have a reservation?"

"I don't," she said. "I'm Dahlia Weathersby. My sister, Rose Weathersby, is staying here?" She couldn't help the lift of her voice that turned an optimistic statement into a question. The Yodel Inn and Tavern was the only lodging in Howling Falls, but relief still flooded over her when the man nodded.

"Yes, she checked in early this week. Would you like a room close to hers?"

Although Dahlia would rather make sure her sister was alive and well and then immediately return to her life in California, she knew she'd need to stay at least one night. The sun had been sinking behind the mountains when she'd finally spotted the "Welcome to Howling Falls" sign. Even if her most optimistic dreams came true and she found Rose chilling in her room at the Yodel Inn, Dahlia would still need a place to sleep, and her sister was a horrible bed hog. Pulling out her driver's license and a credit card, she slid them across the counter. "Yes, please. Just tonight for now."

He entered her information, ran her card, and then grabbed

a key marked with a nineteen off a nail on the wall. She noted that the only missing keys were two, six, and seventeen.

"Which room is Rose in?" she asked, even though she figured she could take an educated guess.

He paused. "Didn't she tell you?"

"She's not answering her cell," Dahlia explained, feeling a sickly dip in her stomach saying the words out loud.

"Well, I don't think I should give you that information," he said slowly. "I take our guests' privacy very seriously."

Maybe you shouldn't keep all the room keys behind the desk for anyone to see then? "She sent me an emergency text yesterday, and I haven't heard from her since."

Bob looked alarmed. "Emergency text?"

"Our private code that we only use in emergencies. 'Tell Mom hi.'"

"Tell Mom hi," Bob repeated slowly.

Practically smelling the skepticism radiating off the man, she repeated, "We only use that in drastic situations."

"What if she just wanted you to tell your mom hello?"

"She wouldn't," Dahlia insisted. "It's our secret code."

"Secret code." He was sounding less and less convinced. "Sure she's not just out of cell range somewhere?"

Dahlia knew it *was* highly likely that Rose was fine, just out of cell range or distracted by new people and places. It wouldn't be the first time her sister had forgotten to check in with Dahlia for days or even weeks. The emergency code couldn't be ignored, however. That brief final text was the only reason she was here arguing with flannel-wearing Bob at the Yodel Inn in Howling

Falls, Colorado, instead of doing a million other things at home in California where she belonged.

A wiry white woman who looked to be pushing seventy entered the office and immediately moved behind the desk to join Bob. She was also wearing red plaid flannel, because that seemed to be the town's uniform—or at least the inn's.

"Would you mind calling Rose's room?" Dahlia asked.

Although he narrowed his eyes in suspicion, he did as she asked while the older woman looked on with obvious curiosity. Dahlia was disappointed but not surprised when he hung up with a shake of his head. "No answer."

"Any chance we can take a look in her room? Make sure she's okay?"

His horrified expression told her that the answer was no. There was zero chance he was going to let her into her sister's room. "Absolutely not. Like I said, I take my guests' privacy very seriously."

"Have you seen her today?" she asked.

"I don't keep track of my guests," he said with an offended huff. "That would be a gross invasion of their privacy."

"Rose? That pretty blond girl in Room Seventeen?" The other hotel employee piped up, making Bob groan. "I haven't seen her for a few days. She's probably off exploring the mountains. She looks like a real nature-lover, that one."

"Becky," Bob huffed. "Don't be giving out guest information."

"Did you talk to her?" Dahlia asked, hope surging. "Do you know where she might've gone?"

Becky shook her head. "But I saw her heading over to the

tavern side a few evenings ago, so you'll want to have a chat with the bartender. Oh, and Glenn too. He's always over there, drinking beer and gossiping. Maybe she talked to them."

"Such a breach of ethics," Bob muttered.

"Thank you," Dahlia said to Becky gratefully, ignoring Bob's grumbling. It wasn't much information to go on, but at least it was a lead. *Someone* in this town had to know where Rose was. It was just a matter of finding the person who could lead her to her sister—her healthy, happy, completely unharmed sister. She had to believe that was true, since the alternative was unthinkable.

———

One side of the Yodel Tavern was connected to the motel, and the other shared a wall with a…*taxidermy shop*?

"That's my place," the fiftyish white man at the bar told her proudly, giving her his business card. "Glenn's Taxidermy. I'm Glenn."

"But why next to a bar?" she asked, pocketing his card, even though she wasn't quite sure why she'd ever need taxidermy services. However if she ever *did* need something—or someone—stuffed in a lifelike fashion, now she knew she could call on Glenn. "There doesn't seem to be much potential for crossover business."

"You'd be surprised," the bartender muttered.

Dahlia blinked, tempted to ask, but her squeamishness outweighed her curiosity, and she let the subject drop. "I'm Dahlia."

"Dulce." The bartender nodded as she continued to slice the lemons and limes on her cutting board.

They were the only three people in the bar, probably because it was still early in the evening. Or possibly because the town of Howling Falls was so *tiny* that Glenn and Dulce very likely made up a large percentage of the local population.

"My sister's supposed to be staying here too, but she hasn't responded to any of my texts since yesterday, and she's not in her room." Earlier Dahlia had even peered through the crack between the drapes into Number 17 but hadn't spotted Rose. Now she pulled up a picture of her sister on her phone and showed the other two. "Have you seen her?"

"Sure," Glenn said, and Dulce nodded. "She was in here a few days ago. Tuesday?"

"Must've been Monday," Dulce corrected. "I was off Tuesday."

"What time?" Dahlia asked, her heart giving a hop of excitement.

Glenn tilted his dark head in thought. "Just after four. I had a meeting with my accountant at four thirty, and it was right before that."

"Did she talk to you? Maybe mention what she'd been doing? Or where she was planning on going?"

Her hope deflated when Glenn shook his head. "Nah, she just swung through like she was checking out the place, but she didn't stay long enough to chat."

"She didn't talk to anyone?" Dahlia asked, disappointed.

"Just Winston," Dulce said.

"Winston?"

"Winston Dane." Glenn winced as he said the name, which sent Dahlia from hope to concern.

"Why'd you say his name like that?" she asked. "Is he awful? Dangerous?"

"Nooo?" The way Glenn stretched out the word doubtfully made Dahlia's worry double. "Just…unfriendly. He's the local hermit. Doesn't care for people much. He wouldn't commit *murder* or anything like that. I don't think. I mean, I couldn't swear on my *life* that he doesn't have a stack of corpses in his basement, but it's doubtful. Sort of doubtful."

Anxious prickles coursed down Dahlia's spine. One of the last people who'd talked to her sister before her disappearance was a people-hating, possibly corpse-collecting hermit. What trouble had Rose stumbled into?

The front door opened, making Dahlia jump. A uniformed cop entered, heading toward their small huddle at the bar. Even though the Silver County Sheriff Department had dismissed her concerns when she'd contacted them last night, Dahlia was tempted to ask this police officer for help. She had a sympathetic face.

"Hey, Dulce," the cop, whose name tag read "Officer H. Bitts," said when she reached the bar. Her dark hair was pulled back into a severe bun, and her makeup-free brown skin was flawless. "I just picked up Mike Tippley's golden retriever on Front Street again. Mike's house is locked up tight, and his car's gone, so I set the dog up with food and water at the shelter."

Dulce sighed. "Thanks, Hayley. That Bailey is an escape artist. I'm working here late tonight, but I'll call Mike, let him know he can pick up Bailey in the morning."

The cop nodded and turned away, giving Dahlia a quick once-over. "Nice outfit," she said.

After a surprised moment, Dahlia smiled broadly. Before her flight that morning, she'd just thrown on some favorite jeans— for emotional support—with a chunky red sweater and tartan scarf, but the unexpected compliment gave her a much-needed boost. "Thank you. You have gorgeous pores."

Officer Bitts blinked. "Thank you?"

"I do makeovers professionally," Dahlia explained. "My clients would kill for skin like yours."

"Okay." Bitts still looked uncertain as she turned toward the door.

"Wait! I'm looking for my sister," Dahlia blurted out, unlocking her phone's screen again and holding it out so the cop could see Rose's picture. "Rose Weathersby. I haven't heard from her since she texted me our emergency code last night."

Bitts glanced at the phone screen. "Emergency code?"

"Tell Mom hi." Dahlia grimaced when the cop's expression flattened to professional blandness. "It's our sister code, asking for help, like when a blind date goes wrong, or my model bailed at the last minute…" She let her voice trail off when she saw the skepticism peeking out of the cop's neutral expression.

"I haven't seen her," Bitts said. "Have you filed a missing-person report?"

"Yes, last night, with the sheriff's department, but they seemed…unconvinced that she was actually missing. I didn't know Howling Falls had a police department."

"It's small. No need to file another report with us, since we'll get a copy from the sheriff. I'll keep an eye out for her."

Forcing a smile, Dahlia held back her torrent of worried frustration and just said, "Okay. Thank you."

"Good luck," Bitts said before heading to the exit.

Dahlia watched her leave and then turned back to Glenn and Dulce, who were watching her with sympathetic expressions. "Do you think the antisocial hermit did something to Rose?" she blurted.

"I'm sure he didn't," Glenn said, although his doubtful expression blocked any comfort his words might've provided. "He wouldn't... I mean, he *probably* wouldn't, although who knows, since they always say serial killers are the quiet ones..." His voice trailed off with a flinch when he saw Dulce's ferocious scowl directed at him. "Excuse me, ladies. I should go check on something." He pushed off his barstool and hurried toward the taxidermy shop door.

Once he disappeared inside, Dulce said, "Winston didn't do anything to your sister. He's a sweetheart."

Dahlia turned to the bartender, some of her worry washing away at the conviction in Dulce's voice. "He's not a people-hating, corpse-collecting grump after all?"

"Well..." Dulce grimaced. "I wouldn't say he's *not* a grump, and he's not exactly *social*, but it's a definite no on the corpses. I can't imagine him hurting anyone. He just really likes his privacy."

"Okay," Dahlia said slowly. "So is this just a guess, or do you know him better than Glenn? Because I got the impression from him that this Winston Dane is part Jeffrey Dahmer and part chupacabra."

Dulce snorted. "Glenn's a drama queen. I'd take everything he—and most of the gossipy locals—says with a serious grain of salt." She leaned over the bar and lowered her voice. "Don't tell anyone, because Winston wanted to stay anonymous, but he made a *huge* donation to the Howling Falls animal shelter. He's the only reason this town even *has* a shelter. Besides, you only have to read one of his books to know that guy's a cream-filled doughnut inside."

Dahlia leaned closer. "Books?"

"Hang on." Dulce came out from behind the bar and crossed to the bookshelf in the corner. She scanned the small collection before pulling out a well-read paperback. Returning to the bar, she handed the book to Dahlia.

"Dane Winters?" The author's name rang a bell. "Oh! I've read some of his books before. Your scary hermit writes cozy mysteries?"

Dulce nodded. "Cozy mysteries with a bumbling, romantic hero even."

"Right." Dahlia smiled as the plot of the books came back to her. "Mr. Rupert Wattlethorpe."

Dulce smirked at her. "See what I mean?"

Scanning the back of the book—on which the author bio was suspiciously absent—Dahlia slowly nodded. "I do, although I still want to talk to your not-so-scary local hermit about what my sister might've told him. Do you have his cell number?"

"No. No one does that I know of."

"How about his address?"

Dulce snorted. "Yeah, but it won't do you much good. He basically lives on a secured compound, and even if you could get to his front door, I doubt he'd answer it."

Resting her chin in her hand, Dahlia gave the bartender an innocent smile. "Oh, I'll figure something out."

———

Picking a padlock with a bobby pin and a lip pencil was harder than Dahlia thought it'd be—which was saying something. She hadn't expected it to be *easy*, but she was slightly irritated at everyone involved in making the movie *Deadly Beauty II*, since the heroine had indeed picked her lock in just seconds. Granted, she hadn't used a Barbara Whitmore Lip Trick in Iconic Rose sharpened to a wicked point, but Dahlia couldn't imagine another instrument making things any easier.

Except maybe a key. Yes, a key would be nice.

With a huff, she put her sadly mutilated lip pencil back into her compartmentalized travel makeup bag, peering at her other options in the dim moonlight. *Lip tint, eyeliner, serum, moisturizer…* She made a face. No one could've predicted that her search for her missing sister would mean sneaking into some local hermit's lair, but not even *considering* the possibility she might need better breaking-and-entering tools when she was packing for this adventure felt like a lack of planning on her part. Sure, she'd look good while failing to pick this lock, but a glamorous fail was still a fail.

Then the slightest bulge in a tiny pocket of her compartmentalized bag caught her eye, and she yanked out her point-tip tweezers. "Hello, beautiful. I'd forgotten about you," she crooned in barely audible celebration. Crouching so she was at face level with the lock, she woke up her phone again. The directions she'd found on the internet filled the screen, and she smiled victoriously as she balanced the phone on her leg above her knee.

"I know, random internet lock-picking instructor person," Dahlia muttered under her breath, "that you said raking the lock is inelegant, but as this is possibly a life-or-death matter, I'm shooting for expediency here. For once in my life—fine, maybe twice—I'm taking the inelegant-but-easy route." That said, even the so-called easy method of picking a lock wasn't really *easy* for her, and it took another several minutes of struggling with her tweezers and bobby pin before the padlock clicked and dropped open.

She stared at the opened lock for several seconds before a satisfied smile curled her mouth. She'd actually *done* it. She, Dahlia May Weathersby, had picked a lock with just the contents of her—admittedly well-stocked—makeup bag and an internet tutorial. Returning her improvised tools to their proper compartments and zipping up the bag, she grabbed her phone and stood, wincing as blood rushed back into her sleeping feet.

"Note to self," she whispered at a barely there volume, "next time you pick a lock while breaking into some weird mountain man's property, don't crouch. Kneel."

With that decided, she removed the padlock and unwove the chain as quietly as she could manage. The eerie silence of the mountain night made every clink of metal against metal sound like an air-horn blast, but she told herself she was being paranoid. She couldn't see a house, which meant the mountain guy couldn't see her...hopefully.

Unless he's hiding behind that pine tree over there, her extremely unhelpful brain offered, but she shut down that nonsense immediately. "Knock it off." Despite her words, her growl was almost soundless, just in case someone *was* lurking close by. "Quit trying to psych yourself out."

Just because this guy had all—well, most of—the residents of the tiny mountain town of Howling Falls, Colorado, terrified of him, just because he lived in the middle of nowhere, just because there was nothing around but snow and dark cliffs and trees and moonlight shadows shaped like monsters and wailing wind and a brutal-looking fence topped with razor wire didn't mean that she should fear for her life. Mr. Winston Dane, Hermit, surely was a rational person who would be happy to talk to her about whether or not he'd played a role in her sister's disappearance.

Dahlia shivered. "Okay, that's enough thinking."

She did her best to shut off her brain as she slipped through the opening in the gate. She mentally debated ease of exit over disguising the fact that the gate was unlocked—just because she couldn't see any cameras didn't mean they weren't there—and decided to rewrap the chain but leave the paddock open. She doubted her ability to pick a lock a second time, especially if she was in a rush.

Turning back to the thick stand of trees, she blew out a breath and straightened her shoulders. "The things I do for you, Rosie-Toes."

She started walking on what she couldn't really call a driveway, since it wasn't even gravel, much less paved with comfortingly civilized asphalt. It was more two strips of dirt about six feet apart, worn down by driving a car—no, not a car, she mentally revised, but a pickup, one of those loud, jacked-up monsters—back and forth until the two grooves were formed. Snow dusted the ground, but she was grateful she didn't have to trudge through drifts up to her knees. Her black boots were, relatively speaking, practical, chosen for breaking and entering, but they weren't anything real mountaineers would wear or anything. Even just a few inches of snow would've made things very uncomfortable for her.

The moon was almost full, just slightly rounder on one side than the other, but as the trees thickened, their branches stretching above the driveway to form a natural tunnel, things got dark. After tripping over a protruding rock for the third time, Dahlia chose comfort over caution and pulled out her phone again. Turning on the flashlight app, she directed the illumination to the ground right in front of her. The edge of the light caught on a sign, and she paused, turning her makeshift flashlight so she could read it. No Trespassing.

There were no threats, no murderous implications, but the sign still felt ominous. Reminding herself that she was doing this for Rose, Dahlia braced herself and walked on. The eeriest part of the walk, she decided, wasn't the dark shadows turning the trees on either side of her into yawning caves where serial killers were bound to be hiding. Instead, it was the silence. Except for the continual groan of the wind and creaking branches, there was…nothing. No traffic, no other humans, no buzz of electronics, no life noises at all. That lack of background sounds was strangely terrifying.

Dahlia bit back a laugh. *I'm confronting a hermit in his potentially heavily armed hideout, and* that's *what I find terrifying? The quiet of nature?*

It wasn't just the silence beneath the drone of the wind that made her uneasy, though. It was the complete lack of civilization. In the city, she was surrounded by people at all times. There, one shout would bring at least *some* of them running if she ever needed help. Out here, it was just her and one scary-ass mountain man. She could scream her lungs out, and no one would ever hear.

"Enough of that," she muttered, needing to stop freaking herself out immediately. She focused on the track ahead, tilting her phone to send the light farther in front of her. All she could see was more snow-dusted driveway and infinite trees. This driveway—as pathetic as it was—apparently continued for *miles.*

Rose, she reminded herself. *My sister needs me. Maybe. Probably. Or she might be perfectly fine, like that time she decided on the spur of the moment to fly to New-freaking-Zealand and forgot to let me know for three days, or that other time, when she spent two weeks at that monastery in Iowa with no cell signal or internet so she could learn how to make elderberry wine. Quite possibly, I'm risking my life for no reason. Maybe Rose's 911 text wasn't an emergency after all.* Despite these optimistic thoughts, just the slight possibility that her sister *was* in trouble was enough to keep Dahlia in sister-rescue mode. With a silent sigh, she trudged on.

Her fingers were starting to ache with cold, so she switched the phone to her left hand, shaking out her right and jamming it into her jacket pocket to warm up. As the light bobbled with the motion, she saw a reflected gleam and came to an abrupt halt.

Was that an eye? Every predatory animal she'd ever heard of living in Colorado—bears, mountain lions, coyotes, wolves… *Wait, are there wolves here?*—flashed through her mind in a second. Aiming the flashlight with a shaking hand, she slowly focused the beam back on the spot where she'd noticed the reflected light.

There! To her utter relief, it wasn't the light bouncing off the homicidal eyeball of a carnivorous beast. It was simply a piece of shiny trash that'd ended up on the ground. Maybe Mr. Weird Hermit himself had tossed his gum wrapper out of his truck window.

That didn't seem quite right, however. Dahlia cocked her head and moved closer to study the object. It almost looked as if it was suspended off the ground. Crouching down, she peered at what was definitely a wire—as thick as a guitar string—stretched across the entire width of the driveway, about six inches off the ground.

"Are you a trip wire, Mr. Shiny?" Dahlia asked under her breath, using the light from her phone to follow the path of the wire. Straightening her legs but staying bent over, she moved to the side of the driveway and between two evergreens, expecting to find the end of the wire tied around a sapling or something similar.

Instead, there was a disconcertingly sleek arrangement of wire and pulleys that looked completely out of place next to the rough trunks and scrubby brush surrounding them. With the light, Dahlia tracked the wire's progress as it moved through the system and up to the dark canopy over the driveway. She turned her phone to the branches above her and had to grin at the sheer campiness of what she found.

"An enormous *net*, Mr. Weird Hermit?" she whispered, trying very hard not to laugh out loud. "Someone's been watching too many Scooby-Doo reruns. Or has a Spider-Man obsession."

Still internally snickering, Dahlia stepped over the wire with exaggerated care. Now that she'd seen the trap, it would be extra humiliating to be caught in a huge net like some cartoon villain just because she'd been careless and caught the wire with the toe of her boot. To make doubly sure, she stayed to the far side of the path, at the very edge of the net suspended above her, and hurried to put that particular trap behind her.

After just a few rushing steps, however, she forced herself to slow, sweeping the light from side to side over the driveway, looking for any sign of another trap. She thought of all those rocks she'd tripped over before she'd decided to use her flashlight app and cringed. It was sheer luck she hadn't triggered something and had sharpened spears flying at her or a giant mace swinging toward her head or stumbled into some other Temple of Doom-like...well, *doom*.

Shaking off her distraction, she focused on the ground in front of her. Every so often, she'd shift the light to the trees lining the drive, but she hated those moments. The light from her phone barely penetrated into the gloom, and it just activated her already overstimulated imagination.

She paused, running the light across the driveway in front of her. It was hard to tell because of the dusting of snow blowing across the space, but it looked like the two tire tracks jogged to the left slightly before returning to the center. For the paths to be worn as smoothly as they were, Mr. Weird Hermit would've had to have taken the same tiny detour every day for months— even years—so it wasn't just that he'd gotten distracted texting one time and swerved slightly off-center. No, this would've had to have been a pattern, and a pattern meant there was a reason.

Moving a little closer—but not too close—Dahlia swept the area with light, searching for anything that didn't belong. Now that she was looking for it, the slight impression jumped out to her quickly, the straight line not fitting the natural surroundings. It would've blended just fine into a sidewalk or building or any other non-natural structure, but here in the curve and waves of the organic world, it looked as obvious as a flashing light.

Once she'd spotted the first straight line barely marking the dirt, it was easy to follow it to the corner, until the entire large square was marked out in her mind. It would've been easier to hide if all the leaves and loose dirt hadn't been blown off, leaving a smoothly swept surface. Even the bit of snow didn't help hide it, instead settling against or in the tiny cracks delineating the square. It was smack in the center of the driveway, so anyone driving straight down the middle would run two tires right over it.

As Dahlia gave the almost-hidden square a wide berth, her imagination ran wild, and the temptation to examine it more closely almost got the best of her. Was it something as innocuous as a sensor, alerting Mr. Weird Hermit that someone was approaching? Or was it something more fun—like a trapdoor that'd drop trespassers into a spike-lined pit?

Okay, maybe not so much fun for the trespasser, Dahlia acknowledged, giving the square a final glance before she pushed forward. She couldn't help the *tiniest* feeling of smugness for sneaking past not only one but *two* of Mr. Weird Hermit's traps. Immediately, she gave herself a mental slap, because getting cocky was how she'd trip her way into whatever came next.

Forcing herself to stay alert, even though this was the longest driveway in the history of driveways, Dahlia pressed on. The flashlight on her cell phone started to dim, and she paused to stare at it, debating whether to preserve the little charge that remained in the battery or use the light for as long as possible. The thought of being stuck in the middle of nowhere with Mr. Weird Hermit and his apparent hatred of trespassers without the ability to even make a 911 call made her turn off the flashlight app and darken her screen.

Once her eyes had adjusted to the small bit of moonlight filtering through the bare tree branches, she started forward again, even more cautiously in the limited light. She made it around a bend in the drive and came to an abrupt stop at the sight in front of her.

The claustrophobic press of forest fell away, and a ten-foot concrete fence rose seemingly from nowhere. It was startling to come upon it, so out of place. Dahlia had expected an Unabomber-type shack, or possibly a single-wide trailer, or—in the best-case scenario—an adorable log cabin with woodsmoke curling from the chimney. This tall, solid fence, so smooth it gleamed in the moonlight, was just…weird.

"You do call him Mr. Weird Hermit for a reason," she reminded herself very quietly as she approached the fence, angling away from the wrought-iron gate. Although she couldn't see any obvious cameras, she had to assume they were there. In fact, he'd probably been watching her progress this entire time, but she still didn't want to be obnoxious about it. There was no reason to throw the fact that she'd outsmarted his traps and made it to…well, this patently unscalable, very tall wall of a fence.

The trees ended a good fifteen feet from the fence, and so did their helpful shadows, so she felt exposed as she moved across the open space. The lack of close by trees was also unfortunate in that there were no helpful overhanging branches that she could use to get over the wall. Once she was right next to it, she sighed. This was going to be tricky.

The painted concrete surface was as smooth as it had appeared from a distance, about twice as tall as she was without any handy toe- and fingerholds. She moved closer to the single gate, hoping for a gap she could slip through if she turned sideways and sucked in, but the wrought-iron bars were so close together that even a Chihuahua would have trouble squeezing through.

Can't go through, so I guess I'm going over. She grimly eyed the wrought-iron spikes at the top of the gate as she moved closer to the hinges, hoping they'd give her a little bit of a foothold. Tossing the strap of her bag over one of the spikes so it hung high off the ground, she backed away, trying to distract herself from the sheer impossibility of what she was about to attempt by planning the lecture she was going to give Rose when she was found safe and sound in some mountain hippie commune, unable to charge her phone because all the community electricity was needed for the grow lamps in the pot greenhouse. Or maybe Rose had decided to become a Rocky Mountain version of Dian Fossey, and she was holed up in a cave with a pacifist family of bears and *no* electricity, about to bed down for their winter hibernation.

Honestly, considering her sister, neither would surprise her. But on the small chance Rose was actually in trouble, Dahlia had to at least *try* channeling her inner parkourist.

She sprinted forward and jumped at the gate, grabbing two vertical bars close to the top. Lifting her feet higher, she pressed them against the bars, her left one finding the tiniest bump of a hinge she could use as a foothold. Releasing her right hand, she grabbed both sides of her bag strap, using it like a rope to help haul herself up as her feet slipped and scrabbled against the bars. The material creaked but held.

"Thank you, Lavinia Holt," she managed to gasp as her left hand grabbed the top horizontal bar between two vicious spikes. "For designing bags that are…not only cruelty-free… but…also…durable." Her right hand grasped the top bar as well, and she pulled her body up high enough that she got her left foot onto the top of the fence. After an awkward twisting scramble, she managed to shift around to the other side of the spikes. Yanking up the bag's strap so it was clear of the spike, she clutched it in her sweaty fist along with the top bar as her feet dangled. Squeezing her eyes closed, she sent a tiny prayer to the patron saint of breaking-and-entering fashionistas, released her hold on the fence, and let herself drop.

Her feet hit the ground with a jarring *thump* before she fell backward. Opening her eyes, she mentally checked herself for any major injuries, but all her parts seemed to be intact.

"Ha!" she exclaimed before remembering where she was and the importance of being quiet.

Standing on shaky legs, she tugged down her top layers and brushed off her butt before looking around. Prior to scaling the gate, she'd just been able to see a few trees scattered around before everything disappeared into the darkness, but from her new vantage point, she could make out a dark shape big enough to be a dwelling of some sort.

Blowing out a bracing breath, she slung her bag over her shoulder and turned toward what, with her luck, was probably Mr. Weird Hermit's torture barn and antique doll emporium.

Although she kept half an eye out for any traps, she marched toward the structure with more speed than was probably wise. The problem was that Dahlia was pretty much over the weird hermit's nonsense. Her muscles were sore and still trembling, her carefully chosen outfit was a definite mess, and the clock was ticking. The longer Rose was missing, the more likely it was that she was seriously hurt or even…

Nope. Dahlia firmly cut off those fatalistic thoughts. Her brain was not allowed to go there. Instead, she focused on the building in front of her, a black shape silhouetted against a not-quite-as-dark sky, and forced her legs to keep walking. *Almost there.* She was so close to completing her quest. All she had to do in this portion of her find-Rose adventure was defeat the big bad—well, perhaps not *defeat,* but more just have a chat with—and then she could move up a level, hopefully to the one that Rose was on.

She walked—fine, *stomped*—closer to the structure, near enough to see that it was indeed a house. The details became clearer the closer she got, and her determined thoughts were whisked straight out of her brain when she saw that there was a man standing on the porch.

No, not a man. A giant. A mountain. A *monolith.*

The guy was tall. And broad. And, judging by the scowl she could finally see once she reached the base of the porch steps, he was *pissed.*

ABOUT THE AUTHOR

A fan of anything that makes her feel like a badass, Katie Ruggle has trained in Krav Maga, boxing, and gymnastics, has lived in an off-grid, solar-and-wind-powered house in the Rocky Mountains; rides horses; trains her three dogs; and travels to warm places to scuba dive. She has received multiple Amazon Best Books of the Month and an Amazon Best Book of the Year. Katie now lives in Minnesota with her family.

Website: katieruggle.com
Instagram: @katieruggle
Threads: @katieruggle